BEYOND THE ENDLESS

BEYOND THE ENDLESS

BOOK THREE

EARTHCYCLES

DONNA DECHEN BIRDWELL

Beyond the Endless: EarthCycles, Book Three

Copyright © 2022 by Donna Dechen Birdwell

Cover design by Robin Vuchnich, mycustombookcover.com
Author photo by Lucero Valle Archuleta

Published by Wide World Home.
8944B Parker Ranch
Austin, TX 78748 USA
wideworldhome.com

First Printing—March 2022

Publisher's Note: This is a work of fiction. Names, characters places, and incidents are either the product of the author's imagination or used fictitiously.

Birdwell, Donna Dechen
Beyond the Endless: EarthCycles, Book Three
330 pp.
1. Science Fiction – Fiction 2. American – Fiction
I. Donna Dechen Birdwell
II. Beyond the Endless: EarthCycles, Book Three
ISBN: 978-1-7355569-5-6

To all the questions we haven't asked yet
and to the future(s) they contain.

"Time is the substance I am made of.
Time is a river which sweeps me along,
but I am the river…"
—Jorge Luis Borges

"Do not say that I'll depart tomorrow
because even today I still arrive."
—Thich Nhat Hanh

1

I'm awash in a blur of color and no-color-at-all, eruptions of intolerable silence. I should never have gone. Already I can barely remember the thrill of sharing the *Book of All Time*, the joy of the Gathering of Melfar and Mundani as equals. Was that only this morning?

"I'm sure the nens are okay, Meri." Damon envelopes my small tawny hand in his dark brown one.

He wants to be my strong, consoling partner, but I'm inconsolable. I shove his hand away, clenching my fists, my face, my orb. "Then why can't I find them?" Tears sting my eyes, but no tears fall. My heart pounds in my chest, reaching, reaching toward emptiness.

Damon pushes the equids harder than he ought to through the gathering dusk, but we have to get home. I won't rest until I'm once again holding my precious twins in my arms, my Naomi and Odilia. I should never have left them. So young and tender, barely three moon-tides old. I'm consumed with regret. What kind of mother am I to go running off to Fayredell like that?

You're the Calumet, Meridia.

In this fraught moment, I don't care about that. I don't care that Melfar call me Calumet, or that many Mundani call me Prophet. I've been away from my nens for nearly three days now, and as I reach toward them, I find nothing.

The cart bounces and rattles and I grip the edges of my seat with both hands, knowing this speed is dangerous, wishing we could go faster. The wind makes a tangled mess of my unruly brown hair and my milk-filled breasts jar painfully. It's almost dark by the time we pass the site of Old Beniford. It won't be long before we reach home. I stretch my awareness outward yet again, imploring the Migrant to show me my nens.

Nothing.

Nothing but a canopy.

Well, of course there's a canopy. There's always a canopy. The main reason my father Abél stayed in New Beniford was so that he could oversee the maintenance of the canopy that protects our Melfar community from danger. This canopy feels different. Thicker. Several canopies at once? Why would Father do that?

Damon reins in the equids and I vault unsteadily from the cart as it jostles to a stop. A wheeled vehicle can go no farther. I take the steep path that leads up to the village in reckless leaps. Damon, with his longer legs, quickly overtakes me.

"Yuli?" As we approach our darkened cabin, I call out for the girl we left in charge of the twins, the young apprentice to our healer Bekanz. "Yuli!" I don't have to step inside to know that the cabin is empty. Hysteria. Is that what this is called? This uncontrolled desperation?

Father is trying to verberate something that I'm too confused to pertange. There! A nen's cry!

"Meridia!" Father's voice.

Father is almost running down the path toward me. Just behind him I see Bekanz. She's carrying Naomi. Where is Odilia? And Yuli? I run toward Omi. She's wailing and I snatch her away from Bekanz, clutching her to my heart. Bekanz is sobbing, her green eyes faded to gray with despair, her pale orange hair flying in tendrils.

"Where's Odi?" I say, demanding that things not be as they appear to be. Jagged crimson fear shreds purpled hope as my orb explodes with futile seeking.

"We were no match for them," Father says, grabbing my gnosic orb with his eyes, forcing me to see what happened. He uses words, too, so that Damon knows.

I require no words. I watch.

A huge, buzzing machine drops slowly from the clouds and two people emerge from it. Are they people? There's something very wrong about them. They're slender with pale skin and straight dark hair. Each one holds some sort of device. They point the little boxes first one way, then another, staring at them. They share a few indiscernible words and head toward a cabin—our cabin.

I'm seeing this through Yuli's eyes now.

Yuli stares out the window, eyes wide as she sings a protection canopy. The strangers come closer. They attend only to the devices in their hands, nodding and pointing, saying words that carry no verberations. Yuli tries to hide, tries to shelter our two nens. The strangers approach the door; Yuli's protection canopy is useless. Clutching Odilia, she grabs up the basket where Naomi is sleeping and runs out the back door. She cowers behind a bush, shoving the basket under its protective branches, rocking Odi and holding her close to keep her from crying.

The strangers are inside our cabin now, still waving their devices around. Through the open back doorway, Yuli sees them go to a high cupboard and take something from inside it.

I know at once what they've taken: It's the mirror fragment the self-exiled Mundani Prophet Amos Quint sent to me. The one I was supposed to give to his son Lambert. The one I did not take to Lambert when I went to Fayredell.

Odi begins to scream, as if she knows something is very wrong. The strangers peer through the doorway and spot Yuli. They exchange more words. Are they laughing? They're laughing. They move toward Yuli and she runs, but they pursue and grab her by the arm. Odi is still screaming and my heart disintegrates as I see what happens next. The strangers force Yuli and Odi into their vehicle and it lifts into the sky, moving rapidly toward the mountains, over the mountains, westward in the direction of Aldbeck and Selbourne.

I'm sitting on the ground, right here in the middle of the path, clinging to my Naomi. I stare in horrified disbelief toward the mountain, still seeing in my mind the flying thing departing with Odilia and Yuli.

I'm sorry, Meridia, Father says, verberating without words. *There was nothing we could do. By the time we got to your cabin they were already getting back into their vehicle. And then they were gone.*

"We have to go there. We have to get her back," I say, my voice trembling purple, verging into crimson.

"I know," Father says. "We've already sent a group up over the mountains to do just that." They sent three Mundani Chanters trained by Gerd at her combat academy. They hadn't attended the Gathering, instead staying here in New Beniford to offer their own form of protection. We'd thought we might need protection from renegade Palinjians. No one expected this.

"What about Brân?" I say. My father's brother twin has been on the western island of Selbourne ever since he returned from his mysterious journey with the Migrant, a strange going and coming that I still find difficult to comprehend.

Father shakes his head. "Brân had already left Selbourne to come back to New Beniford. He made it to a vantage point on the mountainside." He saw it all from there. He saw a ship arrive from the north. He saw people disembark. "He started to go back to Selbourne. But when he saw the flying machine moving toward New Beniford, he didn't know which way to go."

I pertange his indecision, climbing up the mountain and then down again, watching the flyer return from New Beniford, knowing what it held. He's almost back to Selbourne now.

"I have to go, too. I have to go get Odi." I try to rise, but my legs are quaking uncontrollably and I fall back, leaning against Damon, weak with exhaustion and fear.

"Of course we'll go," Damon says. His arms encircle me protectively. Me and Naomi.

But Father says wait. "Rest first," he says. "Even though it's night, the ones we've sent ahead are capable. They'll find their way." Father knows that Brân will arrive back at Selbourne soon. Brân thinks Amos Quint needs his help.

We gather inside our cabin and light a lantern. How can the absence of one tiny person make a place feel so empty?

Damon's hands tremble as he pours tea for all of us. "Who are these people who took our daughter?" he says. There's a tremor in his voice.

We sit around the table—Damon and me with Bekanz and my father Abél—and try to make some kind of sense out of this thing that has happened. We try to make it real. I'm somewhat calmed by Omi as she sucks hungrily at my breast. There's too much milk for one, so I have to pull her away and let the milk drain onto a cloth. I need to stay calm for Naomi, but Odilia needs me, too, and I don't even know where she is. I'm enveloped in a vortex of colors that seem to be cancelling each other out, turning all brown and gray and absent. My heart burns cold as stone inside my chest.

"I've never seen anything like them," Father says. But as he glances toward me, I know he has. He thinks they're like some of the pale people we saw in our visions of a city with flat stone paths and buildings like mirror-clad mountains, a vision we shared when we were searching for the old Prophet Amos Quint and the Ancient Mica Benison.

And then I know what he means. He was unable to pertange these people. He could see them with his eyes, but his gnosic orb was blind to their presence. They were like phantoms. Or patkánies. That association makes me shudder. Patkánies are vicious predators and the only living creature that Melfar cannot pertange.

With my orb, I'd pertanged the movement of the ship as it approached Aldbeck and Selbourne. It had felt empty, with only vague, shadow-like movements within it. I'd told Damon about the ship, but he hadn't really believed me. He believes me now. It was a huge wooden boat hung with shining white sheets like butterfly wings.

"So these people came on a ship? And then in a flying machine." Damon shakes his head in confusion. "What sort of people are they who move about in such vehicles?" Damon's anger sears his broken Mundani heart. "Where have they come from? Why would they come here?"

I want to know why they took our nen. Where they took her. What they want with her. When I thought the twins were in New Beniford, I'd only looked for them here. Now I stretch further, out toward Selbourne.

The ship has begun to move. Odilia wails against Yuli's breast, her tiny head damp where Yuli's cheek lies against it.

Father's head is down, his own tears very near the surface. He hasn't felt this powerless since the time of his unjust imprisonment at Swarthpol. He tries to compose answers to our questions.

"I can't tell you where they came from, though Brân says the ship arrived from the north. And I have no idea why they came." He thinks the reason must have something to do with Selbourne. It's where they landed. It seemed purposeful.

They took one of Amos Quint's mirrors.

"How did they know about the shard of mirror?" *I saw them take it. Their device showed them where it was.*

Father has no answer for that either.

"Why would they care about a piece of broken glass?" Damon says. Doesn't he remember my reaction when he handed it to me along with Amos Quint's request that I give it to his son Lambert? Doesn't he recall how I drew back and refused to take it in my hand?

Father and I both know that shard is more than an ordinary piece of mirrored glass. We try to explain. It had frightened me more than once and I'd intended to bury it, but instead I'd hidden it away and left it in the house despite my promise to Amos Quint that I'd take it to his son Lambert in Fayredell.

"As for Odilia..." There's a catch in Father's voice. "They seemed...amused by her. They kept touching her skin."

"Because of her color? They found her amusing?" I'm horrified that my child could be in the hands of people who only find her amusing, a novelty because of her iridescent skin.

"I think they may have assumed Yuli was Odi's mother." Father is thankful that somehow Naomi was able to sleep through all of this. He's grateful that they didn't take her, too.

I pertange a tremolo of purplish light glinting off Naomi's iridescence. She wasn't asleep when her sister was taken. She knows where her sister twin is and she shows me. Odilia is on the ship, the one that's empty except for her and Yuli. Am I imagining this? I'm so exhausted. I'm hesitant to trust what my orb is showing me. My orb and my heart.

"Have the people you sent in pursuit found anything yet?" Damon asks. "Are you able to communicate with them?"

"Yes, I'm in touch with them. They may all be Mundani, but Vedö is Revelant and Negyed is part Melfar." Father pauses for a moment, eyes closed. "They're past the crest of the mountain. It will still be a while before they arrive at the coast. They'll let us know what they find." He insists that there's nothing more we can do right now beyond what the search party can accomplish. "Rest here for the night, Meridia. You can leave for the coast in the morning."

My heart and mind don't want to delay even one minute, but my body is heavy with fatigue and despair. As we make ready for bed, I try to stifle the little sobs that fall dark red and brown from my aurynx every time I extend my hands for my two nens and find only one. "Odi is okay," I say, not so much to Damon as to reassure myself. "They haven't hurt her or Yuli."

Odi is resting quietly, but Yuli is beside herself with regret. I want to tell her, *It's not your fault, Yuli.* Her eyes are red with crying, her long golden lashes darkened by tears. One tear slides down a smooth cheek, the one where a dimple appears when she smiles.

What will they feed Odi? Do these invisible people understand that nens need milk? Do they have any milk on their ship? I'm overcome with aggravation at not being able to access them, not being able to grasp what's in the minds and hearts of these strange people. Not being able to pertange them at all. At least I can see them through Yuli's eyes.

They think I'm her mother, Yuli says, *but I'm not and I'm so sorry. They think I'll be able to feed her but she needs you and I'm so sorry. I've tried to tell them, but their language is strange and they don't understand me. Oh, Meridia, I'm so sorry.*

It's not your fault, Yuli.

Another sob drops from my aurynx. Damon takes me in his arms. Reaching through his own despair, he offers comfort, support. It isn't enough.

All night long I drift between Naomi, here beside me in the basket woven by her eldfather Abél, and Odilia, sleeping next to Yuli in a little room deep inside that great empty ship. I slide back and forth along entwined fibrous tones of blue and orange that bind these sister twins firmly to one another. Blue from Naomi and orange from Odilia.

I must have slept because when Naomi's cries cause me to open my eyes again, pale daylight is seeping into our cabin. I lay Omi next to me on the bed, between me and Damon, and help her find my nipple. As the milk floods into my breasts, responding to her cries even before she begins to suck, sadness floods my heart. With my orb, I ask Naomi if her sister twin is well.

Odilia's belly is full but distended, distressed. They've fed her something that doesn't agree with her.

"Don't cry, Meri," Damon says. "We'll find her."

Was I crying? I feel the wetness of the tears. There are more tears in Damon's voice. He may not have caused these nens to grow inside me, but he is their father now and he's as broken as I am.

"I don't know how we can do that," I say. "We have no ship. Already they've taken her so far away that Yuli is difficult to find." And then I try to explain to him that only Naomi can show me where Odilia is now.

"There has to be a way," he says. "Have you been able to see whether the ones Abél sent have learned anything?"

I close my eyes for a moment and my face draws into a frown.

2

"The infant is unwell. I knew we shouldn't have brought her." The speaker's small, soft hands probe the crying child's bloated torso.

"I thought her mother would be able to feed her. You know what I mean, Limn. From her teats as mothers among nullions once did." This second person appears younger, her skin taut, her dark hair lustrous.

The smaller, plumper, tawny-colored woman with the golden eyes and frizzle of fair hair is Yuli. She trembles under their gaze. She's powerless to understand the spoken words and finds no pertangible verberations. Her valiant effort to calm herself produces a deep hum in the back of her throat.

"Don't call them that, Tarja" Limn says.

"Why not? Nullions are what they are. They're finished. Failed. Dead." Tarja shrugs in a way Yuli understands. Dismissive.

"Except these, of course." Limn mumbles the words between clenched teeth.

Yuli shrinks from the two strangers; she knows they're talking about her.

"I don't think this one is the baby's mother, Tarja," Limn says. "And even if it is, it's clear that it has no milk in its teats, despite their uncommon size. When we get back home, we can requisition more suitable feedstock from the clonegarten, but until then we'll have to make do with the adult mixture. Try diluting it a bit more. Maybe it's too rich."

Tarja is annoyed. Having the infant on board is a nuisance, but she reminds herself of what a sensation this little iridescent being will cause among their peers at the Institute. Surely they'll be able to find a prominent place for it in the Archaeozón, the museum containing an entertaining array of bizarre relic species. Surely the guide notes will mention the members of the discovery team and include the name of Tarja Ssu. But they need to keep it alive at least until they reach Port Sillick, where it can be handed over to the Institute. Then all of this will be their problem.

Yuli keeps reaching out with her orb for her own people. She reaches for Umet, the man with whom she's promised to partner. She searches for Meridia, wanting to reassure her that Odilia is okay. These efforts are impeded by the leaden sense of guilt that burdens her. Guilt and regret for not having kept Odi safe. This morning she finds both Umet and Meridia inaccessible. Her mentor Bekanz isn't there either. Yuli doesn't want to think about how far away from New Beniford she's come. She's never felt so alone.

She clings to Odilia for comfort, humming softly, too terrified to shed more tears. She had never seen a boat of any kind before and now she's inside one and surrounded by water on all sides. She can tell that the water is very, very deep. Being able to pertange the swarm of living creatures under the water reassures her that her Melfar gnosic orb is still functioning. It's some attribute of these people that makes them impertangible. In that, they're like patkánies and she finds that association unnerving.

Yuli had pertanged Brân where he stood on the hillside above Aldbeck as the ship began to move away. He'd seemed as confused as Yuli herself was. Earlier, she'd briefly pertanged Amos Quint as she and Odi were being trundled into the buzzing machine that lifted them out of New Beniford to carry them to the ship waiting just off Selbourne. She's certain that some of the strangers had been with Amos. Then Amos had gone absent and she'd been unable to pertange him any further. That frightens her, too.

Odilia's distress reclaims Yuli's attention. She wishes she had some silphy root to make medicine to soothe the nen's bloated belly. She holds Odilia close, rocking back and forth, murmuring a verse of the Amethyst Song of Hope like a lullaby.

Yuli has seen perhaps a dozen of the strange people on board. Many of them look the same to her, so it's hard to know how many there might be altogether. Hard to tell if the ones she saw this morning were the same ones she saw yesterday. She thinks of them as "Elossa," because that was the word she deciphered from the side of their boat, this boat that carries her and Odilia across trackless waters.

Yuli is confounded by her inability to discern what these Elossa intend to do with her and Odilia. Her only source of information is what's visible to her eyes and audible to her ears. She finds their odor unusual. It's hard to know what their bodies are like under their loose-fitting garments. They all seem to have breasts—small breasts, even smaller than Mundani women. Their hair is dark brown or black and perfectly straight, cut short all around. Their clothing is not colorful—dull shades of green, blue, or brown are the only colors Yuli has seen. The shirt and trousers of their simple but well tailored garments always match.

Yuli listens intently to the spoken words she hears, searching desperately for meaning. And for names. She thinks maybe one of her captors is called Limn and the other is called Tarja. She tries out the word "Limn" and is reassured when the anticipated reaction occurs. Limn turns toward her and utters a string of vocalizations.

~ ~

"I think it tried to say my name, Tarja."

"Do you think it might have such intelligence?" Tarja looks at Limn askance.

Yuli gestures toward her and says, "Tarja."

Limn's eyes widen. "There. You see? It was looking right at you. If it understands names, maybe it has a name, too."

"Can you find out?" Tarja supposes that could be an interesting addition to the museum notes for the strange little beings.

Limn stands in front of Yuli, taps her own chest, and says "Limn." Then she gestures toward Yuli and tips her head side to side.

"Yuli," Yuli says.

"There. You see, Tarja? Its name is Yuli."

Yuli nods her head and tries to smile as she hears this person say her name. It doesn't sound quite right, but it's recognizable.

"Well, maybe," Tarja says. "I'll record that in our project file. If I can figure out how to spell it. What about the infant?"

Limn goes through the process of naming herself, then Yuli. Then she gestures at the baby, again tipping her head side to side.

Yuli clutches Odi more tightly. "Odilia," she says. And then she adds, "Odi," thinking that the full name might be too difficult for these strangers to vocalize. On impulse she says something else: "Odilia breth Meridia, our Calumet."

"How long do you suppose the baby's been outside the ectogen?" Tarja says. "It looks only a few months out." Tarja knows little of infants, but she likes to appear knowledgeable.

"You know, it may have been gestated in the old way." There's a note of something in Limn's voice that wavers between revulsion and awe.

"Are you suggesting that they may still engage in sexual reproduction?" Tarja's eyes narrow in disbelief. "Random assortment of genes under wild conditions? That practice died out with the last nullions centuries ago. It was terribly inefficient."

Limn rests her arms at her sides, palms outward, and shakes them back and forth. "We can't be certain yet exactly what they are," she cautions, "or what kinds of relic behaviors they might practice."

Tarja pulls her chin into her chest and lowers her eyes. "Yes, of course," she grumbles. Limn's intense interest in the specimens disturbs her. It's inappropriate. Tarja volunteered for this expedition in the hope that it might aid her advancement among the ranks of Ssus. Now she's fearful it might have the opposite effect.

Tarja goes to check on the rest of the artifacts and specimens they've collected on their voyage, but Limn stays a while longer, scrutinizing Yuli. "We'll know more once I can analyze your DNA," she mutters. "I wish I could communicate with you."

Yuli doesn't understand the words, but she's drawn to the wonder in Limn's voice, the curiosity in her eyes. And, for a fleeting instant, Yuli pertanges a wisp of rose-colored light at the crown of Limn's head.

3

Our climb up through the mountain pass and down toward the abandoned site of Aldbeck is more challenging with a nen strapped to my chest. Damon keeps offering to carry Naomi for a while, but I refuse. I need to feel her small body warm against my heart. I need her to keep me connected to her sister twin.

Odilia is unbelievably far away. Though my ability to pertange Yuli frays, Naomi's tie with her sister holds strong and steady. I cling to that. My addled mind calls forth the prayers I heard from the gray-garbed women deep inside the ancient caverns where I first heard the names Naomi and Odilia. I wonder if such prayers could help. I'm touched again by the simple faith I pertanged in Sister Maggie Marie, a faith that "God's angels" and Saint Odilia would protect her and her children from harm. I try to imagine what a such an angel might be like. I think of my eldmother, Avienne.

The Mundani Chanters that Abél sent over the mountains in search of Yuli and Odilia found nothing when they arrived at Aldbeck—no sign of a ship and no evidence of one having been there. I'm frightened by the helplessness that engulfs them, their sense of having failed their Prophet. They're not thinking of the old Prophet Amos Quint. They're thinking of me.

I think perhaps I'm the one who has failed them. Melfar by my father, Mundani by my mother, I'm torn with trying to be the Melfar Calumet, a Mundani Prophet. How can I be any of that when I couldn't even protect my own child? I send a sandy drift of apology to the child I hold here against my chest and through her to her sister twin. So much ocean lies between the two.

I'm reminded of what Father said about the ocean the first time I saw it. Damon had asked him how far it went. *No one knows,* Abél answered. *Some say it goes on forever. Or around to the other side.* Is that where they're taking my nen? Around to the other side? My mind rebels at "forever." Wherever they've gone, I have to trust Yuli to do everything within her power to protect and care for Odi. I have to believe that will be enough.

Vidvana and her partner Willem travel with us. They'd only arrived back this morning from attending the Gathering in Fayredell, but they insisted on coming. Vidvana is the Mundani poet who, along with our Melfar scholar Zara, composed the *Book of All Time.* We'd had such high hopes that the book could heal the ancient rift between Melfar and Mundani. There's nothing in it about people who fly through the air to steal nens.

As I climb, I struggle to maintain contact with that distant ship that carries my beloved Odi.

I search for ships in my memories.

I find the great ships that Brân showed me, the ones that carried Mundani eldpeople from a distant island back to this land. Those are my own eldpeople, too, through my Mundani mother, Maddie. But Brân said those ships are all gone now, rusted away long since at the bottom of the ocean. Another faint memory glimmers through my orb, an image of something in the distance across the water, something with white wings like a butterfly. It's followed by another image. A ship closer at hand and yet less concrete. A photograph of a ship.

"Damon." I lay my hand on the smooth black braid hanging down his back and tug gently. "Damon, were there any pictures of ships in the photographs we took from Fannan's old workshop in Woodclasp? I'm thinking there was an image with a ship." It comes clearer to my mind. An enormous wooden boat with shimmering white wings.

Damon takes my hand and places it on his elbow. The path is too narrow for us to walk side by side. "I'm not sure," he says. "I know none of the pictures we brought back with us contain such an image. Maybe it was in one of the ones we left behind."

"That could be it," I say. "Why would Fannan have printed such an image?" What I really want to know is how he could have done such a thing. Surely there have been no sightings of such ships within our lifetimes. Mundani and Melfar build small boats and rafts of several kinds, but nothing of such a size or design. I know that the photographic process Damon uses can print images summoned up from the past, images Melfar have stored away in our songs. He learned how to do that by studying the process my eldmother's brother Fannan devised. Did Fannan find that ship in a song?

Damon is struck by the sudden thought that he ought to go back to Fannan's workshop and look for such a picture. To see if it exists. To see if it might reveal something that could help recover his daughter.

I shouldn't have suggested it.

We arrive at the sheltered ledge above Aldbeck as darkness falls. We're beyond exhausted and it's too late to think of moving on any farther. We set up a rough camp and settle in to wait for sunrise. I guess we ate something, though I can't recall what it was. I ate it just to keep me and Omi alive, to give me strength to keep searching for Odilia.

Odi is feeling better. The food that disagreed with her has passed through and she's been fed something more tolerable. I can't tell what it is. It isn't milk. Odi is distressed by all the strange, blank people. She cries every time one of them picks her up or prods her. She searches for me and almost pertanges me through her sister twin Naomi here in my arms. She clings to Yuli, to her familiar colors and music. My pertangement of Yuli grows weaker. Through Odi, I know she's singing a protective veil of blue light. Odi adds a few tentative notes in her small, bright orangey voice.

Naomi is voicing concordant notes, sending her own tender blue light to her sister twin. I offer Omi my breast and lay my hand on Damon's arm, trying to hold our little family together.

Already Vidvana and Willem are busy setting out food and packing up their sleeping sheets. Vidvana never adopted the new Mundani style of short hair for women. Her hair is piled carelessly atop her head, a few coarse strands escaping as they always do. She presses at her nose as if to adjust the eyeglasses that aren't there. She only wears them when she's writing.

I lie still, wondering what the people Abél sent ahead might have discovered.

Has Brân met up with them?

No, he's already gone back across to Selbourne. Amos Quint is injured! Why had I not seen that before? I'm so focused on my nen that I never thought to look for Amos Quint. He's weak and barely conscious, his dark face gone ashen. There's a deep gash on his left arm. He's lost a lot of blood. There's a head injury, too.

I try to see what happened.

I see him angry. I see a mirror broken. Amos tries to grab it back and it slashes into his arm. He's pushed. I can't see who pushed him, so it must have been one of the strangers. Amos falls against the wall and strikes his head. Nothing more.

Brân is there with the old Mundani Prophet now, along with Salma and Vedö, two of the Chanters who made up the rescue party. *Amos Quint needs a healer,* Brân says. *He needs you, Meridia.*

He's right. Amos is weak and disoriented. I'm not sure the latter is entirely due to his injuries.

By the time our little company—Damon, me, Vidvana, and Willem—rounds the beachhead and we catch sight of Selbourne, Salma and Vedö are on their way back with the raft to take me to Amos Quint. Negyed is on the beach waiting for us. I'm surprised to see Vidvana run forward to embrace him. Then I see that Negyed is her brother. He has the same soft brown skin, the same coarse, unruly hair. Negyed's is beginning to thin in front.

Damon and Willem help pull the raft in and hold it as Salma climbs off. She and Willem hold it steady as Damon and I join Vedö on board.

As we head toward Selbourne, Vedö tells us what he can about the ship and about the people who took our Odilia. "Brân says that they anchored between Aldbeck and Selbourne and then launched a smaller boat and two flying machines. One of those was the one that went to New Beniford." His sympathetic glance is accompanied by a granular sift of deep brown regret.

I'm startled at the clarity of his verberations. It's unexpected coming from a Mundani man. But then I recall that Vedö became Revelant during the Palinjian attack on Old Beniford, succumbing briefly to his injuries before being sent back by the Migrant.

"Where did the other flyer go?" Damon asks.

"Brân says it appeared to be headed south."

"Maybe they went to Markham." Damon says. "Or Benbridge?"

"Swarthpol," I say. That's what Brân thinks.

"Where?" Vedö knows he's heard this name before and he's trying to place it.

"Swarthpol is near the coast. Not so far as Markham. Father told me about it."

Damon's eyes light up in recognition and then his bushy brows gather ominously. I'd told him at least a little about Father's experiences at Swarthpol. Or maybe Abél himself told him. Either way, Damon knows the misery Father faced there, banished to that strange prison without walls for a crime he didn't commit. "Why would they want to go to a place like that?" Damon says.

I have no answer. I explain to Vedö that Swarthpol was once the site of a Mundani prison facility where my father Abél was kept for many returns—almost two meeds—after being falsely accused of stealing from the temple at Brightlea. Something about Swarthpol drained him of his Melfar powers of orb and aurynx and he was unable to escape until a great storm and flood somehow swept him away from whatever it was that held him. He wasn't fully himself for several more returns. His powers of orb and aurynx came back to him only slowly. It's why he never came back to Mother and me in Temur.

I clench my fists in frustration. This all happened so quickly. The ship came, the flyers flew, and then they were gone, taking Odi and Yuli with them, changing everything. I refuse to consider the futility of our own urgent expedition. How can we pursue these people with their ships and flyers when we have neither? What kind of Calumet am I who cannot even retrieve her own child from invaders? What kind of Prophet who could not foresee and avert such an atrocity?

Our raft bounces unsteadily, tilting side to side as we near Selbourne. Water splashes onto my legs between the logs of its construction. Logs cut by Damon and Brân while I waited on this same island, tending a broken arm. Even though that was barely nine moon-tides past, it seems so very long ago. Before I was ever called Calumet or Prophet. Before I became a mother.

I try to focus on what is near at hand. Amos Quint is injured and needs care. He needs a healer. That is something I can do, though I find little comfort in it. Brân is there with him. My skin prickles with the realization that this will be the first time I will have seen Brân in the flesh since his disappearance, his journey with the Migrant. I have questions about that.

As our raft nears Selbourne, Naomi begins to cry, a plaintive blue cry that is invariably answered by Odilia's orangey voice. Now there is no answer and my heart collapses with emptiness as I hold Omi closer.

4

Yuli tries to focus her orb at the crown of Limn's head whenever Limn speaks. Most of the time she pertanges nothing, but occasionally there are tiny pulses of color—puffs of rosy pink or palest blue, hints of spring green. Yuli isn't at all sure whether the colors mean the same coming from this Elossa person as they would coming from Melfar or Mundani. Yuli also directs her own verberations toward the crown of Limn's head, hoping that this might assist Limn in understanding her more clearly.

Limn completes her daily examination of Yuli and Odi. Some procedures are repeated, but each day there's something new. Yuli finds much of it invasive and all of it distasteful, but she's powerless to avoid it.

This time when Limn departs, she leaves the door slightly ajar, looking pointedly at Yuli, as if to let her know that today she is not being locked in. She speaks and her tone is not unfriendly. It seems to Yuli that she's almost being invited to explore.

Whenever the door has been opened fully, Yuli noticed a window across the hallway. There are no windows in the tiny room where she and Odi are kept. After Limn's footfalls fade away, Yuli rises cautiously and goes to the door. She opens it wider. She glances back at Odi, assuring herself that the nen is sleeping soundly. Yuli peers down the hallway, first one direction and then the other. Seeing no one, she approaches the window, grasps its ledge, and rises on tiptoe to look out.

The water is even bluer to the eye than it appeared to Yuli's orb. It moves in an endless pattern that extends into a distance that is farther away than Yuli could ever have imagined. Mundani call it the Endless Sea and she thinks they may be right. The heaving of the water is what makes the vessel rock back and forth. Odi seems to find the movement soothing. Yuli does not. On the far horizon, there's a line of something darker. Yuli backs away suddenly as a large white bird swoops close. Its cry is the sound she heard earlier this morning. Another bird glides across the sky in the distance. She catches a glimpse of her own reflection in the window glass and recoils from her disheveled appearance. She runs her fingers through her pale curls.

Yuli glances back over her shoulder at Odi once more, then scans the hallway. There are more doors. One of them is open. Should she look? *Just a quick look. It's not far.* Yuli advances a few tentative steps down the hallway and stops at the open door. She rests one hand on the door frame and leans forward.

Inside the room there are oddly shaped boxes made of inert materials, studded with lights and buttons, humming with something that is not song. On one wall there's a glowing rectangle with lines of what must be words. Like most Melfar, Yuli has always found reading difficult. Besides, the words inscribed on this glowing rectangle are no doubt in the strange language of these Elossa people. Yuli focuses on a line of pictures at the bottom of the rectangle. There's one of Amos Quint. And there are a few of herself and Odi. One of those draws a blush of embarrassment to her cheeks. The other pictures are all objects or places. She recognizes New

Beniford. And that rocky island must be Selbourne. She only saw it briefly when she was being transferred from the flyer onto the ship. No, she'd seen it before in one of the photographs Damon printed for the *Book of All Time*. She'd seen it also in Meridia's memories of the place. Meridia loves Selbourne.

There's a sudden loud vocalization. Barked speech.

Yuli's heart nearly leaps out of her chest as she reels to face the speaker. She doesn't understand the words, but the anger they convey is unmistakable.

"I'm sorry," Yuli says, verberating a sandy sift of apology, forgetting to direct it toward the crown of this person's head. Is this someone she's seen before? The individual takes Yuli firmly by the shoulders and marches her back to her room. Odi has begun to fuss. The door closes and Yuli hears the click of a lock. She takes Odi into her trembling arms and squeezes her eyes shut against the tears that want to come, against the frustrating peculiarity of this place and these people. Against the uncertainty of what lies ahead. Against the devastating distance that lies between her and everything she's ever known. She thinks again of her beloved Umet and her tears overflow.

The individual who locked Yuli into her room strides down the hall and up some stairs. She's angry and a little seasick, her face ashen pale against the gray blue of the garments she wears. She's looking for Limn Ssu.

Limn leans on the deck railing, gazing toward the distant land. They'll follow the coastline northward and in another two days they'll reach Port Sillick. Limn is worried about Yuli and the infant. Odi? Yes, that was the baby's name. Limn senses that these are intelligent creatures, but with an odd energy that she can't quite put her finger on.

"Limn Ssu! I'm reporting an infraction. Someone left the door unlocked where the nullion specimens are kept."

Limn turns slowly. "I know," she says. "It was me. I wanted to see what she would do, Windl. What did you observe?"

Windl Wu frowns, her indignant irritation suddenly having nowhere to go. She can't berate Limn Ssu. The Ssu clone set outranks her own. "The specimen was in the hallway and I think it was about to go inside one of the control rooms. I'm not sure why the door to that room was left unlocked either." She stares accusingly at Limn for an instant before lowering her eyes.

"Did she go inside?"

"No, I don't think so. It was just standing there in the doorway, gawking at the computers."

Limn nods. "Thank you for your report, Windl. Now that you've told me in person, there's no need to enter it into the official report."

Windl sniffs and looks at her feet.

"You're excused," Limn says. She watches as Windl returns to her rounds. Limn reminds herself that Wu clones have to be handled with care. They're designed to be guards and their inherent propensity to confront and defend can be dangerous. And you never know when some mutation might manifest. Limn herself has such a mutation. She knows she does. She's confirmed it through DNA analysis. She does her best to hide it, but she thinks Menza Uhr, her supervisor at the Institute in

Port Sillick, suspects that there's something off about Limn Ssu.

She resumes her reflection on the events of the past few days, trying to think how to frame them in her report to Menza Uhr. She'll emphasize the archaeological outcome of the expedition. The recovery of artifacts. There's no need to try and establish any scientific significance for the artifacts or specimens, only their value as entertainment in an exhibit. Their oddness. Limn has her own ideas about the significance of the mirror they're bringing back and about the collection of whitish pebbles her team members found at the old research station. She never intended to bring back any living hominin specimens. She never expected to encounter any. All the official records indicated that her own home territory was the only remaining inhabited region on the planet. Wrong again. She's sorry about the old man.

Limn shoves her hand into a trouser pocket and lets her fingers close cautiously around a shard of glass. The big mirror from the island will be submitted to the Institute for possible display. Limn knows it will be subjected to little more than a cursory analysis. She doubts that the analysis prescribed by the Protocols will reveal anything she would find worthwhile. The mirror will likely end up as one more meaningless oddity in a museum exhibit. If it's not relegated to a storage vault.

The small shard of mirror that Limn holds in her pocket is something she intends to analyze on her own.

Riding the unwieldy raft to Selbourne proved even more disturbing than riding in Amos Quint's tiny boat had been, back when there were as yet no nens to occupy my attention. Today I crouched in the center of the raft, Naomi bound tightly to my chest, while Damon and Vedö used paddles and poles to guide us to safe harbor.

I'm relieved to be on dry land again. I take a few deep breaths and steady my legs in preparation for the climb up the irregular stone stairway toward Amos Quint's retreat.

Arriving in the old Mundani Prophet's living chamber, I reluctantly hand Naomi over to Damon so that I can examine Amos Quint's wounds. The usual mellow brown of his aged skin has gone distressingly gray and I know it's from loss of blood. His long white plait of hair is undone and spreads in a tangle across the pillow. Grizzled brows hover protectively above his closed eyes. The gash on his arm has been skillfully bound and treated with some kind of medicine I don't recognize. Did Brân do that?

No, Meridia, I didn't. I think the ones from the ship treated him. And they must have carried him up here to his dwelling as well.

Amos Quint was injured down there inside his chamber of mirrors. When he struck his head, he fell unconscious and couldn't possibly have gotten all the way up here without assistance. How strange that they hurt him and then tended his injuries. Was it only an accident? Were they sorry?

I focus my attention on Amos. He's conscious now. Mostly conscious. His eyes are open, but they stare off into the distance, unable or unwilling to fasten on the people moving anxiously back and forth next to his bed. The wound on his arm is well wrapped, but blood still seeps through. I'm grateful that I had the presence of mind to bring supplies for making standard medicines. He'll need bartle oil to help restore the blood he's lost and brink thistle to avert infection. The head injury doesn't appear serious enough to account for the old Prophet's state of mind. I think of my own lengthy absence in the months before the nens were born, my travels with the Migrant after a simple fall, a minor knock on the head. Amos may be Mundani, but he is well acquainted with the Migrant.

"Amos? Amos, can you hear me?" I speak gently and place my palm on his forehead, over the spot where his gnosic orb would be if he had one. A gentle spark of fireseed from my palm should bring him together. Another.

"Meridia?" As his eyes find my face at last, they widen in sudden fear. "Your nen," he says, his voice taut.

"Don't try to talk, Amos. I know what happened." There's a catch in my own voice as I fight back the horrifying images.

Amos averts his eyes.

"When you're better you can tell me what you know, but for now we need you to rest while we get the medicine ready."

While Brân prepares the tinctures according to my instructions, I hum a song, generating spirals of healing blue light and directing them into the old man's wounds. I eject more sparks of fireseed into Amos Quint's hands and into his heart, the Mundani vital nexus. I made the same medicines for Brân at Mother's house in Shadham after he'd been killed by Palinjians, after his mother Avienne brought him back to us.

When the medicine is ready, Amos manages to drink it without too much difficulty. I apply more of the brink thistle directly to his wounds and bind them again. We prepare food for ourselves while Quint drifts into healing sleep.

"You saw the ship, didn't you Brân? What can you tell us about the people?" Damon says.

"I was well on my way back toward New Beniford when they arrived," Brân says. "And though I pertanged that something had gone wrong, I wasn't certain what it was until I reached a vantage point on the side of the mountain that gave me a view of the bay. Meridia knew about it before I did," he says. "She tried to ask me about the ship. When I saw them launch their small boat that went to Selbourne I turned back. I didn't want Amos Quint to have to face those people alone. But then I saw their flying machine lift off and head in the direction of New Beniford. At that point, I didn't know which way to go."

His face reflects the quandary he felt at the time. He knew there was no way he could get to New Beniford in advance of the flyer. He turned again toward Selbourne.

"I heard another flyer take off, but I couldn't see which way it went. From the sound, I thought it went south. By the time I was on the coast and within sight of the ship, the first flyer was returning. I watched it land on the surface of the ship."

He'd recoiled in horror as his eyes verified what he'd already pertanged. He saw Yuli and Odilia. "I'm so sorry, Meridia. There was nothing I could do. I was too far away."

My tears begin anew as I suffer all of this through Brân's experience. Through his eyes, I see the strange people more clearly. Busy, expressionless people, gesturing this way and that as they move with machine like efficiency. Why do many of them look so much alike? It's not just that they all have the same pale skin, the same straight dark hair cut in identical fashion, the same monotone loose clothing. Mostly it's the absence of verberations. Mundani are eloquent by comparison.

Damon brushes his sleeve across his eyes and reaches for my hand, interlacing his fingers with mine.

"I knew Amos was injured," Brân says, "so I took the raft and went to him. He was barely conscious, but seemed stable enough, so I went back across to meet the ones sent from New Beniford." A sandy sigh burns through his aurynx. "Of course the ship was long gone by this time."

Much of this is what I had pertanged. I'm grateful that he's described it all in words so that Damon could see it, too.

"Will Amos be okay?" Damon asks.

"He should be," I say. "It will take a while for him to recover from the loss of blood. It would help if someone could catch some fish for a stew."

Damon agrees to search for something suitable.

Brân guides us outside and down the stairs. We discuss details of where the ship came in; he says it had the word "Elossa" painted on it. He indicates with gestures the directions the flyers took. Such details mean little to me. The only thing that matters is that my daughter and the young woman who cares for her and loves her are gone, receding farther away moment by moment.

We walk a while in silence along the narrow stretch of sand. Naomi seems soothed by the ocean, by the repetitive rush and flow of its water. Or maybe it's me. I recall the tide I spent here on Selbourne with Father and Amos Quint, singing with the Ancient Mica Benison, composing its new song while Damon and Brân built the raft to carry the long-lost Benison across the water to be hauled onward to Beniford. It was here on Selbourne that I discovered I was carrying not just one nen, but two.

Two nens. I look down into Omi's face and reach through her to my other nen, to Naomi's sister twin Odilia, taken from me and transported far away by strange vehicles and stranger people, for reasons that baffle me completely.

Odi is still on the ship, rocked gently in Yuli's arms. She turns her head and looks around; I pertange her confusion.

"What was it like, Brân?"

Damon frowns at me, uncertain what it is I'm asking my uncle.

Brân understands. He understands that I want him to speak of his recent travels with the Migrant, of how he was taken from Selbourne to wander somewhere in another time-space for nearly three moon-tides. And he knows that I want him to speak aloud so that Damon can hear what he has to say. "Amos says he experienced my departure as a shaking of the earth," Brân says. He glances at Damon.

Damon's brows shoot up with sudden recognition. He witnessed that shaking from across the bay. He knows now what we're speaking of.

Brân continues, "I'd been trying to reach out to Mother—it had been less than three sixes since her death—when I pertanged what had happened to Maddie."

He turns toward me and I meet his eyes as my heart crumples a bit more, crushed by loss. First the loss of my eldmother Avienne followed by the murder of my mother Maddie. And now one of my daughters is missing.

"As soon as I knew about Maddie, I also pertanged how distraught you were, Meridia. How upset my brother was. So Amos and I went to chant songs in the chamber of mirrors. Knowing how connected Amos feels to the Song of All Songs, I began singing that and he joined in. As for what happened next—how it happened or why—I really have no explanation. My departure was not unpleasant. If the earth shook, I have no recollection of it. I experienced only..."

He stops. And then I feel it as he finds the words.

"A soft wind. A brief tension and then there I was. Elsewhere. It was very easy."

Damon wants to ask, "And where were you exactly?" but he knows that the answer to that question is deep and complicated. He barely comprehends where I was (or when) during my own much briefer sojourn with the

Migrant in the ancient caverns with Amergin and Sister Maggie and the rest.

"And when you returned?" I have to ask that as well.

"I was ready and I'd been searching for a way to come back. Then I heard you singing and I joined you. It felt joyful. Really, that's all I know, Meridia. As for the mechanism of how it occurred, I can't speak to that." He thinks perhaps there is something like music within the mirrors themselves and that singing interacts with that. Like plucking a stringed instrument. Like moving your fingers on the openings of a breath-filled flute.

He doesn't say these things, but I pertange them and hold them in my mind, contemplating what such an experience might be like. It calls to mind my first experience of the mirrors. Before I ever set foot on Selbourne, I walked with Amos Quint in his mirrored chamber and fell briefly into another world, another time.

Damon and Omi and I fall asleep on Selbourne in Amos Quint's living chamber. I take some comfort in the conviction that the ocean that surrounds this small island is the same ocean on which the ship rocks that carries my precious Odilia. How far does that ocean go? Where will their journey end?

Morning comes and I wake with Omi nuzzling at my breast. My heart sinks as I grasp once again the absence of her sister twin. Odilia is even farther away today. If only I could find Yuli. I know she's there. I see her face blurred and unsteady and I know I'm seeing it through Odi's nenish perception.

Amos Quint is much improved and insists on sitting up in his bed. I find what blankets I can to cushion him from the stone that forms the walls of his sleeping alcove.

He's trying to sort out the sequence of strange events, looking for words to explain them to us. And to himself.

"Just show me," I say. Amos Quint is Mundani and although he's not Revelant, he's spent so much time communing with the Migrant that the imagery of his verberations at times approaches the clarity of Melfar.

With carefully chosen words to guide his thoughts, he imparts his vision of the ship as it approached from a distance. "The Elossa," he says. "Such a large ship, with those white wings. I knew at once that this was something never before seen in these parts." He glances toward Brân with a question in his eyes but his story moves forward. "A few people came ashore on Selbourne and I felt that I ought to greet them," Amos says, "so I went down the stairs. They entered my reflection chamber as if they knew what they were doing." There was a hubbub of excited vocalization as two members of the group—both dressed in faded black and as like as simultwins—began to remove one of Amos's mirrors. A third person dressed in dull green directed the operation.

I see that it was indeed the old mirrors that interested them, the mirrors that were here when Amos Quint arrived on Selbourne nearly a return ago. "I tried to question them," Amos says, "but they didn't understand my words. Then I tried to stop them." He chokes on the image of what happened next. They struggled. The thieves dropped one of the mirrors and it broke, slashing Amos's arm as the pieces fell. His blood spilled onto the ground and onto the garments of one of the thieves.

"Why did they want the mirrors?" I ask.

Amos shakes his head and glances toward Brân.

Brân avoids meeting Amos's eyes. "Perhaps they knew somehow what those mirrors are, what they can do," he says. He's thinking about his own experience, how his image was reflected between those mirrors as he and Amos chanted the Song of All Songs, just before he found himself in another time-space. It happened there, in the presence of those mirrors.

"How would they know anything about that?" Amos Quint thinks he has an answer to that question, but he wants to know what Brân thinks.

"I think you're right," Brân says. "I think these Elossa people must know something about the ones who crafted those mirrors. And about this place."

"And then they went to Swarthpol," I say. I let my mind wander toward Father, asking him if he can think of anything that might have drawn them there. He's always resisted delving into his memories of Swarthpol, repelled by the things he experienced during the returns when he was imprisoned there. It was a time when his Melfar powers of aurynx and gnosic orb failed him utterly.

I catch a fleeting glimpse of a pond. A dark pond surrounded by massive broken stones.

6

Limn speaks to Yuli as if the strange little being might understand at least some of what she says. "We've landed at Port Sillick, Yuli. This place is called Port Sillick." She enunciates carefully and gestures toward the land. "In a few minutes we'll be going ashore. Try not to be scared. I'll stay with you if I can."

Yuli had heard some thumping and had felt the ship come to rest. She pertanges the presence of different creatures in the shallower waters. A few birds soar in the air. She nods as Limn speaks. Even though she doesn't understand the words, she thinks Limn is trying to be comforting, so she says, "Thank you, Limn." Yuli wants Limn to continue speaking, wants more opportunities to try and pick up the words and meanings of this disconcertingly empty language. For the first time in her life, Yuli craves words.

Tarja and Limn walk with Yuli—Limn ahead, Tarja behind—as they climb narrow stairs and emerge into the sunlight. Yuli shields Odi's eyes from the brightness and holds her close. They're met by two more people, one garbed in blue and the other in black. They usher Yuli and Limn and Tarja toward one of the two vehicles on the deck of the ship and assist them to climb on board. Limn offers to carry the infant, but Yuli refuses. Once they're seated inside the vehicle, Yuli squeezes her eyes shut, tensing as the craft lifts upward and begins to move forward. She feels the warmth of the sun shift across her face as they fly and turn and fly some more. Limn and Tarja exchange some words. Yuli doesn't open her eyes until the vehicle settles to a stop with a soft bump.

They're on the roof of a low building between two tall, mirrored towers, the sun reflecting from one onto the surface of the other. The glare is blinding.

Everything is a blur to Yuli. There are too many unfamiliar images and sounds and nothing deeper to fasten onto. Her orb encounters only blankness. She'd often wondered what it would be like to be blind or deaf. She thinks it would feel a lot like this.

Limn's heart beats faster as they enter the elevator that will take them up to Menza Uhr's office suite. She reminds herself once again that any requests she makes will have to be couched exclusively in terms of the Protocols. Limn detests the Protocols, the volumes of rules (and more volumes of interpretations of rules) that specify precisely what is to be done. Anything that is not specifically ordered in the Protocols is, by default, something that is not to be done. Something that cannot even be thought.

"This is an unexpected find," Menza Uhr says. Her face gathers into a frown as she rises from behind a heavy desk that dwarfs her slight form. Plush carpet covers the floor, producing an ominous quiet. "Troubling," she says. "There's nothing in the Protocols about nullion survivors anywhere other than Port Sillick's immediate environs. And of course those died out long ago or were exterminated to prevent transmission of their diseases." She directs a sharp look at Limn Ssu.

"They've been thoroughly checked out," Limn says. "We found no evidence of disease."

Menza Uhr doesn't look relieved. "And you say there are other nullions there? Different ones?"

"That's right, Menza-ji. There appear to be two distinct populations. The members of the other population are taller, dark-skinned, and more aggressive, and we... We declined to take any specimens." Limn is thinking of Amos Quint and wonders if "aggressive" is the right descriptor.

"Well, the artifacts you've brought back were the primary goal of your expedition, as I understood it, so, really, that's that. I'm not certain why I agreed to this little excursion in the first place." Menza Uhr is trying to remember the name of the substance Limn Ssu wanted to retrieve from the ancient research station.

Limn restrains her impulse to speak of her curiosity about what another expedition might uncover. She knows curiosity is no justification for the expenditure of scientific funds. Curiosity is a sign of deviance. It's one of the things that the daily supplement is designed to suppress. Limn is not supposed to know this.

Menza Uhr stands in front of Yuli and wrinkles her nose in disgust. "It's so yellow," she says. "Such a silly color." She pats the outer side of Yuli's left breast and watches it jiggle, barely suppressing a laugh. She pokes a finger at Odilia and checks to see if the iridescence has rubbed off. She wipes her finger on the hem of her red shirt.

"I suppose they can be dealt with in terms of the Protocols' guidelines for the display of relic species. We can set up some kind of habitat for them in the

Archaeozón. I'll put Macklin Wu in charge of that. She'll be aided by.." Menza Uhr glances at the glowing screen on the desk behind her. "Oh, a couple of Pas. The Wu will know who. Tarja can arrange interim care of the specimens."

Limn takes in a sharp breath and lowers her eyes. "With your permission, Menza-ji, I would volunteer to take on their care myself, in order to continue the behavioral description we've already begun to assemble for the Archaeozón." Limn is offended that a member of the Wu clone set has been put in charge of the exhibit. Wu are the guard set. Are Yuli and the baby no more than prisoners? Is the primary consideration to be securing them so that they don't escape? But Limn can't object. There are no grounds for such an objection in any of the Protocols. She also can't mention that she intends to carry out a detailed DNA analysis and continue her efforts to decipher Yuli's language. Her suspicion that these clearly intelligent hominins might still be capable of sexual reproduction must also go unremarked. The possibility (theoretical of course) of splicing such genetic information into existing clone sets mustn't even be thought about. But Limn has thought about it and wondered what experiences such changes might make possible. She wonders if it might revive certain relic behaviors that she's found so intriguing in some of the ancient stories she's read, the ones on the shelves labeled "Romance."

Menza Uhr frowns in distaste. "So primitive," she mutters. "I'm not sure why any well-designed human would volunteer to spend time with such creatures. But I suppose the information will add to the entertainment value of the exhibit. Provided it's framed tastefully. Okay, then." She extends both hands about waist high, palms up. "Permission granted, Limn. You are designated as their interim caretaker and adviser to the Wu setting up the exhibit."

During this exchange, Yuli watches, trying to manage her terror by concentrating on what is happening. She listens intently, trying to pick up words, studying facial expressions, straining to pertange any verberations emanating from the crowns of their heads, however faint. And trying to restrain the impulse to hum. She notices how much these people use their hands when they speak. Maybe that could help her gain access to what they're communicating with one another. Yuli is relieved when they finally turn to go. The woman in red frightens her. And Tarja looks annoyed.

"Where do you propose to keep them, Limn?" Tarja asks.

"For now, they can stay in my suite."

There's a barely audible snort of disgust from Tarja as she lowers her chin in acquiescence.

7

Sometime toward the middle of the night, I'm stirred into wakefulness. Naomi is fretting. I offer her my breast, but she refuses, instead beginning to cry in earnest. Not wanting to disrupt our entire group, I take Omi outside and make my way down the stairs toward the terrace in front of Amos Quint's middle chamber, the one with mirrors. The night is cool and clear and the moon bright, though not so bright as to obscure the expanse of stars that stretches from horizon to horizon. Omi continues crying and I think that if I take her inside the chamber, the thick stone will muffle the noise.

The entrance is narrow, and I stand just inside, shushing and rocking Naomi, taking a moment for my eyes to adjust to the deeper darkness within. The luminous stones bordering the chamber come into focus. Omi's attention is also drawn to the stones and she quietens. Her iridescence seems almost bright in this space.

Our images are reflected in the pieces of broken mirror lying at my feet, the pieces left behind by the Elossa thieves. I see clearly that this was not one of the mirrors Amos Quint crafted in his workshop. No, this was one of the mirrors that he found here when he arrived on Selbourne. That dark stain on the floor must be Amos Quint's blood.

I can't look away from the mirror. The pieces are larger than I'd expected. Except for a few small shards, the mirror seems to have broken into only two large pieces. I squat and lift one of them upright, propping it against an empty space on the wall.

It's only when I reach for the second piece of mirror that it happens. I pertange the same piercing sound I felt from the shard that Amos Quint sent to me, the one he intended for his son Lambert. It's a grinding screech that's simultaneously an earthy growl. The sound stabs at the center of my palm with icy bright fibers, pulling my hand toward the mirror. It's what I felt before. It's what made me push the shard away then, hide it, refuse to consider what it might be or the power it might hold.

This time I don't pull away. I take a deep breath, grasp the piece of mirror in my hand and position it carefully on the opposite wall, facing its partner. I wrench my hand away and tuck it protectively into the warmth beneath Omi's small body. My heart thrums loud and fast and my breath comes shallow. Naomi gazes up at me and in her face I glimpse that other face, the face of her sister twin Odilia. I think I hear Odi's orangey cry as it turns almost amber, pulling me, tugging on Naomi.

Do I really want to do this?

I sit down between the two halves of the mirror. Naomi begins to cry again, a mournful whine, oddly tuneful. I join her, humming a lullaby, a fragment of the Turquoise Canopy of Time.

Damon is looking for us, but I keep my seat. My heart beats wildly, filling my chest, my throat, my head, marking the cadence of our song as I rock and hum, singing with Omi, singing to Odi.

Light and sound spark between the mirrors as I open my orb and heart. My song surges full throated and robust as I open wider, and wider still. The song grows brighter, absorbing us as we move with it, through it, following a shimmering, shivering, melodious braid of orange and blue.

My ears resonate with Damon's grief-stricken cry of "Meridia!" I try to send him reassurance, but it doesn't find him.

We're too far away.

Yuli knows at once that I'm here. She was already awake, cradling Odi in her arms to quiet her. "Meridia?" Her question is an awestruck whisper.

Yes, it's me, Yuli. I reach toward her, trying to fathom what it is of me that she recognizes, what it is of me that has made this startling journey.

Yuli's sobs are a sandstorm of regret and apology as she holds Odilia out toward me. The two nens have stopped their crying. A colorful twist of orange and blue still shimmers between them.

I place a hand on Odilia's cheek and shudder with the strangeness. It feels almost like touching the surface of water. Except that it's my hand that is liquid.

What have I done?

8

"I've told you all I know!" Damon's anger and despair fill the little room and reverberate off the stone walls. "She was there and then she wasn't." He's chagrined at how skeptical he'd been when Amos Quint told him of Brân's disappearance from that same spot inside the mirrored chamber. This time he's seen it with his own eyes. And this time it's his own partner and their nen who have gone missing.

Brân sits quietly, gazing through the doorway and across the water. "I can't find her." His words fall like pebbles in a shallow pool. "I'm certain this must be the Migrant's doing." He doesn't look at all certain. "Meridia told me that Naomi was still connected to Odilia," he says. "Surely, wherever Odilia and Yuli are, that's where Meridia has been taken."

Damon groans as he slumps heavily onto a seat next to Brân, feeling awkwardly large and inept next to the old Melfar. "How do we get them back?" Damon's heart wrenches deep, dull purple. He's now lost his partner and both of his daughters. He raises his head and looks toward Amos Quint as the old Prophet stirs and rises into a sitting position.

"Are you saying that Meridia has vanished? Like Brân did?" His deep voice trembles, weak with disbelief.

"That's right," Brân says. "She was in the reflection chamber."

"The mirrors. But they took one of the mirrors. One of the two that were there when I arrived. One of the two that carried you away, Brân. You said you thought that two were required to...do whatever it is they do."

"But the one they left behind broke, remember?" Damon knows that it had to have been Meridia who arranged the remaining pieces to face each other. Did she know what she was doing? Would she have done this intentionally?

Amos Quint's shoulders hunch forward as he presses a hand against his forehead. "It's all my fault," he says. "I should never have come here. I'm just an old fraud who has no idea how to deal with powers such as those mirrors contain. I should have left them be."

"No, Amos." Brân speaks quietly. "This place is important. It holds things we need to know. Our history is here—Melfar and Mundani both. The Migrant has been teaching us and you're a part of that."

Damon would love to blame someone for the loss of his family, but he knows it wouldn't be right to blame Amos Quint.

"Don't try to humor an old man." Amos lies back down and turns to face the wall.

"Does Abél know about Meridia?" Damon appeals to Brân.

"He knows," Brân says. "He just doesn't know what to do."

"Do you know?" There's a note of belligerence in Damon's voice. He wishes he'd paid closer attention to what Brân said to Meridia when she questioned him about his experience, about what happened to him when he was taken from the mirrored chamber. Damon tries to recollect exactly what her questions were. Should he have known from that conversation what thoughts were taking shape in her mind?

"No," Brân says. "I don't know what to do. I wish I did. What I do know is that, Meridia being who she is, she's unlikely to return until she can come back with both of the nens."

"I don't understand any of this." Damon strides toward the door and bounds down the stone stairs, responding to a sudden impulse to immerse himself in this ocean that lies, vast and unfathomable, between him and the ones he loves most in all the world. As he reaches the narrow entrance to the mirrored chamber, he hesitates. He steps inside, just far enough to see the spot where he last saw his beloved partner and their nen. He chokes back a sob and turns away, continuing his descent, not stopping again until he stands waist deep in the surging waves. His eyes close as he tilts his head back and howls at the sky, his clenched fists pounding the water. He does it again and again until his hair is drenched and his eyes burn with the salt of ocean and tears.

He stares upward, then, blinking against the brightness of the rising sun and the reflected brightness of the water, both sky and sea so vast and blue and unknown. Sobs tear at his heart as he falls backward, letting the ocean hold him, rock him, connecting him to...what? To an endless everything. To Meridia and Naomi and Odilia and to these strange beings who came in a ship with white wings and carried Odi and Yuli far away across this ocean, tempting Meridia to follow.

Oh, Meridia, he thinks. *How can I find you? How can we bring you and our nens home?* He trusts that somehow she has found Odilia, that she's now with Yuli and both twins.

At length Damon finds his feet again and walks through the pulsing waves toward the beach. He finds Brân seated there, as if he'd been waiting for Damon.

Brân listens patiently as Damon voices the questions that were already mostly pertangible from the young man's tortured verberations. He responds first to Damon's query about where Meridia might be, wishing he could shape his uncertainty into something reassuring. "I'm afraid I can't tell you where she's gone, Damon. The Migrant took Meridia and me to many different places." He pauses, scratching in the sand with a broken shell. "But there were other places that only Meridia and her father experienced that seemed somehow linked to this location, to Selbourne. They told me about a city with tall, mirrored structures and flat stone paths."

"Do you think that's where she might be? In that place that she and Abél..." Damon doesn't know what word to choose. Visited? Dreamed? Remembered?

"Abél thinks the Elossa may have come from such a place. So if that's where Meridia is, it's a place I've never seen." Brân's mind is jolted suddenly by unbidden images of people hunched over tables, eyes fixed on glowing rectangles full of shifting pictures and lines of words.

Damon sits in stifled frustration. "Then, if you can't tell me where she is, tell me more about what you experienced when you were taken from Selbourne. How it felt to be wherever you were." Perhaps he can at least learn something about the *how* of Meridia's absence, if not the *where.*

Brân tries harder to put his experience into words, verberating as strongly as he can and hoping that Damon's Revelant powers will make it enough. He tries to convey the timelessness he felt after his disappearance from Selbourne, the sense that many different things were occurring at once and that it was simply a matter of which things he decided to attend to. "Similar to what we experience when we use the Canopy of Time but multiplied many times over. More intense. More complete," he says. "Pervasive."

Damon nods as if he understands, thinking of what Meridia told him about how the Canopy of Time enabled her to perceive landscapes as they were in the past. She could move confidently within such landscapes. He knows that his Revelant capabilities do not extend to such experiences of time.

Damon has never felt more helpless. He has a burning need to do something, but what can he do? "We need to build a ship," he says. "Build it and go get them back."

Brân gives him a sidelong glance. "I suppose we could try," he says. "But where would we go? We have no idea where these people came from. 'The north' is not much guidance."

Damon picks up a rock and hurls it out into the water. Suddenly he recalls his conversation with Meridia during their urgent journey over the mountains. She told him that one of the pictures left behind in the ruins of Fannan's old photography workshop in Woodclasp showed an image of a ship. Was it a ship like the one that landed on Selbourne? Might that photograph reveal more than just a ship?

He tells Brân about the picture. "Do you think it might hold something that could help bring Meridia back? Maybe some indication as to where these Elossa came from?"

"Perhaps it could help," Brân says, beginning to reminisce. "Uncle Fannan used to show us his photographs when I was just a boy. Some of them were quite fantastic. Retrieving the rest of his prints seems a good idea. And you think one of them may hold an image of a ship?" He reaches for a little pouch he carries slung under his left arm. He opens it and draws out a small stone.

Damon knows that it's a waif. Its color reminds him of the deep red cover stone on the vault containing Fannan's photographs. That stone is made of jasper.

"No, that one was from the Old Jasper," Brân says, "the one that holds the Song of Burning. It was never dedicated as it should have been, never a proper Benison, though it has its song." He takes the stone from his palm and holds it up, grasped between two fingers. "This is a waif of the Ancient Jasper," he says. "Its song is the Song of the Sea. As far as I know, it's the only Melfar song about the sea. This waif was given to me by my uncle Fannan." It's an unassuming little rock, rough and dull.

"A Song of the Sea? Do you know the song?"

"I don't," Brân says. He thinks his uncle may have sung it to him once or twice. Its images felt remote and exotic. Frightening? He should have asked his mother Avienne to teach it to him. It was too late for that now. "I'm sure Zara knows it."

Damon accepts the stone with a few words of gratitude and places it inside his pouch with his small collection of other waifs. "I'll go to Woodclasp," he says. "I'll leave for New Beniford tomorrow and then I'll go to Woodclasp and I'll find the photograph of the ship."

9

What Abél observed of the strangers from the Elossa stirred something within him, something deep and forgotten. Or at least something he'd tried to forget. It was something about Swarthpol. Abél's brother Brân told him that the Elossa people went southward in a second flying machine like the one that came to New Beniford. Abél is certain they went to Swarthpol. He tries to think why they might go to such a place. What were they looking for?

Abél has refused to think about Swarthpol for so many returns. He mostly says that he's forgotten what happened there, what it was like. Now he finds himself questioning the experience in a new way, wanting to remember. His memories are littered with questions: Was he really at Swarthpol all those returns? Or was he—sometimes—somewhere else? Somewhere far away, or perhaps some time far distant from his own? If Avienne were here, he would ask her about it. But she's gone now and Abél regrets that he avoided talking to her about Swarthpol while she still lived.

Swarthpol becomes an obsession.

Abél knew immediately the moment that Meridia vanished. In a dream, he saw her dissolve into the mirrors. But in his dream, they were not the mirrors in Amos Quint's reflection chamber. No, the mirrors of his dream were underwater, under very deep, very dark water that burned his eyes and orb. He'd awakened coughing, struggling for breath, his aurynx strangled into silence, his heart beating so hard and fast that he'd been unable to go back to sleep. His orb reached for Meridia. He'd seen her go, but he didn't know where she'd gone. He can't find her.

Abél had assured his daughter that it was the Migrant that took her on her strange journeys, took her to those deep caverns where she met ancient people. Melfar had learned so much about their history through Meridia's travels into the past and the songs she brought back. This time Abél isn't convinced that Meridia's absence is the Migrant's doing. But what other explanation is there? He thinks again about the disappearance of his brother twin Brân, about his wanderings in another time-space. He was taken from Amos Quint's chamber of mirrors on Selbourne, just as Meridia has been taken now.

I wish I could help you, Brân says, when Abél shows him his bewilderment and frustration. His fear. *When I was taken from Selbourne, there was...* and Brân shows his brother twin the shattering of space and time that Damon had observed from across the bay as something akin to a small earthquake. *And then I was just elsewhere.* Brân's memories show Abél warm waters with lapping waves, expanses of sparkling white sands, and trees like towering green blossoms. *I felt as if that strange place was where I'd always been. As if it was where I belonged.* He'd had no desire to leave.

That frightens Abél even more. Something stirs inside him as he asks himself: *Is this how I felt at Swarthpol?* It wasn't so much that he'd been physically unable to escape from Swarthpol; he'd had no desire to leave. He'd felt as if he'd always been there. As if time had come to a stop and there was no reason to try and be anywhere other than where he found himself.

That's it, brother. But for me it was also as if all of time was right there. I was able to slip easily from one time to another, one place to another. Except that they were all the same. All concurrent.

Abél's sparse eyebrows clutch at his orb, trying to pertange, to comprehend what Brân is describing. This part doesn't resonate with what Abél recalls of his experience at Swarthpol.

As they commune, the two brothers feel as if they're walking together, though Brân strolls along a sandy beach on Selbourne while Abél meanders a grassy path on the outskirts of New Beniford. Brân hums a tune with an odd, undulating cadence, notes rising and falling and rising again. An image of something bobbing on the water. Something sinking.

What song is that? Abél asks.

Brân sings it again, listening more closely this time. *I'm not sure. It just came to me.* It came with a childhood memory of walking with his uncle Fannan in the forests of Cödweg.

It's only a brief phrase, but Abél requests that Brân sing it once more and this time he tries to follow along. The tune is compelling. The images it suggests feel important.

Abél goes in search of Zara, the Melfar scholar who, aided by the Mundani historian and poet Vidvana, collected the old stories and songs that were compiled into the *Book of All Time*. Zara knows more of the Melfar songs than anyone else. So many of the songs were lost and broken during the Ancient Meeds when

Melfar were isolated from one another in their respective forests and later when they were driven from their ancestral homes by the Great Fires during the Old Jade and Old Jasper Meeds. Many Melfar were compelled to reside among Mundani, where they were scorned and vilified.

"It sounds like the Ancient Jasper song," Zara says. "Or part of it. I can show you what I know of it if you're interested. It was called Song of the Sea."

So that's it, Abél thinks. *Yes, please sing it, Zara.*

As she sings, Abél pertanges the sounds and smells of the ocean, images of a great ship bigger than anything ever built by Melfar or Mundani, stone steps on a barren, rocky island. As Zara finishes singing, Abél pertanges further images of ocean and a village, colorful small boats, and laughing children. *I didn't know your family came from Aldbeck*, Abél says.

They left long ago, in the time of the great floods. I only know the place through my eldmother's stories.

The Song of the Sea shows empty people. Could those be the same as the ones who arrived on the Elossa? The same ones who came here to New Beniford in their flying machine?

I suppose that could be, Zara says. *But if they were here in the time of the Ancient Jasper, what became of them? That was two Great Turnings ago.*

A Great Turning occurs every twelve meeds. The most recent Great Turning, which marked the start of the current New Marble Meed, happened less than six tides ago. Abél thinks of the twelve stones of the sequence of meeds (each meed twelve returns in length) as he cycles through them in reverse. He backtracks through four of the Ancient Meeds to reach all the way back to the Ancient Jasper. *So long ago*, Abél says. *The stone steps in the song's images look like Selbourne.* He hesitates, uncertain, but the thought emerges anyway. *And it mentions Swarthpol.*

In answer to Zara's unspoken query, Abél fights through stubborn layers of shame and regret to remind her of how he was imprisoned at Swarthpol for almost two meeds, falsely accused of stealing from the Mundani Clauster at Brightlea during his search for the Old Mica Benison, now known as the Ancient Mica since the Great Turning. He tells the story of his eventual escape. But as he recites the tale as he's told it before, new memories impinge. His thoughts show him a dark pool surrounded by towering black stones. Broken stones worn smooth by time. Within the pool, something flashes brightly.

10

I didn't sleep. Do I require sleep? I lean on the window glass and gaze out at this bizarre world, still uncertain how I came to be here. The window is huge, sealed shut, and as I look out, I'm also looking down. Far below, I see a flat stone walkway like the ones the Migrant showed me the first time they took me from Selbourne. I see mirrored towers that also remind me of those visions, though these gleam whiter and reach higher. There are lower buildings stretching away from each tower, connecting one to another.

What I don't see are trees. Why are there no trees here? No trees, no bushes, no plants, or flowers of any kind. Every surface is a constructed one. My verberations find no resonance in this place, landing flat and lifeless against the blank surfaces. Even the air is different. At home, the air is tinged with green. It feels alive. There are other colors at sunrise and sunset or when a storm is brewing. Here the air is colorless.

There are people. I see them walking or riding back and forth down there on the flat roads and paths. But these are Elossa people—physically present but otherwise barely alive. I can see that they speak to one another, but their speech generates no verberations, nothing pertangible. The people look so much alike. They all wear the same style of simple clothing in a limited array of dull colors. I can't even tell men from women. Or rather, no one looks particularly like either a man or a woman. I know that sometimes among Melfar and Mundani there are individuals who are neither man nor woman. Or occasionally they're both. But a whole population? And why are there no children?

I gaze down at my Naomi, her sweet face glistening in the pale morning light as she nestles so close against me that we feel almost one again. I yearn to hold Odilia like this. At least Odi has Yuli to cling to.

I crave comfort. Physical comfort. If only I could place my hand in Damon's reassuring grasp. But my present state is not like that and Damon is beyond my orb's reach. Odi and I can pertange one another. I know she hears my voice and recognizes my face. But her sister Naomi and I are not fully physically present here in this space. At least I don't think we are. Does Yuli see me, or only pertange that I'm here?

Yuli shouldn't have so much regret about what happened. Her regret is a sticky gray heaviness that she can't let go of. I feel it in myself when I think of my joyous journey to Fayredell for the Gathering, a journey without Naomi and Odilia. How can we deal with such regret, with the pull of it toward sadness and despair? Sometimes I try to brush it off, to say it was just circumstances, or to let regret stick to someone else, to blame them for my sense of not having what I want to have, not having done what I should have done, doing what I should not have done, hurting other people, not helping when I could have. These are the heavy, sticky things that form our regrets. How do we free ourselves from them?

I envelope Odi in a rosy cloud of affection (tinged only slightly brown with regret) and I'm heartened when she wriggles and coos in response, her eyes fastened on my familiar face.

The door opens suddenly and I freeze as two of our captors enter. Only my eyes move as I search frantically for a place to hide. But their eyes are fixed only on Yuli. I remain motionless, uncertain what to expect. One of the Elossa is dressed in green and the other in faded blue. The one in blue scans the room and I'm reassured when their gaze passes right over me without pausing. I breathe more easily. Yes, I'm breathing. There's a brief exchange of vocalizations. In their facial expressions I detect annoyance from the person in blue and nervousness from the one in green.

Do you understand anything they say? I ask Yuli.

She doesn't respond until after the two people have left, after the door is again securely closed.

I'm beginning to understand a little, Yuli says, verberating wordlessly. *The woman in green is called Limn.* She speaks the name softly. *The other one I never saw before today. I think Limn wants to help us.*

Woman? How can you tell?

I guess I'm really not sure. Maybe it's the way they treat me. More like a woman would. Not like a man.

There are footsteps and the door opens again. The person in green is alone now. She's vocalizing, but she's not speaking to Yuli. She's speaking into a thin box that she holds in her hand.

She knows your name, Yuli.

And Odi's, too. Oh, Meridia, I wish I knew what they intend to do with us. Will you be able to help us? Can you get us back to New Beniford?

I don't know. I'm not even certain how Omi and I got here. There's something about the mirrors in Amos Quint's chamber that made it possible. The only thing I'm sure of is that the link between Naomi and Odilia is what brought me to this place rather than anywhere else. But now that the nens are together... I think about the verse from the Turquoise Canopy of Time that Father taught me, the one that has brought me back home before. Could it also bring back Yuli and Odi? They were brought here not by the Migrant or with mirrors, but in a ship. I'm afraid to try.

I wish the woman in green would leave. Her presence makes me uneasy. My inability to pertange anything from her is maddening. Odi begins to wail and Omi answers in sympathy. Hearing the two nens crying together is oddly comforting to me. Until I turn and see the look of confusion on Limn's face.

11

Damon arrives in New Beniford haggard with worry over the fate of his partner and their nens. Going home has never felt so empty. He surrenders to tears as he enters the little cabin where there is no Meridia, no Naomi, no Odilia. He drops his backsack on the floor and sits heavily on the edge of the bed, a bed that can easily hold four. It's far too big for one. Emptiness weighs on him more heavily than the sack he carried over the mountains.

Thirst draws him back to himself at last and he rises to fetch a drink. On the counter beside the jug he finds a piece of discarded paper. As he drinks, he picks the paper up and spreads it smooth. It's a scrap of photographic paper. Is that an image? It's hard to make out. There's a pale disk that might be the moon. Damon pushes the paper aside and looks toward the food cupboard, suddenly aware that he's hungry.

He finds a few dried guavacots and a piece of very stale nutbread. Still standing at the counter, he gnaws off a piece of bread and chews. It's not the kind of meal that requires sitting down at a table. He sits instead in the doorway, leaning against the frame, one foot outdoors, one indoors. Finishing his paltry meal, he drinks a little more water, wishing it were tea, and walks around to the garden. The garden lies on the north side of the house. From here, he can look in the direction that Yuli and Odi were taken. Meridia and Omi are with them now, too. He's sure of it. Where else would she go? He reminds himself of how diligent and nurturing Yuli was whenever she cared for the nens.

The garden is where Abél finds him. "Good day, Damon," he says. Abél rarely has to greet people verbally and it feels awkward now, but Damon's thoughts were far away.

Damon turns slowly. He finds it impossible to utter the expected response about it being a fine day. "Have you been able to contact her? Do you know yet where she is?" Of course he's speaking of Meridia. He searches for the physical resemblance between his missing partner's father standing beside him and the woman herself, as if the kinship of amber-colored skin, pale eyes, and curly hair might establish the connection he seeks.

Abél moves closer and reaches up to place a hand on Damon's shoulder, gazing northward alongside him. "I know nothing more than you do, Damon. It's like it was when my brother Brân disappeared." Abél knows this is more than a Turquoise journey with the Migrant. Perhaps even something more obscure than Brân's prolonged wanderings in time. He won't share these doubts with Damon.

"But wasn't Meridia in communication with Brân while he was gone? How was she able to do that?" There's a pulse of pale lavender around Damon's heart, a hint of hope.

"I never understood that. Brân was lost to me. I suppose my orb wasn't strong enough to reach him." He's struck by the thought that maybe Swarthpol damaged him more permanently than he knew. His mind swirls in darkness.

Damon's heart shrinks gray and sad. Why does he think that Abél isn't telling him everything he knows? "Brân came back," Damon says, grasping at hope. "How did he do it?"

Abél folds his arms over his chest and turns toward Damon, his eyes on the patch of earth between them. "Again, I'm not sure." He's also not sure how much he ought to tell Damon about what Brân said about time. About timelessness.

"When I spoke with Brân on Selbourne," Damon says, "he tried to explain something about the sense of timelessness he felt when he was...away." Damon's shaggy brows knit together as he scuffs at a tree root with the toe of his shoe. "One thing I do know, Abél, is that as long as the Elossa are holding Odilia, Meridia will never be ready to come home." Damon's voice is taut as a bowstring. A tortured sigh escapes his lips. "At the very least I'd like to be able to communicate with her. To know she and the nens are okay." The rosy pulse around his heart grows stronger and the Quartz bead hanging on its braided cord against his chest feels warm against his skin. The bead was Meridia's gift to him on the day of their partnering. "I don't understand where these people came from. And in such a ship!" He thinks once again about the possibility of building such a ship.

"Zara has told me about an Ancient song that mentions a ship," Abél says.

"The Song of the Sea," Damon says. His Revelant sensibilities caught a fleeting image from Abél, an image of a great ship foundering on the waves. "Brân told me about that song. Well, he told me there was such a song, though he said he didn't know it. And he gave me a waif of the Ancient Jasper that he said holds the song."

Abél tells Damon what he's learned from Zara about the Song of the Sea. His knowledge consists of images and he struggles to find suitable words, hoping that Damon can pertange some of the imagery even if his words are not quite right. He speaks about a ship with white sails like wings, about empty people, about a desperate rescue.

"Meridia told me she thought there might be an image of a ship in one of the photographs we left behind in your uncle Fannan's workshop in Woodclasp," Damon says. He sighs deeply. "I thought I would go and see if I could retrieve the picture." In his mind, Damon is already on his way to Woodclasp.

"Yes, I suppose such a picture might help us." Abél wonders what else Fannan's photograph might contain besides the image of the ship. He turns away from Damon, gazing northward again. "We thought the *Book of All Time* was a complete account of our history," he says. "Apparently it isn't."

12

Naomi and I are solid to one another, which is fortunate. It means I can still feed her from my breasts. Or at least it feels like I'm feeding her and she seems to find it satisfying. But since I'm eating nothing, I don't know how that's possible. What would I eat? Nothing in this world is available to me. I'm not hungry anyway, so this has become one of those things that I don't understand and that I choose not to worry about. As long as Naomi and I stay healthy, I won't worry. Not about that. And for now, we seem to be healthy.

It's afternoon and Yuli and Odi are napping. I watch Yuli for a while, her eyes veiled in sleep yet seeming to search back and forth. The bed Limn has supplied for her looks soft and comfortable. I try to imagine myself lying there, enfolded in its silky softness and lost in the oblivion of dreaming. Maybe all of this is only a dream.

I turn to examine the other furnishings in the room. There are cupboards and chests but whatever is inside them is not mine and would be nothing familiar. I startle with a glimpse of movement over my right shoulder and turn to see...a mirror. My eyes measure the distance and the angle between the mirror and where I stand and my heart shrinks with the realization that my image ought to appear there. It doesn't. I reach a hand toward the mirror and notice a disturbance in its reflected image, like a breath through a cloud of incense. Is that what I am now? An illusion? A breath? I cleave more closely to the solidity of Naomi in my arms. *What have I become?* And then: *What can I do?*

I regret leaving my waifs behind on Selbourne. When I left Amos Quint's sleeping chamber with my crying nen, I expected to be back shortly. Instead I'm here. I have my songs, of course, but the waifs give the songs strength. What waifs would I use anyway? What songs? What effects would a song have coming from a being such as I've become?

Odi begins to whimper and stirs in the odd little bed Limn has supplied. I reach toward her with my hand, but also with a few notes of an Amethyst lullaby. She quiets and settles. At least my singing can still reach my nen.

Limn has provided Yuli with everything she thinks someone needs to care for a nen. The bed where Odi sleeps is actually an elaborate machine. Yuli showed me how it can rock back and forth and make noise that we think must be Elossa music. The sounds are not beautiful; they convey no images. There's a panel of buttons on the side of this nen container, and when Yuli pressed one of them, the machine began bouncing up and down instead of swaying side to side. It was gentle bouncing, but Odi still found it disturbing so Yuli made it stop. One of the buttons causes lights to shine on the ceiling, creating colored patterns. Odi seems to like that. She's still most content when Yuli is holding her. When will I be able to hold her like that again?

Yuli turns and stretches. I watch her, trying to discern the meaning of the pulsing pattern of green and turquoise she verberates. The colors seem to enfold a face. To caress it. There's a hint of a smile and a brief dimpling of her cheek. *Who are you thinking of, Yuli?*

She sits up in her bed and turns toward me with wide eyes, then drops her chin in embarrassment. And then she shows me. He's a fine young Melfar man I've seen often. I think I ought to know his name.

We were just beginning to talk about our partnering, Yuli says. *His name is Umet.*

And then it comes to me. *He's the artist who worked with Elvrid to craft the cover for the Book of All Time, isn't he?* Elvrid printed the book and bound it.

Yuli verberates rosy golden waves like a spring meadow. *It was your design, Meridia. Umet thought it was wonderful.*

Of course you'll see him again, Yuli. We'll find a way. I do my best to convey a confidence my heart doesn't feel.

Yuli's brief surge of pleasant memories lapses into gravelly sadness. She paces, staring out the window. *It's not just that there's nothing I can do about our situation,* she says at last. *Nothing I can do about getting us out of here. There's simply nothing to do here at all. Nothing but tending to Odilia.*

She's right, of course. I'm reminded of a woman who lived near Mother and me in Temur who kept birds in a cage. *Limn seems to want to interact with you, Yuli. She tries to keep you company, to keep you occupied.*

Yuli scowls. *Limn showed me how to operate a machine that speaks in her language, but I haven't used it. It seems so pointless. I could learn to mimic the words, but I'd have no idea what they mean. At least when Limn is speaking I can watch her face and her hands and get some notion of meaning. Words coming out of a box are worse than useless. And the food is so strange. What I wouldn't give for a nice dish of warm guavacot pudding!*

I can't relate to Yuli's hunger. I have no desire for food of any kind. But, like her, I'm restless. Maybe I could go out among these people and learn more about this place where we've landed.

Yuli pertanges my vague longing. *Why can't you do that, Meridia? Go out there and then you can come back and tell me what you see, what you learn.*

I think again about the woman with her caged birds. I sneaked over to her house one day and let the birds out. The woman was furious; the birds were quickly snatched up by a thrushawk. I blanch, thinking of what might happen to us if we tried to escape our cage here. *I'm afraid,* I say. *I don't know whether these people can sense my presence or not. And I certainly don't know what they might do if they did notice me. No, I'm better off staying here with you and Odi.*

Yuli pauses her pacing and takes in a deep breath, expelling it slowly. *You're the Calumet, Meridia. Can't you figure out some way to take us home?*

There's an accusing note to Yuli's query. She knows the answer to her question already. I'm strangled by my silent *no.*

We stand together and watch people and vehicles as they move about on the street below our window. The people walk quickly, not even looking at one another. Some of them go inside one or another of the buildings and sometimes they come out with parcels. I think those are shops, but I can't tell what they're selling.

Limn brings in Yuli's supper and a couple of bottles for Odilia—one for now and another for when she wakes during the night. Again she urges Yuli to turn on the talking machine, which Yuli does. Limn nods vigorously and smiles. She sits, watching Yuli eat, tilting her head and leaning slightly forward each time Yuli takes a bite of something different. I think she's trying to figure out what Yuli likes and what she doesn't like. This time the meal includes something that looks like nabo squash, but when Yuli tastes it, she frowns, swallows quickly, and doesn't eat any more of it. I don't recognize anything else on the plate.

At one point, Naomi starts to fuss and Limn glances in my direction. But then Yuli pats Odilia, as if she were the one making the noise. Yuli finally pushes her plate back to signal that she's finished eating. Limn picks up the plate. She scans the room once more before departing.

Do you think she heard Naomi? I ask.

Maybe. I guess we'll find out eventually. Yuli grins nervously. *Or you could try talking to Limn yourself.*

My heart shrinks at the thought. No, I won't try that. I nurse Omi while Yuli feeds Odi from the bottle. Yuli dozes off, cradling Odi next to her on the bed. I'm glad she didn't put my nen back inside that strange rocking, bouncing contraption.

Yuli's frustration only magnifies my own. She's right. If I'm a true Calumet, I ought to be able to do something about our situation. Of course, I'm still new to being a Calumet. I think again about my waifs. The one waif that surges forward in my awareness is the first one I acquired—the Old Jade with its Song of the Calumet, the song that introduced me to my eldmother Avienne. I didn't know she was my eldmother at the time. I didn't know she was a Calumet. I'd never even heard of a Calumet.

I begin singing the song softly, so as not to disturb Yuli. As I sing, I visualize Avienne as I saw her then, vibrantly youthful, dancing among swirls of color, her hands tracing graceful patterns in the air. Her image congeals and brightens...

There you are, Avienne says.

Avienne? Is it really you? You're here? I reach toward her and our hands almost touch.

I think I'm here, she says. There's a playful look in her eyes that almost brings tears to mine. *I knew you were calling me, but I couldn't tell from where. However did you end up here?* She looks from me to Yuli to the window, which glows with the last light of the setting sun.

Then you don't know where I am either. I show her the mirrors and my despair and the ship carrying empty people docked at Selbourne. I move backward in time through the story, but she doesn't seem to mind. *Can you help us, Avienne?* She's standing by the window and I note that her form doesn't entirely obscure the view. She seems as young as she did the first time I saw her.

I really don't know how I might help, Meridia. It took some doing to gather myself into Avienne when I felt your call. I'm only Avienne now when someone needs me to be. And getting here may have taken me longer than I thought. Time is a fragile thing when you are as I am.

I'm not certain what she means, but I press ahead, hopeful that she can at least bring some clarity to my own confused state of being. *Were you aware of Brân when he was traveling with the Migrant?*

Yes, of course.

Was it you who helped him come back?

No, Avienne says. *That was all his doing. And yours. I wasn't able to help. His state of being was different from mine. I had merged completely with the Migrant. He hadn't. Just as you haven't. You're still a living being wedded to a particular time and place, a particular history. Besides, my son never asked for my help. He seemed content being as he was and never reached out for me, though I know he was aware of my companionship from time to time.*

You brought him back when he was killed by the Palinjians. I call up the image of Avienne singing Brân back to life as Gerd and I searched for him, guided by my avian companion, Duende.

Yes, but I was there to bring Brân back. I was still a living being tied to that time and place. Not as I am now.

Perhaps I understand, eldmother. So maybe this time it will have to be Brân and Father bringing me back. And Damon. I think of the strong heart connection Damon has with me and with Naomi and Odilia.

You may have to do a lot of the work yourself.

What can I do? I feel so powerless. Which songs should I sing, eldmother?

Sing the ones I gave you. She shows me Amethyst, Jade, and Granite. *I can help you with those songs. I can help you sing Hope and Pacification and Firm Resolve. Though even those songs may not be enough.*

13

Orban willingly agrees to accompany Damon to Woodclasp. It was his home, after all, the place where he lived and worked with his Melfar partner Emba, the place where he lost her. Orban adored Emba and marveled at her abilities as a healer. Orban is Mundani, but the lighter brown of his complexion and glints of russet in his dark hair bear witness to his origins beyond the eastern forest of Cödweg. The militant tendencies of western Mundani never appealed to Orban.

Abél advises the two Mundani men to take someone Melfar along with them.

"Who do you recommend?" Damon asks. "Maybe Jalu?" He knows that a Melfar companion would be able to pertange danger along the way as well as raise protection canopies if needed. He also knows how Meridia and Emba had been able to pertange more from Fannan's photographs than either he or Orban could. Jalu is a friend and would be an amiable companion.

Abél has a different suggestion. "Take Umet," he says. "Zara has been teaching him and says he's a gifted singer with a strong gnosic orb. I'm sure he could help you with the pictures."

Damon remembers Umet's work on the *Book of All Time*. Umet is the artist who put Meridia's vision into a cover design. He asked a lot of questions about photography. Damon recalls him as being rather tall for Melfar, with golden eyes, a tousle of pale brown curls, and a smattering of brownish spots across the ruddy amber of his nose and cheeks.

"Yes, that's him," Abél says. "You know, Umet and Yuli have been planning to partner soon. He was in Fayredell for the Gathering but came here to New Beniford as soon as he knew about what happened to Yuli. And of course, being Melfar, he knew immediately. He's as distraught as you are over what happened, Damon. He was asking me yesterday what he could do to help get Yuli and our Calumet back, so I'm certain he'd be more than willing to go with you."

Damon hadn't known about Umet and Yuli, but he feels an immediate bond with this young Melfar man whom he's so far known only casually. He'll be more than a companion in this project. He'll be an ally. "Yes, we should take Umet with us," Damon says.

"Also," Abél says, "Umet has worked with Gerd and Roqu, learning their combat techniques, though hopefully you won't encounter any need for those skills. You and Umet should both speak with Zara before you go. If my uncle Fannan made a picture with a ship, it may well have been a photograph from the Song of the Sea. Zara can tell you more about that song."

Damon watches as Abél fidgets with a scrap of paper he found lying on the table. His hands are unsteady and his skin has grown sallow, his cheeks more sunken than Damon remembers. His eyes are veiled in sadness.

Abél holds up the bit of paper for Damon to see. "Where did this come from?"

"It's just trash." Damon glances toward the trash box in the corner.

Abél smooths the piece of paper out on the table and leans over to scrutinize it more closely. "Did you make any photographs of the Song of Solitude?"

"I don't remember. Or rather, I don't recall that we did. Why do you ask?"

"The image on this print looks like it could be from that song." Abél strokes his beard, inclines his head left, then right, reviewing the imagery of the Song of Solitude. It's about the moon's solitary journey, its faithful repetition of its cycle of growth and loss, its independence from the sun cycle of seasons. At least that's what he thinks it's about. He turns the paper over to examine the other side. There are broken lines of scribbled numbers.

Damon watches him curiously. "I found that piece of paper on the counter over there when I returned," he says, pointing toward the corner with the high cupboard. He had spoiled a batch of photographic paper at his workshop and brought some of it home to use for making notes. But that paper didn't have any images on it.

"Curious," Abél says.

After Abél leaves, Damon picks up the scrap of paper and starts to throw it away. He hesitates. Then he places it into a pocket of his backsack.

14

Damon and Orban and Umet set out for Woodclasp just before dawn, each man carrying a backsack containing basic supplies for the journey. It takes them no more than a couple of hours to attain the main road that will take them to Fayredell, their first destination. Now that the threat of harm from bands of Palinjians has diminished, the three men can travel more safely on Mundani roads. They'll make faster progress than would be possible on Melfar ways, which meander through re-emerging trees and brush and along stream beds that once again flow with water. The men plan to acquire more of the provisions they'll need for their onward journey at the well stocked shops in Fayredell.

The young, intended partner of Yuli was more than eager to join them. He and Damon went together to speak with Zara the evening before their departure. She sang the Song of the Sea for them and Umet joined in, fumbling the notes only a couple of times.

"The images of the song show a ship that may be like the one that took Yuli and Odilia," Zara says. "Brân says that one also had broad white sheets extending on both sides, though I can't tell you what they were used for. There are long-ago stories about ships with sheets to catch the wind but I don't think that's what these did." She mentions some images she saw in one of the books Elvrid brought to New Beniford from his bookshop in Temur.

Damon is grateful for Zara's proficient use of the Mundani language to convey the imagery to him. His Revelant sensibilities don't extend to pertanging detailed images exclusively from song.

As Damon walks along the well traveled road to Fayredell with his two companions, he reviews the images he constructed from Zara's words, trying once more to call up images he may have seen on photographs that are still sequestered in Fannan's ruined workshop in Woodclasp. He finds no ships among his fragmented memories.

The men set a brisk and steady pace, but not so fast as to preclude conversation. "Were you able to stay in touch with Yuli at first?" Damon asks Umet.

"Yes. She kept trying to reassure me that she and your nen were not being harmed. But I could tell how frightened she was. I'm sure she must have been even more frightened once she was so far away that we could no longer pertange one another. Do you think Meridia is with her now?"

"I'm sure that's where Meridia went. She was so desperate about Odilia. Yes, I'm certain that's where she's gone."

"Yuli told me she was very sorry about what happened." Umet's tone is quiet, sad.

"I know," Damon says. "But none of it was her fault. She's so devoted to Naomi and Odilia. And they're very fond of her. I'm sorry Yuli's devotion led her to harm."

As they travel on, Damon fends off the doubts that niggle at him about the purpose of this journey. How can retrieving a photograph possibly bring Meridia and the twins home again? His hand goes to the pouch that hangs around his neck on a sturdy cord. Meridia made it for him when she gave him the Amber waif. She plaited the cord with her own fingers. The waif of the Ancient Amber was for protection on his journey to Temur to retrieve photographic equipment. Meridia used its Song of Turning well.

The pouch also contains Damon's own destiny stone—a fragment of the Old Marble. He's carried that one since he was only twelve passages old, though he was never sure what it was until Meridia told him. He thinks about the waif of the revitalized Ancient Mica with its new song of Calling the Rains. It's there in his pouch. And of course there's a waif of the New Marble. The Song of All Songs belongs to that one and Damon was witness to the ritual dedicating its Benison. No, not merely a witness. He was a participant in the profound experience that they all shared.

The waif of the Ancient Jasper that Brân gave him on Selbourne only days ago is there in his pouch, too. He thinks about its Song of the Sea. Last night he'd added the waif of the Old Jasper that he found when he first excavated the photographs from Fannan's old workshop. The Old Jasper was never a Benison, but it had its song—the Song of Burning, which was meant as protection against the Great Fires.

It's nearly nightfall on the second day when they approach Fayredell at last. Umet consults a waif of the Old Quartz and lets it guide them to a shed just outside the town where they can rest for the night. They're avoiding Mundani inns, uncertain whether a Melfar man like Umet would be welcome there. Prejudice takes a long time to eradicate.

"This is in better shape than I expected," Umet says, explaining how some of the secret Chanters' gathering places are being refurbished and used more openly. "They've always been way stations for Melfar travelers," he says, "but look at this one now. It's almost like a proper inn." He adds that this particular way station has a history as a place where Melfar met with Mundani Chanters to recite songs and poems.

Damon wonders if this might be the place where Ann Landry led Meridia for refuge after she was attacked by Palinjians in Fayredell. Damon's heart stings with the memory of Meridia's solitary journey. He reflects for a moment, realizing that happened not even a full return past. But it was before Meridia knew anything at all about being Melfar, only about being a despised Shoon. And now she's the avowed Melfar Calumet. Damon thinks about how he and Meridia had started out together that day, searching for Brân who, at the time, they only knew as the vagrant peddler who had sold Damon a photographer's bag in which he discovered a waif of the Old Jade. When Meridia sought the safety of this shed, Damon was being held captive by Palinjians. Damon is comforted by the belief that it must be the same shed.

The three men find their needs well supplied. There's a small stove, a supply of cooking blocks, and a stack of bedding that looks clean and comfortable.

"I'm thankful that we don't have to stay in town," Orban says. "After living so many years with Emba, off to ourselves there in Woodclasp, I'm afraid I have little tolerance for the noise and movement of the towns."

Damon agrees. He's become accustomed to the quiet life of New Beniford; it reminds him of the farm where he spent most of his childhood. The last time Damon was in the town of Fayredell was for the Gathering and the presentation of the *Book of All Time*. That was less than two sixes ago. It had been such a joyous event, but that joy is forever tainted for him now, knowing that even as they partook of the feast of celebration, strangers were approaching New Beniford to steal away his precious daughter Odilia. Damon willingly forgets that Odilia and Naomi are not physically his offspring. He finds the fact irrelevant.

The next morning, Damon steels himself for their entry into Fayredell. They plan to pay a visit to Lambert Quint after shopping for the supplies they'll require.

"Should we visit Gerd, too?" Damon says. He feels a certain kinship with Gerd through her close relationship with Meridia's mother Maddie. That and the fact that it was Gerd and her son Fergus who found Damon after he'd been murdered by Palinjians. Restored by the Migrant, but still barely alive, he was nursed back to health with the aid of Gerd and Maddie. And Meridia.

"Gerd isn't here anymore," Umet says. "She's gone to live in Temur. In her friend Maddie's house." He glances quickly toward Damon.

Damon nods toward Umet. *Yes, I know that house well.*

I keep forgetting that you're Revelant. Umet sends an affable wave of orangey goodwill toward Damon and then quickly redirects the conversation. "Gerd has left Roqu in charge of the Fayredell training academy."

After shopping for supplies, they find the son of Prophet Amos Quint in the newly built cabin next to his hall of mirrors. The hall itself is a public space, open for visitors day and night. Damon had noticed Lambert's cabin when he was on the grounds for the Gathering. He thought then that it seemed uncomfortably tiny. Now that it's not crowded around by people, it looks more commodious. It's situated at a short distance from both the hall of mirrors and the tower-like structure that houses the *Book of All Time* and its accompanying framed photographs, the ones Damon printed with the aid of Zara and Meridia and other singers.

Lambert Quint's soft features harden and the silky brows above his pale brown eyes converge as he takes Damon's hand protectively between his. "We were horrified to hear about what happened in New Beniford," he says. "Damon, I know you and Meridia must be sick with worry."

Damon's heart sinks. Lambert is still unaware that Meridia is also gone. Well, how would he have learned about it? Only by being told by someone Melfar. Someone willing to spread the devastating news of their Calumet's baffling absence. Damon looks to Orban, imploring him to explain it to Lambert.

Lambert listens with his head down, pinching his brows together with the fingers of one hand. When he looks up, his eyes are dark with worry. He turns toward Umet and expresses his sorrow for Yuli's abduction. "Such an unfortunate set of events," he says. "Surely Meridia will find a way to come back. To bring all of them back. You can't blame her for wanting to be with her missing nen."

"I'm afraid it's not that simple," Damon says.

"Yes, I was afraid you'd say that. I guess I want it to be just a passing thing. A temporary inconvenience. Oh, Damon, she was so wonderful at the Gathering. Her words inspired so many Mundani here in Fayredell. She's needed." He looks away and his voice goes low and breathy. "This can't be happening."

Damon is still lost in the story, still trying to understand that what happened did in fact happen. To understand how it happened. "The mirror fragment that led the intruders to our cabin is the one Amos had asked her to bring to you, Lambert. Amos thought you might be able to make use of it for your meditations. But when Meridia sensed that it could be something dangerous, she left it behind. She didn't say it, but I think she felt it could have been a disruption for the Gathering."

"Dangerous? She told me about the mirror shard and apologized for not bringing it." Lambert says, thinking back on his conversation with Meridia in the early hours before the Gathering when they'd talked at length about so many things. "She didn't explain to me why she left it. She just said she wrapped it in a scrap of paper and tucked it away in a cupboard. If those people... Elossa? Is that what you're calling them? If those Elossa had come here to Fayredell in their flying machine, who knows what might have happened? Though I doubt it could have been any worse than what transpired in New Beniford. And now Meridia herself gone!"

Damon is scowling. "Would you say that again Lambert? What Meridia told you she did with the mirror fragment."

Lambert tilts his head to one side and answers slowly. "She told me that she hid it. She wrapped it in a bit of paper and hid it in a cupboard." Lambert watches, bewildered, as Damon fumbles for something in his backsack.

Damon holds up what looks to Lambert like a corner torn from a printed photograph. "I think that's what this is," he says. "I think this is the paper the shard was wrapped in." He turns toward Umet. "Could you ask Abél if that would mean anything to him? Remind him that it's the scrap of paper he found on my table."

Umet wants to ask, "Why?" but instead he closes his eyes and goes to Abél. After a moment his head jerks back. Then his chin drops to his chest, his ear tilted upward as if he's listening. He nods.

"Well?" Damon says.

"If I understand Abél correctly," Umet says, "he thinks the mirror shard could have left the imprint you see there because..." Umet takes a deep breath. "Okay, here's what he remembers: Meridia took the shard to Abél one day and he wanted to see what kind of thing it was, so he laid one of his waifs next to it and...and there were fibers of sound. And somehow he thinks the mirror shard drew the song out of the waif and that it was that song that was later imprinted on the paper. That's what I understood anyway." Umet shakes his head and flicks his sleeve across his eyes and orb. This is all more complicated than he'd realized.

"What? How could all of that be?" Lambert says. "Why does Abél think that's what it is?"

"Oh." Umet clears his throat and composes himself. "He says he's sure the image on the paper is from the Song of Solitude, which belongs to the waif of the Ancient Granite that he set down that day next to the mirror shard."

"What a remarkable artifact!" Lambert says. "How did an ordinary Prophet like my father manage to craft such a thing?"

"He didn't," Damon says, sounding apologetic. "There were two mirrors already in the cavern when your father arrived on Selbourne. The shard was from one of those. And it was one of those original mirrors that the Elossa carried away." What Damon wants to know is how a piece of his photographic paper could be imprinted in this way. He tries to recollect how it was exactly that he'd spoiled it, making it unfit for his process. Too much ecphorite in his emulsion? Was that it? He calls to mind what Meridia and Abél explained to him about how ecphorite is used in the crafting of Benisons, about how it encodes the songs into the structure of the stones.

They sit in silence for a while, absorbing this new information. Then Lambert asks what he is convinced is the most important question: "Do you have a plan for getting Meridia and Yuli and the twins back?"

"Not yet," Damon says. "But if these Elossa have been here before, we think learning more about that incident might help. Before she left, Meridia told me that there may have been a photograph of a ship among the prints we left behind in Fannan's old workshop in Woodclasp.

You know that Fannan's photographs are far more than simple pictures. Anyway, Woodclasp is where we're going. We intend to collect the rest of Fannan's photographs." Saying it aloud makes Damon realize that this is really more of a vague hope than anything that could be the start of a viable plan. He falls silent.

Orban reminds Lambert that Fannan was the Melfar photologist who devised the method Damon uses to print images from the verberations of Melfar songs. "For all the returns Emba and I lived at Woodclasp, we never knew what was left there in the ruins of Fannan's old workshop. When we found the cache of his photographs, Damon and Meridia weren't sure what they were or what anyone might be able to do with them. We all agreed that it was best to leave some of them stored away there."

Damon rejoins the conversation. "Abél and Brân think there may be some connection between the Elossa and a story relayed in one of the old Melfar songs. It's called Song of the Sea."

"A Benison song? What was the Benison? When was it dedicated?" It's clear that Lambert finds the Song of the Sea to be a more promising lead than a buried photograph that may or may not show a picture of a ship. Possibly a ship that will prove to be totally unrelated to the one that took Yuli and Odilia away.

"It's not a song that I've printed on any photographs. Zara told me what she knew about it." When Damon expresses uncertainty about the provenance of the Song of the Sea, Lambert suggests that they take a look at the *Book of All Time* to see what's said about it there.

Just outside the shrine where the book is kept, they encounter Ann breth Keira and Fergus breth Gerd. "Good day," Ann calls out.

"Fine day," Damon says, his flat tone giving the lie to the verbal formula.

"We were just going inside to consult the book," Lambert says. "Would you mind assisting us in searching for something?" He turns to Damon and continues speaking. "Ann has become a sort of guide and caretaker for the book whenever she's here and not at the school or out planting trees. I think she's read it all the way through several times."

"What is it you're looking for?" Ann asks.

"A reference to a Song of the Sea," Lambert says. "They think it may make reference to the same people who recently landed at Selbourne."

"The ones who kidnapped Yuli and your nen? We're just devastated about that Damon. I can only imagine how upset you and Meridia must be."

"There's more to that story, Ann, but I'll tell you about it later," Lambert says.

Damon is grateful for Lambert's unwillingness to discuss Meridia's plight openly. "Zara says the Song of the Sea belonged to the Ancient Jasper Benison," he says, bringing the conversation back on track.

The building that houses the book is not large, little more than a long hallway, with the book itself secured inside a glass structure just inside the central doorway. The central tower has windows on all sides so that the space is always well lighted. Some of the windows have panes of brightly colored glass. The halls extending in both directions are lined with photographs that Damon produced using the process he learned from studying Fannan's work.

Lambert takes a key from around his neck and unlocks the glass lid of the box to access the book.

"The Old Jasper was never dedicated as a Benison," Ann says, "but it had its Song of Burning. The Old Jasper Meed began in passage 618. The Ancient Jasper would have been 144 passages before that." Ann is clearly proud of her developing knowledge of Melfar calendrics.

Ann opens the book carefully, touching only the edges of its pages as she turns them gently, almost reverently. "Here it is," she says. "The Ancient Jasper. Song of the Sea. Dedicated in Mundani passage 474." She does a quick calculation and announces, "That would be 192 passages ago." She studies the page, then turns back a few more pages. "That was a relatively peaceful time for Melfar, while they were living undisturbed in their forest towns and villages. Oh." Ann turns a page back and forward. "Here's the page where Vidvana and Zara have put images from the Song of the Sea into words. Shall I read it?"

"Yes, please do." Damon listens expectantly as he and Orban hover over Ann's shoulder to see the printed words as she reads. Umet stands to one side and closes his eyes.

"'In the region where Cesta meets Serani, Melfar built a boat and set it on the waters of the sea in the care of empty people. They spoke words that none could either comprehend or pertange. They took ecphorite from a place the empty people called Swarthpol. The boat with its great wings was swallowed up by the sea, but the sea gave back its occupants. They climbed the stone steps and were never again seen by Melfar. The place called Swarthpol harbors great danger beside the dark sea. Let this song be a warning.'"

"That sounds ominous," Lambert says, glancing over his shoulder at Damon.

"That's definitely not one of the songs that we printed in any of the photographs," Damon says, wishing that it had been. His Mundani mind supplies images to go with these words—images of the ship, but also images of flyers, though there was no mention of flyers in the song. He has no way of knowing whether his mental images match up with the Melfar images that constitute the song, much less with the reality of the things and events themselves.

Ann is frowning. "Is that what you wanted? Does it make sense to you, Damon?"

"Some of it does," he says. "The part about empty people speaking words that couldn't be pertanged. That's how Abél described the people who took Odilia and Yuli. And the description of a ship with wings sounds the same. Do you suppose such people may really have come here before? Could this song be about Elossa people?"

Umet is frowning. He'd experienced the imagery of the Song of the Sea from Zara, but he'd also heard the song from his own eldfather. He's not certain that these words convey it properly. His memories hold some notes of the song, some tones that don't match up with the images he's pertanged in Ann's verberations, which of course were scripted by the words in the book. And those likely came from the song as Zara sang it. Translation is so imperfect. He tries to identify those mismatched notes, but they slip away from him. "What else does the book say about the song?" he asks.

"There's nothing else written here. No interpretation. No attempt to link the song with any events in Melfar or Mundani history beyond noting the passage 474. But of course, that was the passage—the return—when the Jasper Benison containing the song was dedicated. The events referred to could have happened any time during the twelve returns of the previous Jade Meed. Or even before that, I suppose." Ann flips back a few more pages, back past the dedication of the Ancient Jade in 462 to the Ancient Obsidian in 450. "It says the Ancient Jasper was dedicated in Túl."

Umet nods, his mind suddenly filled with images from his eldfather's accounts of visiting Túl, the most remote of all the Melfar communities.

Ann closes the book.

Abél was right, Damon thinks. *The Book of All Time is incomplete.*

As they walk past the photographs that hang on the walls of the shrine, Damon sees Fergus take Ann's hand. Ann leans into his shoulder. Damon knows that look on Fergus's face. His heart shudders with longing for Meridia. He glances toward Umet and the two men's eyes meet in a moment of shared loneliness.

In the yard, a small group of Mundani men and women have gathered near the entrance to Lambert's hall of mirrors. Lambert walks toward them, acknowledging their respectful half-bows with a nod. As Lambert and the visitors exchange words, Ann explains to Damon that these are Lambert's students. "They come to meditate and chant together and to discuss the deeper meanings of the Sidaya," she says. "Sometimes I join them. Some of them are old Sidayens, though they don't wish to be called that anymore. They oppose the distinction between Sidayen and kinren." The pride on Ann's face is easy to read. The group enters the hall of mirrors and Lambert returns to Damon and the others.

"I don't want to keep you from your students," Damon says. "From what Ann was telling us, I'd say that your work with them is important."

"It's also important that they know they can meditate and chant and discuss without me," Lambert says with a slight smile. "Will you stay the night with us, Damon? We have rooms at the Pickle School where you could all rest comfortably."

"Where?"

Ann explains. "We're opening a school at my parents' old pickle factory. It doesn't really have a name yet, but people have started calling it the Pickle School. I thought Fayredell needed a school where women and other former kinren could learn to read. Elvrid Conif has promised to print books for us. We intend to teach from the *Book of All Time*, too. And we'll teach forestry, of course. In the proper season, students will accompany me in planting trees to restore the forests." She adds that Roqu continues to use parts of the building for the self-defense academy that Gerd started.

Damon expresses his admiration for Ann's projects as well as Lambert's work. He declines the offer of overnight accommodations. "Umet knows a place where we can rest tonight that will put us well on our way toward Woodclasp."

Lambert understands Damon's eagerness to get on with his mission. "At least stay and have a meal with us before you go." He directs a questioning glance toward Umet, who holds a waif of the Old Quartz in one hand.

Umet nods assent. As long as they don't tarry too long over their meal, he's sure they can reach the place the Quartz's map has shown him, arriving there before nightfall. Or at least before it's fully dark. He glances toward the clear sky; the moon will be still be near half tonight and rise early. There's no need to hurry.

15

Limn gives up trying to teach Yuli her language. Although Limn understands nothing at all about verberations, she could tell that the project was going nowhere. Instead, Limn concentrates on learning Yuli's language. She sets up a computer with a microphone and manages to convey to the girl that she should speak into the device, responding to pictures displayed on the screen. All day long, the machine exhibits objects and activities, and Yuli explains what she sees. Her spoken language, of course, is Mundani. Melfar traditionally communicate with one another only through verberated images, so as Yuli records comments into the machine in Mundani, she sometimes does it in a sing-song, verberating different images that make Meridia laugh. Hearing Meridia laugh brings a smile to Yuli's face and a dimple to her cheek.

When the computer finishes showing things for Yuli to describe, she's free to drift off into her own thoughts. Sometimes when Yuli holds Odilia, feeling the warmth and delicateness of her small body, she imagines a child of her own, a child she might one day have with Umet. Provided Meridia can find a way for her to get back to him. Or maybe Umet will find a way to come and rescue her. He'll build a boat just like the Elossa...

Yuli and Meridia are surprised one day when Limn's machine starts asking questions in the Mundani language. The project becomes more engaging.

Soon Yuli and Limn are able to converse, with the computer serving as translator. Meridia listens, occasionally prompting Yuli with verberated questions.

"Is Tarja your sister?" Yuli asks Limn. "You look so much alike."

"No, not exactly," Limn says after the computer has rendered Yuli's vocalizations into her language. "We're the same clone set."

"Clone?" The translator has no Mundani word for that. "What is 'clone'?"

The Mundani words that come out of the machine seem to be telling Yuli (and Meridia, who is listening) that Elossa nens are composed in glass vials and nurtured in big jars until they're ready to be born. This sounds so outlandish that Yuli and Meridia both burst out laughing. Meridia quickly stifles her own laughter in response to Limn's startled look.

"You must think I'm a very foolish person to believe such a tale," Yuli says, still laughing. "Every nen—not just people, but animals as well—is composed by the union of substance from two parents, one of each sex. A father deposits substance into the womb of the mother to create offspring."

"We have no parents," Limn says. "We have no sexes."

Yuli scowls in disbelief, her amusement dispelled.

Limn had suspected that Yuli's people were still capable of sexual reproduction and she now has reasonable confirmation of that. It makes her even more eager to get the results of the DNA scans she's ordered.

Leaving Yuli alone (or so she thinks) Limn goes to check her main home computer to see if those results are available. As she waits impatiently, she tries to suppress the nagging recollection of two voices laughing. She tells herself that there is absolutely no conceivable way that there could be another person in there with Yuli. It has to be some effect of the unusual vocalizations that the girl seems capable of producing. But it certainly sounded like two people laughing. And Limn has thought a couple of times that she heard a second infant crying. Or maybe it's all just her imagination. That combined with the effects of too many hours of work and too little sleep. Still, the sounds pique her curiosity.

Curiosity. That's what is eventually going to get Limn into trouble. Well, more trouble. Irreconcilable trouble. She's been getting into trouble ever since her earliest years in the training pods, asking questions that weren't the right ones, the prescribed ones. By the time she was eight years old, she'd learned to keep such questions to herself. She stored them up in her mind and took them to the Library, where she discovered shelves and shelves of old books that were supposed to be just for display. But Limn looked inside a few of the dusty books and found them filled with all kinds of enchanting stories and astonishing information. Sometimes she'd go missing for hours at a time, but since no one expected her to be in the closed off rooms of the Library, no one thought to search for her there. Later, when Limn was in her teen years, she found similar relics through her computer— massive numbers of files of material stored long ago and forgotten. Hidden among a vast amount of silliness, Limn found reports and pictures that caused her to think of questions that nobody had thought to ask for centuries. Eventually, she began thinking questions about the Protocols themselves. And she began to understand why nothing had changed in the past seven hundred years or more. What she didn't understand was why so much was so meticulously preserved when nobody ever looked at it. She was just glad it was there.

Limn checks her wrist communicator. Still another fifteen minutes until the DNA analysis will be available. She clicks a few keys on her computer and calls up an image of the interior of her dwelling suite. She clicks from room to room until she finds Yuli and the baby. Yuli appears to be engaged in animated conversation, though she doesn't seem to be speaking. Limn toggles the camera to scan the room and finds no one there other than Yuli, who startles at the camera's movement and glances toward...what? Or whom? There's no point in turning on the audio; there's no language translator on Limn's work computer. It's on her other computer, the portable computer she's not supposed to keep here in her suite. Besides, Yuli seems to be communicating without moving her mouth. Without speaking.

A reminder pops up on Limn's wrist communicator with an annoying buzz. "Damn," she says. Limn had forgotten about her scheduled meeting with Macklin Wu, the woman in charge of the museum habitat that will house Yuli and the baby. She taps out a quick message: "Running late this morning. Can we delay meeting for a half hour?" Limn would like to cancel it altogether, but her capricious behavior since returning from the expedition has already resulted in one reprimand from Menza Uhr's office. After a brief delay, her reprieve is granted. She consults her watch again. She wishes that her clandestine access to the DNA analysis machine could accommodate more than two specimens at a time. The two she's waiting on are from Yuli and Odi, but she has a third specimen ready for analysis. That one is derived from the blood-stained garment of one of the individuals who was with her when they took the mirrors from the island. She'd furtively retrieved the discarded garment and kept it hidden, carefully wrapped in plastic. *One of these days, Limn.* Sometimes Limn curses her curiosity, that compulsion to do research that is not specified in the Protocols, to seek answers for inadmissible questions. And yet she knows that such research is—always has been—the most exciting and satisfying part of her otherwise monotonous life.

A soft ding announces the completion of the DNA analysis. A few seconds later, the results begin to scroll across the computer screen. The leading summary reads, "Specimen 1: 97.4% normal, 2.6% unidentified. Specimen 2: 98.2% normal, 1.8% unidentified." Limn scowls. She'd expected this gross level analysis to be identical. She begins skimming the detailed results, not sure what she ought to be looking for. She stops. Sits up straighter and clicks on the submission details. Specimen 1 is Yuli. Specimen 2 is the baby. Limn checks the time again and groans. She saves the information quickly into an encrypted segment of her computer and then copies it onto a smaller device, which she tucks behind some papers in the back of a drawer.

Limn doesn't want to go to this meeting. She's been delaying progress on the museum habitat repeatedly. This time she knows she's going to have to agree to let them get started on their construction. Limn is offended by the idea of Yuli and Odi having to live in a glass cage where they can be stared at for the amusement of even the lowest ranking clone sets. They're human beings, for god's sake. If she submits the DNA evidence of their humanity, would that sway Menza Uhr into providing Yuli with a suite instead of a glass cage? She can already hear Menza's angry retort: "Who authorized you to do DNA analysis? It's not in the Protocols!"

16

Meridia has been gone an entire six and Abél feels just as helpless now as he did in those first shattering moments when he knew she was gone. He keeps going over what little he knows and he keeps coming back to the mirrors. And to Swarthpol.

His memories of Swarthpol are a constant torment. He fends off the obsession successfully enough during the day, but every night he's back in that dreadful place, assaulted by cacophonies of sound, pulled this way and that without purpose or intent, and always, always, he senses the flash of sunbeams reflecting off...what? Is it only water? It feels like more. In his dreams, he sits all night long next to a pond, hardly moving, drawn toward the deep, dark waters, while simultaneously repelled by what lies within them.

Last night's dream was like that and he awakens frustrated and restless, an anger coalescing within him against this Swarthpol that stole so many returns of his life, returns that he ought to have spent with his beloved Maddie and their daughter Meridia. But it's also anger at himself, anger at his idleness and weakness during those returns. What was it about that place that left him so bereft of perception and will, so impotent in both aurynx and gnosic orb?

Without even a thought of breakfast, Abél steps outside his cottage. The day is still new and the light lies sepia-soft across the sleeping village of New Beniford. He knows where he's going.

When he steps into the green glen that everyone calls Meridia's Temple, his eyes fill with tears. There are bunches of fall flowers everywhere. The blooms that were cut yesterday are barely wilted after the cool dampness of the night. Were the donors mourning Meridia's absence or making offerings to petition her safe return? Probably both.

Abél tries to recall what Meridia told him about her experiences on the day Brân returned. She had let the Migrant guide her in selecting waifs, which she laid out on the ground in front of her. The waifs prompted her to sing certain songs. Abél has never been as grounded in the Migrant as Meridia is (at least not since Swarthpol) but he follows his daughter's example, taking from his own pouch of waifs—how many was it? —three stones.

He lays the stones out on a kerchief spread on the dew-wet grass. He arranges them to form a triangle.

One of the stones is an Obsidian and for an instant Abél fears it might be the Old Obsidian with its Song of Embracing Death. But, no. This is an Ancient Obsidian. It contains a song Abél doesn't know well. It was called Overwhelm With Splendor.

The New Marble is there, too, and this one brings a fleeting smile to Abél's eyes. He crafted this Benison himself, with Meridia's aid. Its Song of All Songs incorporates so much of the history of the Melfar. *So much hope for our future,* he thinks. It feels like a blessing.

The third waif is smaller than the others and worn smooth on two sides. It's a deep red, shot through with darker veins. This is a Jasper. Tentatively, haltingly, the notes of its song manifest in Abél's mind and begin to verberate in his aurynx. This is the Ancient Jasper and its song is the Song of the Sea.

Abél tries to empty his will, asking the waifs to teach him what he needs to know, to show him what he ought to do.

And then he lets go of trying.

Abél sputters and coughs and inhales deeply just before his head is pushed once more beneath the water. He wants to cry out with voice and aurynx, but this water has choked the life out of both.

It very nearly choked the breath out of him forever.

He remembers lying on the ground and retching. The dark water that spews from his mouth has a foul taste and stinks of something Abél cannot name. It smells purple, almost black. He struggles to rise and can only teeter weakly on hands and knees. Raising his head, he sees where he is: Dark stones, black as the blackest obsidian lie tumbled all around him, mingled with occasional tiny pebbles of something white. The pool where he nearly drowned is even darker than the stones. But somewhere, just below the rocks that surround this pool, he senses a steady hum and the pull of something brighter. He collapses back onto the ground and releases his despair in great sobs.

Tears roll down his cheeks with the painful memory. *This is what happened at Swarthpol. This is what they did to me. And they left me there, satisfied that I was a broken man.*

The three stones on the kerchief in front of Abél shimmer in the morning light and he pertanges delicate tendrils of sound connecting each to the others. As the tendrils dissolve, he resolves to open up his mind to more memories of Swarthpol. He needs to know why these Elossa wanted to go there.

He'll start by trying to learn more about these three songs. He'll take his questions to Zara.

Can we talk about the song called Overwhelm With Splendor? Abél starts with that. He's come to Zara with a new determination to find some course of action, something he can do to aid in getting Meridia back.

Ah, the song of the Ancient Obsidian. That Benison was erected in Lindmor, during troubled times near the forest of Cödweg. Zara reminds Abél of the Melfar forests as they once were, verdant stretches of towering trees dotted with villages and towns. She sings what she knows of the song.

The forests were so healthy then, Abél says. *And there were so many Melfar towns.*

Maybe too many. Melfar prospered, but they were outgrowing their forest homes and moving into new territories, founding new settlements. Vidvana says that at the same time, Mundani were becoming fragmented. Ever since the death of their Prophet Razak Pherson, they'd been quarrelsome and competitive, trying to out-do one another building great temple complexes with clausters, fortifying their towns with walls. Being mostly concerned with one another, they left Melfar pretty much to their own places.

Abél pertanges all of this through Zara's verberations. He wants to know more about the song itself.

Overwhelm With Splendor was meant to be sung whenever new settlements were founded. It told about the splendor of the village that would take the place of the splendid trees that had to be removed to make way for the people.

Abél muses over the cycle of meeds celebrated by Melfar, thinking of the colors and qualities of each. The Ancient Obsidian was followed by the Ancient Jade, with its Song of Pacification. *Wasn't that song's intent much the same?* It was about living at peace within the disturbed forests and with one another.

Yes, in that period of our history, our songs were for ourselves. As long as Mundani weren't interfering, Melfar were mostly content, seeking only to live at peace within our own communities. The Ancient Jade was dedicated here at Beniford.

Then came the Ancient Jasper.

Zara folds her arms and furrows her brow. *The Song of the Sea.* She pauses and then begins using words to structure what she wants to say to Abél. "After you asked me earlier about that song, I searched through some of the notes that Vidvana left with me to see if there might be anything more about that song or about the Ancient Jasper Meed."

Abél leans forward in anticipation.

"There wasn't much."

His shoulders slump.

"The Ancient Jasper Benison was erected in Túl," Zara says, "and that may be part of the problem. You know they've always been somewhat secretive."

Abél tries to summon up what he knows about Túl, the primary Melfar community within the great southern forest of Cesta. It's the one Melfar community that kept mostly to itself, always a little removed from the main circuits of Melfar singing.

"I did find Vidvana's notes from a conversation we had with a woman from Túl. She was called Boovez breth Noita and she was here in New Beniford for the celebration of the Great Turning, the dedication of the New Marble." Zara has a dazed look and struggles to find words as she recalls her experience of the conversation. "The woman wasn't very forthcoming. According to Vidvana's notes, Boovez mentioned that Mundani from around Markham were interfering with the Túl communities. Vidvana assumed she was talking about something recent, likely a reference to Warreth Pherson and the Palinjians."

Abél knows that Markham was Warreth Pherson's stronghold before he died, the place where Gerd and her crew of adventurers encountered his younger brother Saami.

Zara frowns and presses her palm against her forehead. *As I think back on the conversation, I think Boovez was more likely referring to something that happened long ago. Or maybe both? The woman was a bit awkward with Mundani words, but the images I pertanged when she spoke of this seemed...ancient. And complicated. I'm sorry I didn't pursue it. I think Boovez and her family probably know a great deal about the history of the southern regions.*

And about the Song of the Sea, Abél says. *We should definitely ask this Boovez more questions. Perhaps we should go to Túl and see what more we can learn about the Song of the Sea.*

You may be right, Abél. Boovez told us that her own mother and, if I'm not mistaken, even her eldmother are still living there. Zara suddenly finds herself thinking of the distance from New Beniford to Túl, of what might be the best route to arrive there, of how long such a journey deep into the heart of Cesta might take.

"Will you go with me?" Abél says. *How soon can we leave?*

17

This city is perhaps the quietest place I've ever experienced. Yes, during the day there's noise from vehicles and other machinery whirring and clanking and swishing, but almost nothing for the gnosic orb to experience. No trees. A few birds flying in from the sea. If I reach out toward the ocean I can pertange the fish and other creatures living in its coastal waters.

I've been here more than a six and I understand very little more about this city than I did on the day I arrived. I don't belong here but I don't want to be anywhere else. I don't want to be apart from Odilia.

It's good that Yuli is able to communicate with Limn through the machine, but when she asks the questions we really want to know about, the machine falls silent. Mostly we share thoughts and images with one another.

How did you first know you were a healer, Meridia?

I'm a bit startled by Yuli's query. I've never really thought much about how I became a healer. It seemed to happen so naturally, so gradually. I think back and share some memories with Yuli about a time when I was just a child and my mother was ill. *I was thinking about her, worrying about her, as I walked among the trees gathering firewood. My attention was drawn forcefully to a particular plant and I felt compelled to take it home and offer it to Mother. As it turns out, the plant was moon laurel and Mother was suffering with her moonflow. So the plant helped her. When I remember that incident, I hear the song of moon laurel and I wonder if I also heard it then.*

You had no one to teach you? Yuli says. *That must have been difficult for you, learning about different plants and how they're used with no one to show you.*

The hardest part was figuring out how to prepare the plants and how much to use for different illnesses. I learned to pay attention to the quality of the plants' tones and the intensity of their colors and how that seemed to match up with the symptoms a sick person was experiencing, how they verberated to me. Of course, I didn't understand at all that that was what I was doing. Or rather...I think I knew, but I couldn't speak about it. I had no words for it. And besides, no one would have believed me about the colors and tones of plants and illnesses. There were only Mundani in Temur. But when people got well, they believed that what I knew about plants was good. I experience the stickiness of regret over a few cases that did not go so well. *What about you, Yuli? How did you become Bekanz's apprentice?*

I was given to her as apprentice when I'd completed hardly more than five returns. My parents had noticed how I would take injured birds or small animals and care for them and how quickly they were healed in my care.

She's thinking of a particular incident in which a stillborn lamin was left for dead. She brought it back to life. Does she know that I saw that? That's a very special sort of gift. I see that Yuli also collected small healing stones—waifs. *Yes, I did that, too.*

Later in the evening, after Yuli and Odi are sound asleep and Omi drowses here in my arms, I turn my thoughts toward Avienne's advice. I wish she were here with me. But she said that if I wanted to get back to where Damon and Father are, I might have to do most of the work myself. She suggested I try using the songs of the last three waifs she gave me as she lay near death—songs of Hope, Pacification, and Firm Resolve.

I sway gently, rocking Omi to sleep, and begin softly voicing "ahhh" to the notes of the Old Amethyst Song of Hope, the notes that became part of the Song of All Songs. The music surges from my aurynx, all lavender and violet, and I think of old Prophet Amos Quint, chanting among the mirrors of his meditation chamber. I look into the mirrors. Or I try to. Everything feels brittle, hissing and crackling with something that isn't song. Tension creeps into my aurynx and orb, choking out both song and images. Omi's eyelids flutter.

I shift to the Ancient Jade's Song of Pacification. In my mind, that song is forever wedded to the Old Jade Song of the Calumet. Isn't a Calumet a peace-bringer? Those two songs belong together. Nevertheless, I focus on the Song of Pacification. Its notes also prove elusive. Powdery, crumbling like dried leaves. Dissipating on my own breath.

What is wrong with me? Why can't I sing?

I turn to the third song that was part of Avienne's final gift to me—the Old Granite's Song of Firm Resolve. Its notes are angular and solid. Heavy. As I sing, each note drops deep into something I cannot fathom and as I sing the last note, I know the song is gone. Does it even belong to me anymore? I shiver with trepidation.

The shiver turns into a wave that vibrates my whole being from the soles of my feet right through the crown of my head and I remember. I remember how it felt as I sat between the two mirrors in Amos Quint's chamber, as I found myself all at once with Odilia and Yuli and I know that both things happened at the exact same moment. I quiver with this sense of discovery, but as I grasp for it...it's gone.

I embrace Naomi more firmly.

I need to remember this.

But already, the memory fades.

18

"I'm afraid I've never been very good at judging distances," Umet says by way of apology. Darkness has overtaken them well before he and Damon and Orban reach the Melfar way station he'd pertanged through the maps stored within the Old Quartz.

"Never mind," Damon says. Despite his fatigue, he's glad they didn't stay the night in Fayredell.

When they arrive at last, they find the place well supplied with comfortable beds and a stack of clean sheets. There are cooking implements and a pile of fireblocks, too.

"Is there any news from Abél?" Damon asks as the three men settle down to consume the stuffed bread and fresh wilderfruit they brought from town. Damon knows he didn't really need to ask Umet for news. If Umet knew anything, he would have shared.

"I'm sorry," Umet says. "Abél is still unable to contact them." Umet almost says something about Abél's desire to learn more about the Song of the Sea, but since he's unclear how Abél intends to do that, he says nothing.

Damon pours a second cup of tea and walks outside the shelter to sip it in the gentle light of the moon. He knows he needs sleep. He doubts he'll get much. It's been like this ever since Meridia became lost. Whenever they've been apart in the past, the quiet of nighttime was when Meridia came to him. Now the nights bring only crushing loneliness. And doubt. Why does he think that finding an old picture of a boat can possibly help bring back the woman he loves? He sits there much of the night, doubting himself, eventually dozing under the stars on a bed of soft leaves. He doesn't even receive the comfort of Meridia's presence in his dreams.

By late morning the next day, Damon and Orban and Umet are approaching the town of Blanton. "Will we go through the town?" Orban asks. "Would it be safe?"

"It's my understanding that Palinjians still hold the clauster there in Blanton," Umet says, "but there's a strong weftred of Chanters as well." Umet muses silently for a moment. "Biding their time. Did you ever meet Daedal and Shifra breth Ilda?"

"I think I met them once," Damon says. "Gerd introduced us in Fayredell." He remembers the two strong and lively Mundani women and their enthusiasm about the Gathering.

"They'd likely provide us with a good meal if we went to their house."

"No delays," Damon says. "We need to press on." When he and Meridia traveled this way less than a return ago, there were no well supplied way stations or friendly houses offering cooked meals. He's grateful that things are calmer, but that's no reason to become complacent and sluggish. "Do you think we might stay tonight in Shadham?"

Shadham is where Meridia's mother Maddie tended to Damon after he was murdered by the Palinjians. It's where Meridia found both of them after... Damon's heart wrenches in his chest with the memory, but he forces himself to acknowledge it. *After Meridia was raped by that bastard Malaki.* But Malaki is dead. *The twins will never know any father but me.* These memories make Damon even more painfully aware of the absence of his partner and their nens. He stops himself before the next thought, the one questioning whether he will ever see any of them again.

"We can go to Shadham if you like," Umet says, "though it would take us out of our way. Maybe by quite a lot."

"Then we should move on." Damon thinks that if they press hard, they might be able to reach Woodclasp by tomorrow.

A night of exhausted sleep in a spot that provided little protection from the elements and less comfort is followed by another day at an unrelenting pace. The sun is low in the sky as they arrive at Woodclasp.

Damon is unprepared for the sight of Orban's burned cabin. He'd only thought of how helpful Orban would be in pursuing Damon's own project, in helping to recover the remaining photos from Fannan's destroyed workshop. He turns toward Orban and sees the man's pain engraved on his face and weighing down his body.

At the end of such an arduous trek, Orban has no energy left to withstand the flood of emotion. He falls to his knees, overcome by the memory of what occurred here, how the Palinjians attacked, how they made him watch while they tortured his beloved Melfar partner Emba. While they slowly killed her. His tears fall hot and silent.

Damon and Umet keep a respectful distance, heads down. Umet never knew Emba, but he knows her sister Bekanz and Bekanz told him the story of what happened at Woodclasp. Emba was a gifted Melfar healer and Orban's beloved partner, as Yuli will one day be Umet's.

Damon's heart breaks for his friend. He cautions himself against identifying too closely with Orban's sense of loss, thinking surely his own loss—his and Umet's—will not be so permanent, so absolute. His breath is hot against his face and his eyes burn.

At last Orban rises stiffly to his feet. He approaches the edge of what was once his house. There are a few fall flowers there where Emba planted them. He picks some and, with halting steps, makes his way toward a low mound of scorched earth by the stump of a bartlenut tree.

Damon and Umet follow, and as Orban places the flowers atop the mound—atop the grave holding Emba's ashes—Umet begins to sing. Damon knows the song must be the Old Obsidian Song of Embracing Death. He heard it at Avienne's funeral and again at Maddie's. He refuses the thought of ever singing it for his own partner. He knows Umet is not singing it for Yuli. He looks at the young man and sees tears, yes, but tears tinged with hope.

There's little conversation as the three lonely men make a camp for the night and cook a simple meal. There will be time enough tomorrow to discuss the details of their plan to recover the last of Fannan's photographs from the vault beneath the ruins of his old workshop. Tonight is for Emba.

19

Vidvana is more than willing to join Abél and Zara on their journey to Túl, their quest for more information about the Song of the Sea. She and her partner Willem had returned to New Beniford from Selbourne only two days previous. Vidvana recommends that her friend Salma accompany them as well.

"Do I know Salma?" Abél tries to remember when he might have met members of Vidvana's Mundani weftred.

"She was with me at the Markham Clauster when you and I first met, Abél." It's not a pleasant memory, but Vidvana knows it's something Abél is unlikely to have forgotten. It was the day Keira Landry was murdered.

"Oh, of course." The azure wave of comfort he sends toward Vidvana is flecked with the crimson anger he felt that day. The Mundani women had been chanting poetry inside the Clauster, and for that crime Lambert Quint's only daughter Keira was killed. Abél recalls, too, that Salma was one of the members of the Mundani group who went in pursuit of the ones who abducted Yuli and Odilia. He can't summon to mind the woman herself, but at least now he knows what manner of woman she is.

"Has Salma returned from Selbourne?" Zara asks.

"Yes," Vidvana says. "She came back with Willem and me. Vedö and my brother Negyed stayed behind to keep watch over Brân and Amos Quint."

"And you think Salma would be willing to go with us?"

"I'm sure she would. And she'd be helpful. She's trained with Gerd and Roqu," Vidvana says.

Abél hopes there will be no need for the fighting skills that Gerd has been teaching to Mundani Chanters, but it's reassuring to know Salma possesses such skills. That was why she had stayed with the Mundani protectors in New Beniford rather than attending the Gathering in Fayredell.

"How long should we plan to be gone?" Vidvana asks.

"Túl is well to the south of Brightlea, so I expect it will take us at least a six to get there," Zara says, trying not to verberate her doubts about Abél's fitness for the journey. "And I have no idea how long we might decide to stay there. We'll be able to pick up additional supplies in Temur or Brightlea." She pauses. *We might also see about securing an equid for you to ride, Abél.*

I made it to Selbourne and back not so very long ago, Zara. I think I can manage this trip to Túl.

Vidvana doesn't know the meaning of the look Abél and Zara exchange. She does know that Melfar are prone to these shared moments to which she is not privy. She's learned to accept it and not ask questions. But she can't help feeling left out.

On the day before they're due to depart, Abél feels a sudden tug from his brother twin Brân. *I hadn't forgotten you, brother,* Abél says. *I've just been...*

I know, Brân says. *You're consumed with Meridia's plight. You want to help. But are you sure traveling to Túl is what you ought to do?*

I need to do something. Zara says they may know more there about the Song of the Sea. Its Benison was erected there; the song belongs to Túl.

But wouldn't it be just as well for Zara and Vidvana to go on their own? You know Zara can learn songs quicker than a flash of fireseed. And Vidvana is more than meticulous about writing everything down in Mundani words. Surely it's not necessary for you to go.

Abél rubs his forehead, seeing in his orb's eye the frown of worry on Brân's face. He tries to verberate reassurance to his brother. He can't explain why it's so important to make this journey himself. He just knows he wants to listen to whatever stories the people of Túl might tell, to witness the telling directly. But there's something more. He coughs in an effort to prevent his brother from knowing what else he's considering.

Swarthpol? You're thinking of going to Swarthpol? But you barely made it out of that place before, brother. Why would you want to go back? But Brân knows it's because Swarthpol is mentioned in the Song of the Sea. And they're both reaching the conclusion that the Song of the Sea is about people like the ones that took Odilia and Yuli. Brân suspects that song is also somehow about the forces that took Meridia and Naomi, the same forces that flung him through a breach in time-space only a few tides past.

Abél acknowledges Brân's concern. *It's not that I want to go, brother. You well know how terrified I am of that place. But if the Song of the Sea mentions people like the ones that took Meridia, if such people were once at Swarthpol, then maybe Swarthpol holds something that could help us figure out how to get Meridia back.*

Do you have a waif of the Ancient Jasper? Brân is thinking about his own waif that he gave to Damon.

"I'm glad you gave yours to Damon," Abél murmurs, letting the spoken words focus his intentions, mask his worries. *Yes, I have a waif of the Ancient Jasper. What I need is the full song to go with it. I'm not sure that what Zara knows is all there is.*

20

As the sun breaks the horizon the next day, its beams fall on Abél's little group, already well on their way toward Temur. Abél is gratified to find Salma an amiable companion, gentle in spite of her imposing stature and reputed skill as a fighter. She's even taller than Vidvana and considerably darker. In fact, she may be the darkest Mundani person Abél has ever seen. Her cropped hair shines black as obsidian and her dark brown eyes are flecked with gold. She and Zara lead the way, with Vidvana staying close by Abél. Too close, he thinks, though he grudgingly accepts her protective concern.

They arrive in Temur in late morning on the second day of their journey and make their way toward a small house near the edge of town, the house where Gerd resides. Once it belonged to Maddie and Meridia. And to Abél. Now it's where Gerd runs combat training sessions for Chanters and where Elvrid convenes poetry readings with a couple of Melfar singers who recently moved to Temur.

Abél is happy to see Gerd, or at least he tells her that he is. Although he'd never admitted it, he had felt occasional twinges of jealousy over the fondness his estranged partner Maddie had developed for Gerd. Or maybe it was just the residue of regret for Abél's own failure to reunite with Maddie and their daughter Meridia after his miserable sojourn in Swarthpol. He thinks Gerd's short hair has more streaks of gray now.

She used to wear her hair in a long plait down her back as most Mundani men still do.

Gerd listens anxiously as her guests provide details of a story she's only heard hinted at in rumors. "I don't understand how such a thing could happen to Meridia. I guess I didn't really believe it had happened to Brân until he came back. I'd convinced myself that he'd just wandered off and fallen into the sea. But Damon saw it this time? Poor Damon. He must be frantic with worry." Gerd is worried, too. Meridia is being hailed as a Prophet among the Chanter weftreds and her absence could be disheartening to them. Besides that, Meridia is the daughter of Gerd's beloved Maddie. She's family.

"Damon is in Woodclasp," Abél says, following up with an explanation of his reason for that journey, his search for a photograph of a ship in Fannan's destroyed workshop.

"What can I do to help?" Gerd says. "Should I go with you to Túl?" Gerd never thinks she's doing enough, even though her work played an important role in finally permitting Chanters to take their place openly in Mundani society, pushing Palinjians into the background.

"Oh, Gerd, what you're doing here in Temur, what you did in Fayredell... Surely that's the most important work for you right now," Vidvana says. "And as for protection, we have Salma."

"Vidvana's right," Zara says. "We need you here, Gerd. Without our Calumet, it's even more important to have strong leadership among Chanters. Keeping Palinjians at bay."

"It may be best not to confirm the rumors about Meridia's absence," Salma says. "I haven't even told my partner about it."

Zara senses Abél's question before he asks it. *Her partner is a brother of one of the Palinjian arsonists. He's one of Lambert's students now, but he does still have a few Palinjian kin.*

Abél knows how dispirited the Melfar in New Beniford are over the absence of their Calumet so soon after the loss of Avienne. It's been barely five tides since Avienne's death. *Yes, I'm sure it's better if the Palinjians remain uncertain about any news regarding Meridia.*

"It's good that you have Salma traveling with you," Gerd says. "She's a canny fighter." Gerd smiles at the tall woman, recalling training bouts with her. Gerd came out the worse in a few of those.

They spend the rest of the afternoon sharing information, as well as thoughts and worries, with one another. In the evening Elvrid arrives with a newly printed book of poetry to share. As night falls, Gerd lays out blankets for her guests and offers Abél her own bed, which he gladly accepts. His old bones are aching and weary. He knows this bed. He crafted it himself when he and Maddie were recently partnered young lovers.

When Abél is at last overtaken by sleep, it's a fitful slumber. He feels the slippage beginning and he wants to resist. He's not as certain as he once was that all this to-ing and fro-ing is the work of the Migrant. He felt lost to the Migrant when he was at Swarthpol and he's begun to feel that way again.

He sees once more the vision that Brân shared with him, a glimpse of glowing rectangles filled with pictures and lines of words.

He's seen those before. Somehow, sometime, he saw them when he was at Swarthpol.

He saw a whole line of the glowing rectangles.

He sees them now and, seated in front of each rectangle, there's a person. The people are neither Melfar nor Mundani. They're as short as Melfar and as sturdily built, but they mostly have straight black hair and their skin is a deep golden brown.

A sudden commotion disrupts their work. A child runs toward one of the women and she turns to embrace him, cooing comfort into his ear as she strokes his hair.

"What is it, my son?"

The words are strange, but Abél pertanges clear verberations.

"They called me a thief," the child sobs.

Abél knows what that feels like. It's what banished him to Swarthpol.

The woman turns toward the man who pursued the child into the room. "My child is no thief," she says, clutching the child to her breast, her eyes flashing anger.

But he is a thief. He took something he shouldn't have. He only took it because it was pretty and now, because he doesn't want to give it up, he refuses to admit that he has it. It's just a small thing, a pebble of milky white that gleams blue and green and rosy orange in the sunlight.

The child shrieks with despair as he's torn away from his aggrieved mother.

"I will always love you, m'hijo!" The woman cries out, struggling helplessly against those who hold her fast. Lasaro knows that his mother means it. Her arms stretch toward him as the wheeled vehicle carries him away.

Abél awakens with a sharp pain between his brows and an ache in his throat. What are those strange glowing rectangles? And how did that child come to possess a piece of ecphorite?

21

I experience a sudden longing for Father accompanied by memories of Temur. I think of how, growing up in Temur, I was despised and disparaged and called "Shoon." I felt as if I was less than no one.

Here in Port Sillick I barely exist at all. Yuli and Odi know I'm here, and sometimes I think Limn suspects something when she hears two nens crying and sees only one. Avienne would be here if I called on her, but she says she doesn't know how to help, so I don't call. I only try to follow her instructions.

Although I'm unable to experience Avienne's songs in the usual way, I'm convinced that they've helped me to become more solid to Odilia. She reacts to my touch in addition to pertanging my face and voice. I find this both gratifying and frightening. Would other people here be able to touch me as well? I don't know, but I'm sure it's best that I remain silent and keep my distance from others.

My days are filled with an emptiness that exhausts me. My eyes and ears work too hard and easily grow weary. My orb and aurynx are only useful in communicating with Yuli and the nens and a few birds and fish.

Without the physical presence of Yuli and Odi, I think I would have no touchstone to tell me whether this experience was occurring now or sometime in the past. It would be little different from watching Amergin and his Naomi in those ancient caverns where they wandered without being aware of my presence except when I verberated to them with my aurynx. They, at least, could pertange my verberations. These people are impervious to verberations and incapable of generating them. They're nothing more than a physical presence uttering unpleasant noises, garbed in dull colors.

Sometimes I doubt that the Migrant has anything to do with my presence here.

Then how do you think you got here? Yuli wants to know.

Of course Yuli knows my concerns. I send her a brief rosy burst, grateful for our kinship as Melfar. *It was because of the mirrors.* I show her again the moments before we came here, our last moment in Damon's presence. I sense once more the elusive vibrations that shook me away from there and into this emptiness that is now the sum of my existence.

Limn sits in stunned silence, trying to process what Macklin Wu has just told her. The words still echo in her head: "Menza Uhr has decided that the live display would be too complicated, given all the delays we've experienced thus far. She says you're to hand over the specimens to the cryoplastics facility before close of business tomorrow."

That is not going to happen, Limn vows to herself, though she's not at all certain how she's going to prevent it. "Of course," she says. "I agree that the live display would entail a great deal of work to make it realistic and adequate to the ongoing needs of the specimens. But surely you'll want them in peak condition before the cryoplastic processing. The adult has been ill and the infant has some sort of rash on its face. It will take a couple of days to clear that up."

The project chief sighs mightily and shakes her head as if she knows Limn is just stalling again. But Limn Ssu outranks her and the argument is logical, so she raises her hands, palm upward and lowers her head in agreement. "Two days, then." She raises her eyes and glowers at Limn. "But I'm sure Menza-ji will allow no more than that."

Limn gestures her agreement, her frantic heartbeat calming only slightly with this small reprieve.

As Limn makes her way back toward her residence, she formulates and discards one plan after another. In a society such as this, defying authority and escaping surveillance are supposed to be impossible. Impossible because they're unthinkable. Limn smiles slightly as she thinks that. She appreciates irony. Here in Port Sillick everyone knows their place and their duty. The Protocols are followed to the letter and without question.

Except among the entertainment clone set. Members of the Qi set are expected to engage in outrageous behavior without it ever being taken seriously.

Limn recalls a brief encounter she had last year with an entertainer. The individual had overstepped the boundaries of tolerance, performing something that Limn's subsequent research identified as satire but that members of the technocrat set saw as a threat to social order. Limn had helped the entertainer avoid punishment. She'd also taken a specimen of her DNA and analyzed it. The entertainer carried a mutation on the same gene as Limn's, leading Limn to hypothesize that the mutation made both of them resistant to the drugs that were supposed to constrain their behavior within the limits of what was acceptable under the Protocols. The drug was meant to constrain curiosity and, sadly for the entertainers, creativity.

Limn decides that it may be time for the entertainer to repay that kindness by doing a favor for Limn. If only Limn can remember her name. Last name Qi, of course.

"Jack," Limn says, as she closes the door of her residence behind her. *Jack Qi. She's the one.*

"Hello?" Yuli makes tentative use of a word of greeting in Limn's language. She's not sure what "Jack" means.

"Yes, hello to you, too," Limn says, leaning over her computer to switch on the translation program. She wonders what she'll say to Yuli to explain what's about to happen. What she hopes is about to happen.

22

Damon and Orban work in silence, shoveling away the dirt concealing the vault that holds the last of the photographs printed by the Melfar photologist Fannan. Umet watches. Sometimes when Damon glances toward Umet he detects an expression on the young man's face that suggests he may already be examining what's inside the vault.

"There it is." Orban's implement scrapes against stone beneath the remaining thin layer of earth.

Damon is surprised. In his memories of their initial discovery, the stone covering Fannan's secret cache had been buried deeper. But back then he was still recovering from injuries. Fatal injuries. He hadn't been at full strength.

Umet joins them at the rim of the pit as they finish unearthing the blood-red cover stone. "Jasper," Umet says. "Song of Burning."

"That's what Emba told us," Orban says.

Damon had pocketed a fragment of that stone and left it in the backsack that Meridia carried when they left Woodclasp. He'd been unaware of the power it held to send her into terrified flight, driven by visions of blazing forests.

It takes them only a short while to haul the covering stone aside. Damon has prepared a container and secure wrappings in anticipation of the removal of the photographs. Gently, he lifts them from their resting place and lays them out on the wrappings. "What do you see, Umet? Do you see a ship?" Of course he does. Even Damon can see the ship, although it's indistinct, as if it's shrouded in mist.

"It's sinking," Umet says. "Is that Selbourne behind it? If so, that's a very large ship. And it does have white sheets extending on both sides like wings."

"The Song of the Sea tells about a ship sinking. Do you think this is it?" Damon tries to recall the words Ann read from the book.

Umet quotes it for him. "'The boat with its great wings was swallowed up by the sea.' The song also says that 'the sea gave back its occupants,' but I don't see any occupants in this picture."

Damon is quiet for a moment, staring at the photograph, wishing he could see it as Umet does. "If they were Elossa, maybe they can't be printed by this method. I mean, if they can't be pertanged, maybe they can't be verberated and so can't be printed."

"That could be," Umet says. He's not sure he understands how Damon's photographic process works, but he knows that Abél was able to show him what the Elossa people looked like. Maybe the people are absent only because the song defines them as empty people. He adjusts his position to study the rest of the picture. "There's another boat there. Just a small one, an ordinary one like the kind we build. No wings. The front of it is pointed toward Selbourne. It's empty, just like the large ship. Well, at least there are no people in it that I can pertange." Umet squints at the picture and then raises his eyes to meet Damon's. "I've been thinking about the Song of the Sea," he says. "What if some of the words are out of order? What if it's supposed to begin with the sinking of the ship with wings?"

"With the arrival of the empty people?" Damon rests his chin on his fists and furrows his brow. "I guess that likely would have been the start of it," he says, not certain what "it" refers to exactly.

Umet studies another picture. "This one shows a pond," he says.

Damon wonders if it might be the same pond where Fannan found the luminous slime and the billbugs that caused the nacreous fever. "Is it in the forest?"

Umet stares intently at the picture, his head slightly cocked, his eyes moving as if he's following something. "No," he says. "No forest. Stones. Piles of huge, dark-colored, jagged stones." He leans in closer to the photograph.

"What else?" Damon is certain Umet sees something more.

"It's almost as if I can see through the waters of the pond," he says. "It's unclear, but something about it reminds me of Lambert Quint's hall of mirrors."

Or Amos Quint's chamber, Damon thinks.

"I've never been in Amos Quint's chamber of mirrors," Umet says. "But you may be right." He hands the photograph to Damon. "There's something else about the Song of the Sea that's been bothering me. The image in the Melfar song that Vidvana translated as 'sea' in the last line is not really the ocean. I think it may be the pool that's shown in that picture." He tries to remember if there was a pool in the imagery he learned from his eldfather. He's almost sure that there was.

Confident that they've learned as much as they can from Umet, Damon assembles the photographs and wraps them carefully. "Well," he says, "I think we need to get back to New Beniford and show these pictures to Abél as soon as we can. Maybe there's something here that can help him figure out how to get Meridia and Yuli and the nens back."

"Abél is not in New Beniford," Umet says. "He's on his way to Túl."

In the clear light of dawn, Abél is increasingly convinced that the vision of his dream—the glowing rectangles and the child who stole the tiny lump of ecphorite—is a memory of something he's been shown before. It feels like a memory from Swarthpol. He seeks out Brân.

I've seen it, too, brother. I think it's a memory that belongs to that place. I shared something like it once with Meridia. She said the boy Lasaro ended up at the children's home with Amergin and Naomi.

So you think it is about Swarthpol?

Yes, I do, but from a time long before you knew the place.

Abél considers the time during which he knew Swarthpol. The memory of it feels unstable, unmoored from any customary experience of time.

He turns the images over and over in his mind as his band of travelers bids farewell to Gerd and departs Temur. They head toward Brightlea with the rising sun in their faces. Using a Mundani road, it takes them only a day to reach the town. Brightlea is where Abél was seized on the grounds of a temple where he'd been searching for a piece of the Ancient Mica Benison. He'd found nothing, taken nothing, but the Mundani who found him there accused him of theft just the same. They sent him to Swarthpol, that strange prison without walls.

It's late when they arrive in Brightlea. Zara pertanges a lodge that would accommodate them safely and comfortably, but Abél—because of his own unpleasant associations with Brightlea—insists that they camp instead outside the town, beside an obscure Melfar way leading toward Túl. At least it used to lead toward Túl, back in the Old Quartz Meed when the maps and instructions were imparted to the Quartz waifs.

The region to the south, beyond Brightlea and westward all the way past Benbridge, was once the great forest of Cesta. It burned during the Old Jasper Meed shortly after the forest of Cödweg burned for the second time and just before the burning of the southern reaches of Serani, on the slopes of the western mountains. As they leave Brightlea behind, it becomes clear that the fires that took Cesta were not recurrent like the ones that burned Cödweg. Even Serani burned more than once. But as they enter Cesta, they encounter tall trees, old trees. Survivors.

"Boovez told us that after Túl was destroyed in the Cesta fire, they rebuilt it in some surviving wooded areas to the southeast," Zara says as they tread a path that is all but invisible to their Mundani companions. "I'm sure the Quartz can guide us as far as the old site of Túl, but I'm still a bit unclear beyond that."

Salma is crestfallen. "How will we find it then?"

Abél already knew that Túl had moved, of course, and Vidvana is not surprised. Zara has brought two waifs of the Old Quartz, and she explains that one shows roads originating from Beniford in the northwest and the other starting from Lindmor in the northeast. "They all contain the same maps," Zara says, "but the orientation is a little different. I'm sure we'll be able to find the current location."

Though Abél trusts Zara to guide them, he keeps seeing a different way, a way that approaches from the southwest.

Without smooth Mundani roads to follow, the group makes slower progress. Their encampment for the night is none too comfortable, but they're tired and well fed and Abél is soon sleeping. The others take turns standing watch. Other than the calls of a few night birds and what might have been the distant squealing of a patkány's prey, nothing disturbs the silence here at the verge of Cesta.

Next day, as they move deeper into the forest, Salma glances nervously about. Zara knows that she's thinking of her journey into Serani with Ann and Yuli, searching for furtivine, searching for a cure for nacreous fever.

"Do you think the nacreous fever made it all the way to Túl?" Salma says. Her hand goes to a small pinkish scar on her neck and her thoughts to the son she lost to the fever in Fayredell. Their discovery of the medicine hadn't come soon enough to save him.

"I don't think there were any cases of nacreous fever in Túl," Zara says. *I'm sure they had the medicine from the furtivine.* She feels confident about this information, though she can't say why.

It's late afternoon when they enter a broad clearing dotted with rambling bushes and tall fruit trees. "This is it," Zara announces. "This is the old site of Túl. Vidvana, if you and Salma can set up camp, Abél and I will work to see if we can pertange where the new site of Túl lies."

Abél and Zara move to a spot in the shade of a wilderfruit tree. As they spread a blanket over the lush growth, they're met with scents of several different herbs.

You can tell this was once inhabited space, Zara says. Almost all of the plants growing here give either food or herbs or medicines.

Abél takes his pouch of waifs and holds it between his hands, listening. He tries to think which Benisons were erected in Túl, supposing that their waifs might resonate most strongly with its people in their present location. Back when customs were followed more closely, the dedication of Benisons cycled among the three main Melfar towns—Lindmor, Beniford, and Túl. Of course, Túl Melfar weren't always constrained by custom. Abél is certain that the last Benison erected in Túl was the Ancient Amber, with its Song of Turning. Three meeds before that, the Ancient Jasper was dedicated in Túl. That's the one they're seeking to learn more about, the one with the Song of the Sea. What else? It would have been three meeds before the Ancient Jasper, which was the Ancient Granite.

The Ancient Granite held the Song of Solitude, Zara says, responding to his thoughts. It's one of the strangest songs in the entire Melfar cycle. The people of Túl were already becoming reclusive and... She fumbles over the images, searching. *Well, they're different. When the Ancient Granite was dedicated, instead of large parties of families arriving from all the Melfar communities, the people of Túl only permitted one representative from Lindmor and one from Beniford.*

Avienne told me about that. And the song is for unison voices, isn't it?

That's right. No harmonies, no counter melodies. Everyone sang the same notes, almost like chanting. I've only heard it performed a couple of times. It has a strange effect on the gnosic orb.

I'm not certain I've ever heard it performed, Abél says. *Where did you hear it?*

When I was a young girl, Avienne brought a group of her students to a meeting house north of Brightlea. I went with my mother. There were people from Túl and they sang the song for us. We should ask Vidvana what she knows from Mundani history about that time period.

After communing with the three waifs from the three Túl Benisons, Zara is satisfied that she knows where to search for the new community. All three seem to orient toward a common destination. Zara and Abél rejoin the others and approach Vidvana where she and Salma have erected a shelter. Salma prepares food while Vidvana adds sticks to a struggling fire. After assuring the two Mundani women that they now know what course to take to find Túl, Zara asks Vidvana about Mundani history around the start of the Ancient Granite Meed.

After a quick calculation, Vidvana says, "That would correlate with the Mundani passage 438, more than two hundred passages ago. At that time it may have been prudent for the Túl Melfar to restrict attendance at the dedication of the Benison." She adds a more substantial stick to the fire as it begins to blaze. "It had been fewer than forty returns since the final death of Razak Pherson and there was a great deal of discord and division among Mundani." She sits back, watching her fire with satisfaction. "Although it was a period of passive peace between Mundani and Melfar, Mundani didn't like it when Melfar strayed too far from what they considered to be Melfar's assigned homes," Vidvana says. "Large groups of pilgrims might have caused concern."

Zara settles herself near the fire next to Abél. "Under such circumstances," she says, "an affirmation of the virtues of solitude could have been beneficial to Melfar as well."

Abél recalls what Zara shared with him when he'd asked her about the Ancient Obsidian's song called Overwhelm With Splendor. The Ancient Obsidian Meed followed after the Ancient Granite and Zara had said that the Ancient Obsidian Meed had been a period of unprecedented Melfar expansion into previously unsettled areas. Abél's mind follows his gaze into the darkening woods surrounding Old Túl and, as he contemplates what Zara said about the Song of Solitude, he's seized with sepia loneliness.

24

As the little company proceeds toward where they hope to find New Túl, Abél is soothed, almost spellbound by the deepening forest. So many memories of his childhood and youth are filled with forests such as this, steeped in their songs. No, those forests were even more magnificent. Older. Wise with all of the songs that the trees relayed throughout the three great Melfar forests. Abél is certain that he can pertange fragments of old songs still held in the roots beneath his feet here in Cesta. He listens for the three Túl songs—the Song of Solitude, the Song of Turning, and especially for the Song of the Sea.

"Are you sure we're going in the right direction?" Salma glances back over her shoulder and peers into the woods to right and left. "I feel like we're going in circles."

Zara laughs. "That's because someone is using a Song of Turning to try and get us lost."

"So even though it looks to me like we're going in circles...?"

"We're right on course."

"Why would they try to make us lose our way?" Vidvana says. "Can't they tell that we're Melfar? Well, some of us are Melfar."

"They're unsure about us," Zara says. "I've sent messages to tell them that we mean no harm, that we're friends of Boovez. I'm sure they pertanged that. But they've also pertanged the presence of Mundani. They're confident that if Melfar are leading the way we'll arrive in spite of their efforts. You might call it a kind of test. To see who's in charge."

Abél had been inattentive, lost in his own thoughts and the enchantment of the forest. He's chagrined as he belatedly notices the effects of the Song of Turning and thanks Zara for her vigilance. He chuckles, reminding himself that Túl is where the Ancient Amber and its Song of Turning originated. It's hardly surprising that the people of Túl are expert in its use.

Zara hadn't expected the new site of Túl to be such a distance from the old site. Though she can't see the sun through the forest canopy, she knows that it's already past its zenith.

She stops suddenly, motioning the others to stop, too, and to stand silent. She cocks her head and opens her orb. *Someone's there.*

Just ahead. Abél pertanges them, too.

"Boovez breth Noita!" Zara calls out, vocalizing the name so that Vidvana and Salma know who this woman is who seems to have materialized from behind a tree that is no longer there.

Zara breth Itzal, Boovez says. *How nice to see you here! And here is Abél breth Avienne. Welcome to our forest home.* "I see Vidvana has come as well, but this other Mundani is unknown to me."

Zara introduces Salma as Boovez makes gestures of welcome to each of the travelers. A young boy steps out from behind (or from within) another tree. "This is my son, Kimsa," Boovez says.

Together, the group—now six in number—makes its way confidently toward Túl, toward the place where Túl now exists. Kimsa evaporates into the forest and reemerges with handfuls of berries, which he shares with everyone before disappearing again and reappearing with more berries.

"Here we are," Boovez announces suddenly.

Without this woman's guidance, Abél wonders if they wouldn't have become lost after all. There's no clearing such as the one that marked the old site of Túl. Here there are only small houses lodged against the trunks of undisturbed trees and so shrouded in still-living vines as to be almost invisible. It's not what Abél was expecting.

Boovez chuckles at their confusion. "We've built as Melfar once did, without disrupting the forest and safely away from the eyes of strangers." *You're not strangers,* she adds. *You're welcome here.* She invites them into one of the houses and offers tea.

In the dim interior, an old woman sits next to the only window, mending a garment by lamplight. "This is Noita breth Idös," Boovez says, after first naming each of them to Noita.

This is your mother? Zara nods respectfully toward the old woman, who continues concentrating on her work.

"Yes, my mother." *I know you have questions for her. Of course I know why you've come. But wait a while. Let her get accustomed to your energy first.*

They drink tea and exchange pleasantries. It becomes clear that Boovez doesn't know the full reason for their arrival in her veiled community. She knew there had been trouble in New Beniford. She knew that they wanted to talk about the Song of the Sea, but she didn't know why. Patiently, they try to explain to her in images, using words hardly at all. It's evident that Boovez finds words awkward and tiresome.

Where did such people come from? Do you think Meridia is among them now? What a tragedy! Boovez clasps her fists in front of her face and blinks furiously.

Abél watches Noita. As she absorbs the story, a knowing look steals across her face.

So they came back, did they? she says.

25

"We're going to have to get you out of here," Limn says. Or rather she utters some incomprehensible vocalizations and her machine produces the message in words that Yuli and Meridia can understand. Limn has been tapping away at her machine ever since she got home. Odilia is fussy and Yuli knows it's because she's hungry. Meridia knows, too, and she's annoyed that there's nothing she can do about her nen's discomfort. She's already nursed Omi, but now she's getting fretful, too, in empathy with her sister twin.

"Odi is hungry," Yuli says. She's been instructed not to interrupt Limn when she's working, but she does it anyway.

"Of course." Limn taps more of the little squares on her machine. "We'll have to take a supply of the supplement powder with us. I've made a note." She stares at the screen on her machine and then glances back toward Yuli. "Oh, you mean right now. I'm sorry. Yes. I'll get her bottle."

Yuli thanks Limn and almost apologizes for bothering her. Limn looks even more anxious than usual. And she looks tired.

Limn is very tired. She's been at her office and in the laboratory trying to finish up her research, determined to learn what she can about everything she brought back from her expedition into the southern hemisphere. She received the DNA analysis of the old man who had tried to keep them from taking the mirrors. Even a cursory assessment was sufficient to show that he was not as distinct from Yuli as she'd anticipated. She noticed that a couple of the genetic deviations were the same ones she'd detected for the baby. She promises herself that she'll examine the data in more detail when she has the opportunity. If she has the opportunity.

As for the mirror fragment, she'd been surprised at the radiation it emitted. It was a very low level, but still unexpected. The component she'd been most interested in, however, was a silicate that the lab's X-ray fluorescence analysis returned as "unidentified." Nonetheless, it matched perfectly with the composition of the substance she'd been searching for, the one she'd learned about from ancient data files. Its presence in the mirrors had been a surprise. An intriguing surprise. Limn's team had recovered several small chunks of the pure substance from Swarthpol. She hopes to be able to snatch one of those on what she knows will be her final visit to the lab.

Limn had read about the "unidentified" silicate in a couple of relic lab reports she'd recovered last year from some previously inaccessible data servers—solar powered computers into which data had been reflexively copied and recopied for generations without anyone ever bothering to see what it was. This complete absence of curiosity among her people has become intolerable to Limn. It was these reports that launched her on the risky adventure from which she's only just returned. According to the relic data, the silicate is called ecphorite.

Limn brings the bottle for Odi. She's disturbed by the nagging suspicion that her occasional perception of two infants crying is not just her imagination. And, yes, she's curious. She'd been so worried about Yuli during the nights she spent working at the lab that she'd left the surveillance camera switched on. She was certain that, more than once, she'd seen Yuli communicating with someone. Not talking, but there were facial expressions and gestures. Intent and response. She decides it's time to ask. She pushes her chair back from the desk and turns toward Yuli. "Yuli," she says, "is there someone else here with you?"

Yuli looks up, her eyes wide, her heart lurching wildly. She glances toward the spot where Meridia stands. Meridia clutches Naomi closer. "Would you mind so much if there was?" Yuli says.

"No," Limn says. "I know your people are different, capable of things we rational scientist types don't understand. But if we're going somewhere together— and we are—it might be useful to know how many of us are going."

"Meridia is here," Yuli says. Her voice is breathy and barely audible. "Meridia and Naomi."

"And is one of them a nen? Are they kin to you?"

"Meridia is Odi's mother. Naomi is Odi's sister twin."

Limn stands for a moment with her hand over her mouth, staring at the spot where Yuli's eyes fell when she spoke of Meridia. Meridia isn't there anymore, but no matter. "Well, you're welcome to come with us, Meridia," Limn says. Then, turning back to Yuli, she asks, "Can she hear me?"

"Yes, I can hear you," Meridia says.

Though the computer translates the words without difficulty, Limn is taken aback. The voice sounds like nothing she's ever heard before. It's muffled and distorted, as if it's filtered through a thinly vibrating metal wall, its texture shredded into separate strands. It reminds her vaguely of the warbling of a bird she heard once. A recording of a bird. In a museum.

"So I really was hearing two nens crying!" Limn is overcome with excitement about this discovery. She takes a step toward the spot where Meridia's voice came from and she's stunned when she feels someone take her hand. The weight of the touch dissipates almost at once and yet she continues to feel it. Tears well up in her eyes.

There's a knock on the door and Limn raises a finger to her lips. "You can't let Jack know," she says. She toggles off the translator, straightens her shoulders and, taking a deep breath, she walks toward the door, calmly and deliberately.

My heart pounds and my hands shake. *Was it a mistake to let Limn know I can communicate with her?*

No, Meridia, Yuli says. Her heart is beating almost as rapidly as mine. *Whatever she's planning, I think you may be able to help. It's better that she knows.*

Limn opens the door to let this person called Jack inside, closing it quickly and locking it three ways.

Jack is dressed in dull yellow garments. Her face is exceptionally pale and I think it may be an artificial coating of some kind. There's a dot of bright red on the end of her nose.

I'd heard Limn talking through her computer to Jack. She'd forgotten to turn off the translator. Or maybe she wanted Yuli to hear. What she'd told the woman in yellow was that she and her friend were going to play a prank on someone and needed to dress up as entertainers. I'm not sure what a prank is, but it seems to be some sort of performance. Something amusing. They laughed a lot as they talked about it.

They're laughing now.

Limn had tried to explain her plan to Yuli. "These entertainers are outrageously truthful," she said. "If we tell Jack what we're really doing, she'll be incapable of keeping it to herself. We have to make it into a performance. That's something she understands."

I'm sure I don't understand what we're really doing any better than Jack does.

"Is this the one you want me to dress up?" Jack says. She stands directly in front of Yuli. She's too close and Yuli instinctively takes a step back. Jack stands with her hands on her hips, elbows forward, her chin drawn in awkwardly. "She's a strange-looking one, Limn Ssu, but with the right makeup I think I can make it work." Jack turns back toward Yuli. "What's your name, girl?"

Yuli's eyes widen. She knows she's been asked a question, but she doesn't know what it was or how to respond.

"Her name is Jules, Jack. But she's shy. She probably won't answer you." Limn places a finger to her lips and sends Yuli an urgent look. "Besides, you can tell by the clothes she's wearing that she's Pa clone set. You know they don't ever talk much."

The entertainer sets her bag down and takes out some garments—two sets of clothes in the same color as her own. She holds the shirt up in front of Yuli. "You didn't tell me she was so fat. And short. Not like any Pa I ever met. Never mind, I think we can squeeze her big teats into this." She grabs for the shirt Yuli is wearing.

Yuli takes hold of Jack's wrist and gently pushes her hand away. She picks up the garments and begins to undress, her back turned toward Jack and Limn.

"Kinda pushy for a Pa, isn't she? Why's she wearing that yellow makeup? We'll have to get that off before we put on the white."

"It's not makeup, Jack. She…uh…she was exposed to some chemicals that turned her skin that color." Limn grimaces. She should have thought this out in more detail ahead of time.

"Oh." Jack sucks her teeth. "Hunh." She turns toward Limn and whispers, "Probably due for elimination soon, right? Poor thing." Jack's eyes fall on the contraption in the corner where Odi is sleeping. "Is that the baby you mentioned? Don't know why you want to take a baby along on this gag, but if it's in the script…" She takes a couple of steps toward the crib.

"Don't worry about the baby." Limn doesn't want Jack to see Odi. If Jack thinks Yuli looks strange, what might she say about Odi's iridescent skin? "We'll just carry the baby along in this bag." Limn holds up a large bag.

Yuli's eyes flash with alarm, her gaze darting toward the spot where Meridia is standing. Limn holds her hands facing one another and then moves them apart. She hopes Yuli and Meridia understand that she's saying the bag will remain open at the top. Yuli's shoulders slump in helpless acquiescence, even though every muscle in her face remains tense.

The yellow garments make Yuli's amber skin look even yellower. The shirt is too tight and the trousers too long. Jack does her best to pin the pants legs up so that Yuli won't trip over them when she walks. She begins applying a pale cream to Yuli's face. It turns her skin almost white. Finally, she adds a touch of red to the end of Yuli's nose. While Jack is busy applying the makeup, Limn takes the opportunity to slip the sleeping Odi into the carrying bag.

Jack picks up Yuli's tawny-colored hand and turns it over and back again. "We need gloves," she says, "and we need to do something about her hair. Whatever made it go all kinky like that? More effects of the chemicals, right? Do you have a wig?"

"No, I'm sorry," Limn says.

"Never mind, she can use mine." Jack grabs the top of her head and yanks. The hair comes away—the wig—revealing hair underneath that is just as black and straight as the wig. She shakes the wig out and puts it on Yuli, tucking in stray amber curls and arranging the black hair to hide Yuli's ears.

Limn finds some gloves that are too small for Yuli's plump hands, compressing them so much that she can barely move her fingers. Limn has put on yellow garments, too, and coats her own face in the white makeup.

Jack adds the red dot to Limn's nose. "Oh, you look smashing, Limn Ssu! Whoever you're pranking will never know it's you!" Jack's laugh makes Limn smile in spite of her worries.

Limn takes a deep breath and goes to her computer. She taps on it for a moment. Waits. Taps once more. "Okay, we have seven minutes to clear the premises," she says.

Jack giggles, clearly relishing this risky performance.

Yuli follows Limn and Jack out the door. They enter the elevator and the doors begin to close, then suddenly pop open again. Limn smiles, confident that Meridia is with them. She punches a button to force the doors closed and the elevator begins its descent.

When the doors open, Jack stands at the front of the little group and spreads her arms, throws back her head, and shouts "Ta-dah!" She laughs and the group of people standing in front of them laugh, too, and slap their hands together. They exit with Jack doing a little dance and Limn and Yuli awkwardly copying her movements.

Being out on the street, surrounded by so many strangers, Yuli is clearly unnerved.

Odi begins to cry and a shadow of panic flashes across Limn's face. But Jack pretends that it's her making the noise. The crying continues and people barely notice, but if they do, they grin at Jack and slap their hands together a few times as they pass.

When they reach an old building far down a lonely side street, Jack opens a door by tapping a small light with a card. There are stairs. They climb several sets of them before Jack opens another door into her residence. Limn tries not to show how appalled she is at the cramped and dilapidated space. The rooms are tiny and the furniture drab and worn. There's only one window. It's a tiny window, but its view of the ocean is expansive. There are several ships lined up at docks along the shore. In the fading evening light, Limn searches for the one she intends to commandeer. She turns back toward Jack with a conspiratorial smile. Jack has no idea. Neither do Yuli and Meridia.

26

Abél turns to address Noita, the old woman who is Boovez's mother. *You know about these people, then. These Elossa.*

Is that what you're calling them? We just called them empty people.

Abél experiences a rush of images—a ship, rocks, frantic workmen digging. The impressions pass so quickly he struggles to process them.

Noita has put down her handwork and squints into the dim light of the cabin toward Abél. She slows her verberations, making them more deliberate. *That song was meant as a warning. You want to know about it because they came back. And because your daughter is gone. Your Calumet.*

Noita's images are brief but vivid, vibrant, each thought verberating with intense clarity and detail. Abél is overwhelmed as he struggles to pertange it all. His own orb and aurynx feel shamefully slow and sluggish in comparison to hers. He knows Noita must have found the imagery he verberated cumbersome as he attempted to show Boovez how the Elossa came first to Selbourne and then to New Beniford, how they took Yuli and Odilia, and then how Meridia and Naomi vanished from Amos Quint's mirrored chamber.

"He shouldn't have messed with the mirrors," Noita says, gazing at Vidvana and Salma with amber eyes so clear they almost glow. *Mundani don't know what they're doing.*

"What do you know about the mirrors?" Abél says, hoping Noita will continue to use words.

"It's what the empty people wanted when they came among us before. That and the ecphorite. But you should ask our Calumet about that. Idös knows more than I do."

Abél's eyes go wide in amazement. "You have your own Calumet?" *How could I not have known that? And if your name is Noita breth Idös... is the Calumet your mother?*

We've always had our own Calumet, though we honored yours as well. Especially Avienne breth Meridia. And yes, Idös is my mother.

Abél turns toward Boovez. He continues using words for the benefit of Vidvana and Salma. "Could you take us to your Calumet, to Idös?"

"We have to ask her first if she's willing to see you." Boovez looks at Vidvana and Salma as she says this. It's clear that these Mundani women are a potential obstacle.

"We understand," Zara says. *Why didn't you tell me these things when you were in Beniford?*

You didn't ask.

Zara smiles in acknowledgment. "Please tell Idös that Vidvana is the Mundani scholar who wrote down all the words for the *Book of All Time*."

Boovez isn't sure that will help. *Idös isn't entirely convinced that the book was a good idea.*

Zara feels chastened by such skepticism. She shouldn't have been so proud.

Boovez closes her eyes for a moment and then says, "While we give Idös time to consider your request, I invite you all to share a meal with us. Our food is simple, but I can assure you that it's fresh and healthful."

The meal is delicious. Abél is already well satisfied, but then Boovez passes around slices of a starchy root drenched in honey and spices and he has to try it.

As they conclude their meal, Boovez announces, "Idös will receive Abél breth Avienne and his companion Zara breth Itzal."

Abél sees the disappointment on Vidvana's face. More than disappointment. Annoyance. Annoyance at being treated with such prejudice. Then she purses her lips and lowers her chin. Abél knows she has just reminded herself how Melfar have been consistently treated by Mundani. Vidvana will acquiesce without protest.

The boy Kimsa waits at the doorway as if he expects to accompany Boovez and Abél and Zara to his eldmother's house. There's a flurry of verberations between him and Boovez and then Kimsa steps away, returning to sit next to Noita.

As they walk among the almost-living houses, Abél wonders which one shelters Idös, the Calumet of the Melfar of Túl. She must be even older than Avienne was at her death. *Did Idös know Avienne?*

Yes, they met. Boovez verberates a series of fleeting images that Abél finds impossible to follow.

They keep walking. Soon Abél sees no more houses, only forest. *Have we left the village?*

Yes, Boovez says. *Our Calumets have always lived apart. It will be a while yet before we reach Idös.*

Abél tries to think if such was ever a custom among the Melfar of Lindmor or Beniford. He can't recall Avienne ever mentioning it to him. These Melfar of Túl definitely have their own ways.

Boovez chuckles as if in acknowledgment of Abél's thoughts. He's discomfited by the fact that she can pertange him so perfectly and yet seems capable of shielding her own verberations from him when she chooses to do so.

If Idös likes you, maybe she'll show you how it's done.

The forest is taller here, the ground more open the further they go. Abél hears birds that sound familiar, though he can't name them. Tiredness drops away from his limbs as his mind summons up youthful rambles in such forests. The scent of moss, decaying leaves, and flowering vines is intoxicating, the buzz of insects mesmerizing, the hints of song entrancing.

Boovez takes his arm to draw his attention to the fact that they've arrived. She's stopped just a few spans from a little house. It's built of stone and resembles a large anthill rising from the ground. There's a woman in the doorway.

The woman is tiny, as if the flow of time has whittled away at her body until there's little left of her beyond her essence. That essence, however, is huge and her eyes are as bright and golden as two drops of honey. She doesn't beckon them to enter. Instead she gestures toward an arrangement of benches fashioned from logs. They sit there. She knows why they've come and launches immediately into a sequence of evanescent images. Abél is enthralled.

It happened in the Ancient Obsidian and Ancient Jade Meeds. Melfar spread all throughout Cesta. Many villages. A few large towns. Destruction of many, many trees to make space. Time passed and some went even farther. They went all the way to the edge of the sea, over there beyond Markham. Too far. They changed. We lost them. They were no longer Melfar. Many returns later, some of them came back to us broken. Broken from serving the Mundani and the others who came, the empty ones. The Song of the Sea is a story they brought.

Idös begins to sing.

At first Zara doesn't recognize the song. But soon she begins to hum along with Idös. When the song finishes, she says, *That's different from the way we learned it in Beniford. It starts in an entirely different place. That's why I didn't recognize the tune at first. But I see now that this is the way the story really goes. It begins with the great winged ship sinking near Selbourne and the empty people being rescued by Melfar.*

Some of those rescuers were our eldpeople, Idös says. *They couldn't communicate with the empty ones, but they helped them. They pitied them. Such sad people, stranded far from home among people they couldn't understand. They wanted ecphorite and Melfar helped them find it. They wanted mirrors.*

Idös stops, her brow furrowed, the images in her mind going all topsy-turvy. She nods and the images sort into a new sequence. *They had questions for the ecphorite. No answers were there at Swarthpol. They wanted to take the ecphorite and the mirrors home. Back to their own home. Melfar built them a boat, but it was too small. They went only as far as Selbourne and stayed there.*

Did she say Selbourne, or does Abél only recognize the island she showed him?

Those who brought us the story say the empty people disturbed something at the place they called Swarthpol.

It was bad for Melfar but they didn't leave. They were ignorant of their altered condition. Helpless.

Abél shudders, recalling such a feeling of impotence. Recalling ignorance.

You've been to Swarthpol. I'm sorry for you. What a terrible place for Melfar. The song was meant as a warning. She's asking him why he went there, chastising him for his foolishness.

Abél wishes that he could shield the story of why he was at Swarthpol from Idös, but he knows he can't.

The old Calumet shakes her head in sympathy. *I've never personally been in the presence of someone who survived that place. And now you're thinking of going back.*

Abél acknowledges that the thought has been there in his mind. *What about the mirrors?* He asks this instead of pursuing the question of his future course of action.

I know nothing about the mirrors. What you've told me about your daughter Meridia and your brother Brân surprises me. I don't know what the mirrors are, what they're for. I don't know how they came to be at Swarthpol. I only know that the empty people wanted them and took some of them to the island. And now it looks like they still want them. Mundani never should have disturbed those mirrors.

Maybe. But I think the Migrant has used them to show us stories about our eldpeople.

Idös's verberations become so fleeting and complex that Abél is unable to make sense of them. She's trying to sort out how the Migrant and the mirrors connect. She's troubled.

Boovez showed me what Meridia learned about our eldpeople, the stories that Zara and the Mundani scholar set down in their book. I sometimes wonder if it does us any good to know so much about our past. Melfar and Mundani should each just keep to their own path. Each go our own way.

She begins humming a simple tune that Abél knows at once must be the Song of Solitude. It draws their orbs together with a singular clarity that feels like moonlight. Images become shadows and dissolve into light and then even Abél's perception of the place where they sit dissipates and there is nothing left but pure white light and the silvery sound of Idös's voice. When Idös finishes singing, they sit in purified silence for a while. Finally the old Calumet speaks, using words that still resonate with song. "Other Melfar are not like the Melfar of Túl. They're losing their attunement to the natural songs of the endlessness of forest and water and sky."

Is that what it is?

We've learned to be still and listen, to channel all the songs that the trees know. Our Benisons are strong, too. What we encode in our Benisons is vivid and everlasting.

Are your Benisons still standing?

Yes, of course. You passed one of them on your journey. She chuckles.

Abél knows she's talking about the Ancient Amber. That was why the Song of Turning had felt so strong. That was why they almost lost themselves.

The Granite is a day's journey northeast of here, but the Jasper is nearby. Do you want to see it?

Abél does want to see it. He follows the old woman as she guides them toward the Benison with slow but certain steps. Unhurried, as if she's swimming through the ocean of sensory experience along the way, through trees and plants and scents and colors embroidered with the songs of birds. Abél loses himself in the immediacy of so much aliveness.

Idös stops.

At first Abél thinks she's only stopped to catch her breath or to rest aching knees. But then he sees it. Why had he expected that there would be a clearing? No, the Ancient Jasper is right there, covered in moss and vines and the excrement of forest creatures. The stone is barely visible, little more than a shape, but Abél pertanges its resonance as Idös begins to sing. He joins her and his will collapses into the detailed imagery the old Calumet evokes.

There is the great ship, one of its brilliant white wings torn, its hull canted and sinking. The waters are roiled by the desperate efforts of spectral people, silent and blank. Melfar drag them to shore, tend their injuries, feed them, and offer safety. There are no verberations from the rescued sailors. Their mouths move, but nothing comes out. In Swarthpol, the strangers build their own dwellings and day after day dig into the earth and move stones to unblock passageways. They show the Melfar white pebbles of ecphorite and beg them to search for more, to dive beneath the waters of the pond. There they uncover huge white rocks of ecphorite. Using gestures, they entreat Melfar to bring back other treasures from the dark pool. The Melfar divers find two mirrors and many pieces of obsidian, a strange obsidian that glows intense purple at its heart. The strangers take the mirrors and some ecphorite and obsidian and, in a small boat built by Melfar, cross the water to a stony island, never to be seen again.

Abél coughs and draws in a sharp breath, overwhelmed by the memory of how he was nearly drowned. Was it in the same pool the song speaks of? Although the song doesn't say it, he knows what happened to those Melfar who once lived at Swarthpol. He knows that there is something there that changed them. Something that changed him. And in the mirrors, there is also a power to move things. A power that took Brân away. And now it's taken Meridia.

Idös thinks it can also bring her back. The old Calumet takes a deep breath, inhaling the song back into herself. *Yes, Abél breth Avienne, you may have to go back to Swarthpol.*

27

Damon feels a nudge of nostalgia as he and his companions approach his old photography shop down a side street of Temur. The town seems busier than it used to be, more prosperous. The little shop still belongs to Damon, though it stands shuttered and nearly empty. He moved the bulk of his equipment to New Beniford. As long as he's here, he thinks he'd just as well to retrieve the last of his printing paper to take back with him. He'd hoped to find a source for it in Fayredell, but photography is not in high demand these days. Damon thinks about the fact that he has no photographs of Meridia or the nens. He'd been kept too busy making the special pictures for the *Book of All Time*.

"We ought to go see Elvrid while we're here," Orban says, watching Damon as he places the box of paper into his backsack next to the bundle of Fannan's photographs. "He said he'd be coming here after the Gathering. I think he may be planning to move back to Temur."

"I liked working with Elvrid on the book," Umet says. "It would be good to see him again."

They've already agreed to visit with Gerd at Meridia's old house. Damon doesn't look forward to visiting Gerd, and it has nothing to do with Gerd herself. He's fearful of the memories he'll find at the house he knew as Meridia's house. Fearful of what such memories might evoke. Damon knows he's in a fragile state. He's grateful to delay by visiting the bookseller.

Elvrid's shop is down the next street. Damon thinks about how many times he passed it by without ever stopping to investigate what kinds of information and curiosities it might hold. The books Elvrid took to New Beniford have piqued Damon's interest and he's curious now to see what else he might find in Elvrid's extensive collection. Elvrid claims his family has printed and sold books for at least seven generations.

The bookshop is open but devoid of customers. Elvrid sits in a tattered chair, absorbed in the story he's reading. He places a scrap of paper inside the book to mark his place and looks up with a scowl to see who dares to interrupt him. His face is transformed when he sees who it is. "Damon! Umet! And Orban, too. Welcome! What brings you fellows to Temur?" His face falls as he anticipates their answer. "Gerd told me about your alien visitors in New Beniford. And about what happened to Meridia. Is there any news?"

"No," Damon says. "No news." He doesn't want to talk about that. He doesn't want to face the hopelessness that engulfs him whenever he thinks about it. Instead he explains that they're coming from Woodclasp and he describes what they've brought away with them to show to Abél.

"Abél came through here on his way to Túl," Elvrid says. "You should stay until he returns on his way back to New Beniford."

"Perhaps we'll do that," Damon says. "I don't suppose you have any more books about ships, do you? The one you brought back to New Beniford didn't have anything in it about ships like the Elossa." The ships described in the old book Damon saw had sails, but their sails were designed to catch the wind. The wing-like sails of the Elossa and of the ship pictured in Fannan's photograph look altogether different. They seem to be designed to adjust around a horizontal axis rather than a vertical axis.

Elvrid scans the shelves on the far side of the shop as he taps his chin with a forefinger. He points and nods. A few quick steps take him to the book he wants.

"Do you know all of the books in your shop?" Orban says.

"I think so. I've lived with them all my life. I've read most of them. Many of them more than once. Mother finally stopped selling the oldest books, you know, only lending them to trusted friends. Or maybe it was my eldfather started that. Mother was so fearful that some Palinjian would buy books just to fuel one of their ashing bonfires." He hands the book to Damon. "Take a look and see if this has anything useful. You can sit here. I'll bring you some tea."

Damon opens the book. It's an old one; its faded cover hangs in pieces and its pages are yellowed and brittle. And yet the pages are still smooth and tight along the spine, suggesting that the book has had few readers. While Elvrid fetches tea, Damon flips through the pages, looking for pictures, but catching a few words here and there. At the center of the book, he finds a series of illustrations. One of them shows a ship. He leans in closer to study it. The ship has two great white sheets, one on each side like the wings of a butterfly. The sun is depicted in one corner of the picture and there's a pattern of bright spots on the sails that look like small suns. He reads the caption under the drawing: "This is the ship that reportedly sank off our western coast in the passage 472, as described by a Shoon man of that region."

"That's it!" Damon says. "Look, Umet. Isn't that the same ship as in the photograph?"

"It certainly looks the same," Umet says. "Except the one in the photograph had one of its wings torn. And it was sinking. But definitely the same sort of ship. What does it say about it in the text?"

Damon scans a few pages and finds no mention of a ship. He flips back to the cover, searching for the title of the book. The words are too faded to decipher. He opens to the title page: *Shoon Tales and Legends.* No wonder no one read the book. Mundani have never found anything Melfar said to be of any importance. And Melfar don't read. He searches for the name of the book's author and finds only a ragged line where it ought to be, as if someone had tried to scrape away the name with a knife point.

"What do you know about this book, Elvrid?" Damon reaches for the proffered glass of tea with a nod of thanks to the bookseller.

"That's actually one that I never read," he says. "But I had opened it to the center to see if there were any pictures and I thought there might have been a ship there. Lots of books put a collection of illustrations at the center. I didn't even know the name of the book, only what the cover looked like."

Damon wonders how that's possible. So many of the books on Elvrid's shelves have equally tattered covers. "I'd like to buy this book from you if you're willing to sell it. How much?" Damon has spent most of the coins he brought with him for the journey, but he'll gladly sell some of his possessions in order to acquire the book.

"Take it," Elvrid says. "And maybe bring it back when you're done with it. Or not. I know you'll make good use of it."

Damon expresses his gratitude and tucks the book into his backsack with his box of papers and the bundle of Fannan's photographs. The little group lingers a while longer in Elvrid's shop, drinking tea and avoiding talking about what's really on their minds. When Elvrid learns where they're headed next, he volunteers to close up his shop and accompany them.

The closer Damon comes to Meridia's house, the more intensely he feels her absence. Doubts and regrets plague him as he contemplates all the things they might have done differently that would not have ended in this painful state of affairs. He touches the Quartz bead that hangs around his neck and takes a deep breath to quell the despair gripping his heart.

Gerd welcomes them with open arms, holding Damon quietly for a moment to let him know that she, too, misses Meridia.

Damon is comforted to see that Gerd has rearranged the sparse furniture to suit her own needs, making the space seem somewhat less familiar. Somewhat less empty of Meridia. Gerd insists they join her for supper, and over a delicious repast of scurfpea stew and fresh nutbread, they exchange stories. Damon notices that Elvrid seems to know where all the plates and utensils are kept; he brings a jar of tea from outdoors without Gerd asking.

As soon as courtesy permits, Damon excuses himself and finds a spot outdoors where he can settle comfortably to read his newly acquired old book in the waning evening light.

There's no list of contents and the book isn't arranged in anything like chapters. It's just a collection of stories—"tales and legends"—printed sequentially according to no discernible plan. He reads a few of the stories and quickly realizes that whatever Mundani person wrote these down had very little understanding of Melfar capacities and customs. They're written as if Melfar (who are consistently referred to as Shoons) are illiterate fools who believe all sorts of fantastical nonsense. The book may not be as helpful as Damon had hoped.

He flips through more pages, scanning without really reading anything, until a name catches his eye: Swarthpol. It's a brief entry and Damon reads it eagerly: "A Shoon man from a village called Swarthpol tells a strange story of a ship sinking off our western coast. He claims that his own eldfather helped rescue people from the ship and that those people came from a land far to the north where people flew about in machines driven by power sucked from the sun. According to a resident of Markham, Swarthpol may once have been called Harilun. The Shoons who live there are exceptionally dull and slothful. Their belief in alien sun-beings from a northern land does not appear among any of the other Shoon groups I've contacted." The next entry is about a Shoon from Lindmor who "worships talking trees."

Damon knows this is something else he will want to share with Abél. He hurries inside to tell Gerd and Elvrid and Orban. They're enthusiastic, but Umet has that faraway look that makes Damon ask, "What is it Umet? Do you know something?"

"I know nothing about your book, Damon. But I know that if you want to share it with Abél, you won't meet him here. Abél is on his way to Swarthpol."

28

Limn explains to Jack that there have been some changes in plans that must unfortunately force a delay in the launch of her prank. "You go on to work, Jack. We'll be okay from here." She thanks Jack profusely for her assistance.

"So long, then," Jack says. She leans back inside the door and, closing one eye and thrusting a thumb into the air, she says, "Break a leg!"

Limn is relieved to be alone at last. *Hardly alone,* she reminds herself. Yuli, after all, is the reason why she's about to leave behind everything she knows. And all because there's so much more she wants to know. She wants to know more about these people—and they are people, just as much as she herself is. And she knows they have not just one infant, but two. The infants' mother is here as well, though not exactly here. Limn is slightly amazed at her own credulity about these things.

She sets up her portable computer and begins tapping away. She has two goals in mind: First, to facilitate their departure from Port Sillick. And second, to arrange cover so that no one will realize she's gone until it's too late to do anything about it. She has a plan in mind that she's convinced will meet the first goal. She's less confident about the second.

As night falls, she prepares a bottle of infant supplement and hands it to Yuli. "We'll need to keep the nens as quiet as possible, so make sure Odi is well fed. And when we leave, just try and copy whatever I do."

"Where will we go?" Yuli asks.

"We're going to get on a boat." Limn's tone of voice makes it clear that she has too much on her mind to answer any more questions.

Soon the little group is out the door and down the stairs and back on the street. Yuli divides her attention between Odi and Limn and Meridia. Limn walks quickly and quietly down the street, staying out of the most brightly lit areas. Suddenly she leans down and whispers into Yuli's ear. "Is Meridia still with us?"

Without the assistance of the translator, the only word Yuli understands is "Meridia." She nods. "Yes," she says, using Limn's language. She pronounces the word oddly but Limn appreciates the effort.

They arrive at the dock and as Limn makes her way toward one of the ships with wings—a considerably smaller vessel than the one that brought Yuli to Port Sillick—she begins to gesture broadly and sing: "Free beer! Free beer! At Wembly's Pub you'll find good cheer! Free beer! Free beer!"

Her performance at first has little effect. She repeats the little ditty again and again, and as she sings more loudly, people begin to take notice. They turn and chat with one another. And then they move away, all going in a common direction.

Limn approaches the ship that is her intended target; it bears the name "Pequod." She almost laughs, knowing that the name likely means nothing to anyone but her. It's meaningful only to a child who once perused dusty books and forbidden stories, dreaming of great white whales in closed-off sections of old libraries.

Limn continues singing as she crosses the little bridge onto the ship, dancing as she makes the rounds of the ship's deck. Yuli dances, too, doing her best to follow Limn's lead. Members of the crew laugh and clap and then, in twos and threes, they depart the ship, joining the growing crowd of people moving in a direction that Yuli assumes must be toward Wembly's Pub.

On her next circuit of the deck, Limn leans down and casts off first one and then another of the ropes that had secured the ship to the dock. Then she stops singing and runs to the ship's helm, starting up the engines and pointing the little ship out toward open water. With a jerk, it surges forward.

"What are you doing?" A sailor has suddenly emerged from below deck, rubbing her eyes as if she's just awakened. She casts about, looking for companions and explanations. "Who are you?"

Limn frantically pushes buttons on the lighted panel in front of her. The engines rev faster and the ship surges through the waves.

"You have no business…" the woman starts, as Limn turns and points a device toward her. The woman's mouth is still open, but before any more words can emerge, there's a spark from Limn's device and the woman falls to the deck, silent.

Yuli's eyes fill with horror as she crouches against the wall in disbelief. "Is she…?"

"Probably," Limn says, turning back to the vessel's controls. Sometimes communication is possible without understanding the language.

Yuli's hands shake as she removes the constricting gloves and lifts a wailing Odi from inside the bag.

Limn reaches for her mobile computer and turns on the translator. "Did Meridia make it?" she asks.

"Yes. She's here. Limn, where are we going? Where are you taking us?" Yuli's voice is faint with fear.

"Home," Limn says. "Your home. I'm taking you home."

29

Abél and his group depart Túl early in the morning, after a restless night on an uneven floor that, for Abél and Zara, resonated with a symphony of songs from the many trees whose roots seem to converge there.

Vidvana at last gives in to her suppressed curiosity. "What did you learn from Idös, Abél? Can you tell me?"

Abél reflects for a moment on Idös's unwillingness to include his two Mundani companions in their meeting. Idös didn't exactly say he shouldn't share what he learned with them. *If she knew Vidvana as I do, she'd understand.* He begins tentatively: "Well, she told us that Melfar once lived in the region of Swarthpol. She said that it was these Melfar who brought to Túl the story that's contained in the Song of the Sea, the story of the empty people who arrived in a great ship. Idös said the empty people were searching for ecphorite, just as the song says, but also for mirrors."

Salma shakes her head in confusion. "Mirrors? But Vidvana told me it was Amos Quint made the mirrors there on Selbourne."

"He made several mirrors," Vidvana says. "But he also found two mirrors there when he arrived. Are those the ones Idös was talking about, Abél?"

"I'm sure it must be. Idös said that the empty people—the Elossa—took the mirrors from Swarthpol to Selbourne in a small boat built by Melfar." At least that is what Abél experienced from the imagery emanating from the Ancient Jasper Benison itself when he stood in its presence, drenched in Idös's song. And it fits the narrative held in the Song of the Sea even though the song itself doesn't mention mirrors. At least there are no mirrors in the version of the song that's come down to the Melfar of Lindmor and Beniford.

Abél thinks about the bit of glass that Amos Quint wanted to give to Lambert. Of course it came from one of those original mirrors. Meridia had known at once that it was nothing ordinary. That's why she didn't take it to Lambert. And it was that shard that led the Elossa to Meridia's house. Abél had asked Meridia to leave the shard with him. He regrets that he didn't insist.

"What is it about those mirrors that makes them different?" Vidvana says. "What makes them able to do what they've done?"

"I can't answer that," Abél says.

The perplexity on Vidvana's face deepens. "I wish we knew exactly when the events recorded in the Song of the Sea took place," she says. "All we know for certain is that it had to be before Mundani passage 474 when the Ancient Jasper was dedicated in Túl. It could have happened any time during the twelve preceding passages, any time since the dedication of the Ancient Jade. Or even earlier." She continues speaking, trying to organize in her own mind the details she can recall about that time, not sure why it should matter whether the events referenced in the Song of the Sea occurred in 460 or 470. She reminds her Melfar listeners that the period throughout the 400s had been an unsettled period for Mundani and a time of isolation for Melfar.

Abél nods, remembering how Zara had explained this period to him when he questioned her about the song called Overwhelm With Splendor.

"Most construction during that time was in stone," Vidvana says, "but in Benbridge and Markham, where stone was scarce, they used wood."

"Yes," Zara says. "There are stories about Mundani in that area recruiting Melfar to cut wood for them. That always struck me as odd, knowing how Melfar feel about trees. Why would Melfar agree to cut trees for Mundani buildings?"

"They wouldn't," Abél says, a hardness glazing his amber eyes. "Unless they had ceased to be Melfar."

"What do you mean?" Vidvana says.

"Idös mentioned that Melfar from that region became broken, that they were no longer Melfar. I'm certain she meant that those who lived near Swarthpol lost their powers of orb and aurynx. I told you about what I experienced when I was there. Idös said that Swarthpol became dangerous because of things that the empty people disturbed." Is that what she was telling them? Abél can't bring himself to mention the dark pool.

"If it's so dangerous, why do you want to go back there, Abél?" Salma asks.

"I'm very sure I do not *want* to go back there. But I must. That place is connected to the Elossa and to the mirrors that took Meridia away. If that place holds anything that can help us get her back again, well, of course I have to go."

When they're back at the old site of Túl, they stop to share a light meal, taking advantage of the bounty of fruits and berries that grow in the abandoned gardens.

Abél reaches inside a pocket of his shirt and takes out something wrapped in cloth.

"What's that?" Zara says. As soon as it's unwrapped, she knows. The stone is almost as large as a gallekrel's egg and, as she gazes at it, focusing her orb, she's engulfed in a murmured dissonance of images and sounds, as if everyone and everything that had ever existed in this place were here all at once, in this very moment. She turns away. "It's ecphorite." She speaks aloud so as not to exclude their two Mundani companions.

"Pure ecphorite? Such a large piece!" Vidvana draws a pair of eyeglasses from a pocket and puts them on so that she can examine the stone more closely.

"What's ecphorite?" Salma says. All she knows is that the stone is very pretty, glistening gold and blue and green as light plays across its surface and penetrates its milky depths.

"Ecphorite is a material that we use in crafting our Benisons," Abél says. "It's what holds the songs and images." He tries to explain the process to Salma but finds he doesn't really understand the exact mechanism himself. He only knows what it does and he knows where to find the ecphorite and how to use it in making the Benisons. Melfar have traditionally sourced ecphorite along the streams and beaches west of the coastal mountains, south of Selbourne. Near Swarthpol? They never find it in large quantities and generally collect only small fragments, mere pebbles in comparison to the piece that shimmers here in Abél's hand.

"What are those other stones?" Salma says.

Abél rearranges the other four stones that rest in the palm of his hand, clustering them closer to the ecphorite. "Those are pointing-stone," he says. "The pointing-stone works to mute the effects of the ecphorite." *Yes, I know, Zara. It's more complicated than that.* He's thinking about how pointing-stone is used along with ecphorite in the crafting of Benisons in order to encode the songs in the desired way. Was there pointing-stone at Swarthpol? Abél can't recall. "Storing ecphorite together with pointing-stone is a practice I learned from our eldpeople."

Abél wraps the ecphorite and pointing-stone securely and hands the bundle to Zara. *I don't wish to take this with me to Swarthpol,* he says. *I'm going to trust you to care for it.*

"Where is he now?" Damon says. He relies on Umet to know where Abél is.

"They've left the old site of Túl," Umet says. "They're following a way that will take them well north of Benbridge. I believe they intend to stop somewhere for the night before they cross to the western side of the main road."

Damon's own little group of travelers is on that main road—the one that leads from Temur to Benbridge—walking fast and steady. They relax their pace, confident that they can easily encounter Abél the next day.

Damon knows this road well. He lived in Benbridge before leaving his photography apprenticeship there and moving to Temur to open his own shop. His family had moved to Benbridge in the aftermath of the fire that took their farm when Damon was just a boy. Thinking about his past, about moving from one place to another, he yearns for home. But where is home? *Home is with Meridia and our nens.* Home is nowhere Damon can go.

30

The boat Limn has stolen bounces across the water at a terrifying speed. I'm not sure how Limn can see where we're going. The little room from which she seems to be operating the craft has only one very small window and outside that window there's nothing but darkness, no lights at all other than small patches of stars between clouds. Limn stares at one of those glowing rectangles she calls a screen. Her fingers tremble as she pokes at a couple of buttons.

Then she smiles and says something we don't understand. She opens her portable device and turns on the translator. "I said, 'This is exciting, isn't it?'" She shakes her head and says, "Not so effective warmed over."

I'm not sure what that means. Yuli looks a bit pale, and I know it's not just because of the makeup that still streaks her face. I think the movement of the boat may be making her ill. It's not affecting me at all.

After a while, Limn slows our speed. "I don't want to use up all of our power before sunrise," she says.

I'm not sure what that means, either, but, for Yuli's sake, I'm grateful that we've stopped bouncing so much.

"You can go inside the cabin down below deck and rest," Limn says.

"I don't think I could rest right now," Yuli says. "We'll stay here if that's okay." Yuli is sitting next to me on a bench across from the only window. Her gaze is fixed on a single bright star just above the horizon.

"Limn," Yuli says, her voice tight with apprehension, "what happened to that woman? The one who was still on the boat when we left? The one you..."

"Overboard. Unfortunate, but I did what I had to do." She shrugs. The woman was a clone and easily replaceable. It's not as if she was a unique individual. Nevertheless, there's a line between Limn's brows, a softness in her dark eyes, a brief pulse of brown from the crown of her head.

"There's something I've been meaning to ask you," Limn says. "About the bracelet you wear. The beads on your wrist."

"Oh. This?" Yuli holds up her arm. "My mentor Bekanz gave it to me."

"Does it have any special meaning? I'm asking because I saw one just like it on the wrist of the old man we encountered on the island. He seems to be different from you in certain ways and I was just wondering if the bracelet indicated some kind of interaction. A connection of some sort."

"Well, we give them to Mundani who are our friends, people who share our desire for peace between Mundani and Melfar. The beads are from the Ancient Carnelian Benison." Yuli glances toward me, wondering if she's said too much.

I shrug slightly and turn my attention toward Limn.

Limn's eyes are wide with some combination of surprise and confusion. The translator has been forced to use the words "Mundani" and "Melfar" and "Benison" since it finds no equivalents in Limn's language.

"Mundani. If I'm going back to where you live, I'd like to learn more about you. More than just scientific data. So the old man was Mundani? And you must be...what did you say?"

"Melfar."

"Are all Mundani your friends?"

"Oh, no. Some Mundani want to kill us. They have killed us. The Mundani Palinjians killed Meridia's partner." Yuli's eyes dart toward me. She's uncertain whether she should have shared this information.

It's okay, Yuli. I think she really wants to know about us.

"Oh, I'm so sorry, Meridia. I didn't know your partner was dead," Limn says.

"He isn't," I say. "Well, he was, but the Migrant brought him back."

Limn lifts her scant eyebrows in astonishment. "Brought back from the dead?" She chuckles softly. "Well, I never. You people—you Melfar—are quite the ticket. It looks like I have a lot to learn. Tell me more about the bracelets."

Between us, Yuli and I tell Limn about the Carnelian beads, about the Song of the Wide Path, and then try to explain about Chanters and Benisons and waifs.

"Meridia helped craft our newest Benison," Yuli says. And she stops. Limn is no longer paying attention to her. Instead, she's staring wide-eyed at one of her screens.

"Oh, shit!" Limn says. "Fuck." Those are the sounds she makes. The translator remains silent.

"Is something wrong?" Yuli asks.

"Go. Go down into the cabin. I'll deal with this. There's a drone coming and I'm going to have to try and evade it. Just go down there and hold onto something. It's going to get rough."

Odi is disturbed by the change in mood and starts crying as Yuli hurries down the narrow stairs. Omi and I are right behind her. We barely sit down before the boat lurches crazily, first one way and then another.

I think it's one of their flyers, Yuli says. *Oh, Meridia, I wish there was something we could do to help.*

Maybe there is. No, not a protection canopy. Yuli and I both know that didn't work at New Beniford. I'm not sure whether it's the perception of the Elossa that's unaffected or whether it's their reliance on devices. I just know such canopies are of no use.

What about bringing up a storm? You know how to do that, Meridia.

Yes, a storm might bring down the flyer, but it could sink our boat as well.

Maybe use the Song of Turning?

If the protection canopy doesn't affect their perception, then I doubt a Turning would affect it either. They use devices to find their way.

We sit in fearful silence, buffeted first one way and then another as the nens' cries grow louder. I shush Naomi by placing her at my breast. With my orb, I look inside the pouch that no longer hangs at my side, passing my attention from one waif to another. There's the Old Lapis with its Song of Liberation. That might inspire us if we needed to fight, but how can we fight a flyer? The Old Turquoise. Could that work? I hum a few notes, uncertain what verse might help us. I settle on the verse that only shifts time a short while.

There's an untranslatable shout of astonishment from Limn.

Meridia, I'm not sure that's working. Meridia? Where did you go?

There's a strange buzzing in my orb and a dizziness that I know is not caused by our reckless path across the waves. I stop singing. I hear Naomi and Odilia crying. The buzzing slows and I take a deep breath. *If only Avienne were here. Avienne would know what to do.*

Avienne. Our Calumet. And suddenly I'm consumed by the song of the Old Jade, the Song of the Calumet, and I begin singing it, not tentatively, but loudly and lustily, letting the exquisite green notes of Avienne's song expand to fill our space.

Yuli recognizes the song. *Are you sure, Meridia? Why that one?*

I continue singing without acknowledging Yuli. But I hear her join in, our two voices taking different parts of the song. I attend only to my own part.

And then I realize that I can no longer hear Yuli. I can no longer hear Odi's cries. What I do hear is altogether astonishing.

I don't want to take this with me to Swarthpol, Abél says. *I'm going to trust you to care for it.*

I know he's talking about ecphorite, though I don't know why. *Father? Father, can you pertange me? I'm on a boat. Limn is bringing us home.*

But Abél is gone and I'm enveloped in a cloud of cool green that stretches toward a pulsing wave of something that's a deep, scorching red, pressing against it as the colors collide, turning all brown and absent. I keep singing and singing until the red wave grows faint and finally dissipates.

I hear Odi again. Odi and Omi have stopped crying and whimper softly as Yuli and I continue humming the pale green notes of the Song of the Calumet.

We're still humming, more to soothe the nens than to accomplish anything, when Limn comes down the steps carrying her translator device. "Well, that was a close call," she says. "For some reason the drone got way up ahead of us and kind of lost us for a few minutes. And then their radar failed. Let's just hope we're a lot farther away by the time they try and send another one. We might not be so lucky next time."

"What color is radar?" I say.

31

Abél's eyes are glazed with bewilderment. "I'm sure it was Meridia," he says. "And I'm sure she said that she's coming home. No, I don't know how we managed to pertange one another, but I'm certain it was her doing and not mine." He thinks it may also have something to do with his mother, Avienne. Or perhaps the large piece of ecphorite he was holding in his hand when it happened. Zara now holds that ecphorite and its attendant lumps of pointing-stone.

"How?" Vidvana says. "How is Meridia coming home?"

Is there anything we can do to help? Zara hushes her doubts, the thought that Abél's frustration and his fatigue from so many days of travel might have something to do with this inexplicable and unlikely vision. She experienced nothing. No, there had been a brief glimpse of Avienne. She'd thought it was just a transient memory.

Abél turns away from Vidvana's questions, Zara's doubts, Salma's skepticism. His eyes go unfocused and his hands twitch as his orb opens toward his daughter. He only pertanged her for a fleeting moment, but there was something about her presence, something fluid. "She... I think she's on a boat, Vidvana." *No, I don't think there's anything we can do to help. And no, I'm not imagining this, Zara. It was Meridia.* The notes of a song rise verdant into Abél's awareness, and he recognizes the Song of the Calumet.

"So should we go back to New Beniford instead of going on to Swarthpol?" Vidvana says.

Salma looks from one to the other of her companions, trying to fathom what is happening, perplexity drawing her dark face into a deep scowl.

Abél stops mid-path and turns to face Vidvana. "Oh. I'm not sure," he says, suppressing the impulse of his aurynx to sing Avienne's song, the Song of the Calumet. It's Meridia's song now. *Zara, I'm so disoriented. What do you think?*

We know Swarthpol is a dangerous place. If Meridia is on her way back, as you say, then surely there's no need to go there now. We can return to New Beniford.

Abél is mystified by his experience of Meridia. And Avienne. Yes, she was there, too, wasn't she? He's also relieved. *I think you're right. There's no need to go to Swarthpol. But not back to New Beniford. We should go to Selbourne. That's where their ship arrived before.* "We'll go to Selbourne, Vidvana. We'll meet Meridia there."

32

"We need to stop," Umet says.

Damon continues striding ahead. "I'm not hungry yet, Umet. I think we can go a while longer before stopping to eat." They're on the road that leads from Temur toward Benbridge, hoping to intercept Abél on his way to Swarthpol.

Umet has already stopped and he has to raise his voice to catch Damon's attention. "It's not that. Something's happened. Something's changed."

Damon turns and makes his way back toward Umet. "Changed? What is it?"

Umet holds up his hand, asking for the silence that will help him pertange more clearly this alteration in Abél's orientation. His intention. Umet's eyes close. His hand trembles and then a smile creases his face. "Abél contacted Meridia. Or she contacted him. He thinks she said she's coming home."

Damon freezes in disbelief, his heart lurching fiercely, hoping against hope that this might be true. "Are you sure?"

"As sure as Abél is. And he seems convinced. His group has changed their plan and they're heading toward Selbourne."

"That's wonderful news," Orban says, trying to quiet his own doubts. "Surely Yuli is coming, too, Umet."

Umet's tense smile is his only response to Orban's comment. He had quickly reached out for Yuli and found nothing.

"How soon will she arrive?" Damon says. "How long will it take us to get to Selbourne?" Of course that's where they'll go. Damon's heart quivers with suppressed joy, unwilling to give itself over to the expectation of Meridia's imminent arrival, fearful of disappointment.

"Abél doesn't know when they might arrive," Umet says. He wants desperately to believe Yuli will be with Meridia. "They must still be too far away to pertange in the usual way. As for your other question, Damon, I'm guessing that we should be able to get to the coast across from Selbourne in about three days, maybe four. If we can join up with Abél tomorrow," Umet says, "he may know the best way across the mountains from here. I've never been to the seacoast, you know. And the Quartz can't show us how to get to Selbourne."

Damon is familiar with the path to the coast that goes through the mountains above New Beniford and down into the abandoned Melfar town of Aldbeck. He gazes toward the line of mountains barely visible on the western horizon, wondering how they'll get across them this time.

By evening, Damon's group is approaching halfway between Temur and Benbridge. They don't stop until darkness is nearly upon them, hurrying to arrive at the way station Umet identifies. It's not much, but at least it provides a roof over their heads. An ominous line of clouds has formed in the northern sky.

"Why would they send rain at this time of day?" Orban says as the first drops patter down.

"This isn't Melfar rain," Umet says. "Haven't you noticed that the rains have started rising on their own lately? I think that's because the land has stopped being so dry. Moisture has started to feed into the formation of rain without Melfar help."

Damon hadn't noticed. "And that's good, right?"

"Back to normal, I guess." Umet accepts his share of the supper provisions from Orban. So little seems normal now.

"Do you think we'll be able stop in Benbridge and pick up some supplies when we get there? Maybe get a good meal?" Orban says.

"It might be better to bypass Benbridge and go to Markham," Umet says. "There are more friends there. Abél will probably go that way, too. I'm thinking we can meet him there."

After supper, Damon walks by himself along a line of young trees toward a tall peppertree, an old and gnarled thing with many dead branches and only a few living ones. Its leaves have turned golden orange with the shortening days. He sits among seed-heavy grasses and leans his tired back against the tree. With his eyes closed, he feels the darkness closing around him. "Oh, Meridia," he whispers. *Please come home safely.* He opens his heart, searching for her, for Naomi, for Odilia. He finds nothing but memories of a happiness that lies beyond his reach. He thinks about the pale image of the ship in Fannan's photograph and about the words of the Song of the Sea. *This world is bigger than we thought. Bigger and more dangerous. I need to be careful. Meridia may be coming home, but is she coming with friends?* Damon's heart wrenches deep red in his chest with the sudden thought that she might arrive with more of the

Elossa, people intent on doing even greater harm to Melfar and Mundani.

The beds in the way station are less than comfortable and Damon tosses restlessly most of the night, rising just before dawn. Breakfast is only hard bread and dried fruit.

Now that Abél has no need to go to Swarthpol, he doesn't even want to travel close to the place. He insists that his little group move directly toward the mountains, avoiding not only Swarthpol, but Benbridge and Markham as well. It's a very old Melfar way that he follows, a way he's never seen before and that is unmarked in the Quartz map he carries. He thinks it must be Idös who is guiding him through this unfamiliar landscape with such unwarranted confidence. He wishes he'd had the time to stay longer and learn more from her.

You can come back another time. And bring your daughter. I'd like to meet your Calumet.

Does Idös know that Meridia is coming home? A weeping bluebill whistles from a high branch, and Abél realizes that he's seen the same bird repeatedly since early morning.

Thank you Idös, he says. *I'll do that.*

Damon and his companions arrive in Markham just past midday, tired and hungry. They make for the home of Mundani Chanters they know from Fayredell. Teagan and her son Rio welcome the little party, spreading a hot meal of soup and fresh bread, pungent tea and sweet cake. "We've been so worried ever since we heard what happened in New Beniford, but we didn't want to believe the rumors of Meridia's disappearance. As you say, it's good that news such as that is not spreading. Or at least not being confirmed. Except among Melfar, of course." Teagan nods toward Umet. She knows it's next to impossible for Melfar to keep secrets from one another.

"We're hoping to catch up with Abél and accompany him to Selbourne." Umet frowns. "But I've been having some difficulty today pertanging Abél's location. He's much farther to the north than I would have expected." He stops for a moment, his head cocked to one side. "And already traveling due west. We may have to find our own way over the mountains."

"What? Why haven't you mentioned this before?" Damon does not relish the prospect of another exhausting climb over the mountains, even with Abél to guide them. But without his aid, searching for a way through the mountains could prove treacherous. They could easily get lost.

"The mountains to the north of Markham are steep and rugged," Teagan says. "If there's a pass, it's not something I've heard anyone speak of. Mundani fishermen from here still go to the coast occasionally, but they take a route that follows the Lubak River south until it comes to the sea. That might be the best way for you, too. It might be a few fellspans farther, but you'd only have to cross through some low hills and then onto the broad plain that stretches along the coast. Or so they say. I've never been there myself."

After they've consumed their supper, Teagan pours glasses of steepberry wine and tries to distract the three men with the latest gossip.

"There are hardly any Palinjians left in Markham and not that many in Benbridge, either" Rio says. "At least there aren't many who acknowledge being Palinjians."

"There are a few, though," Teagan says, "and I hate to think what they'd try to make of Meridia's absence. Did you know the Chanters here have begun asking for Saami Pherson to come back and become spiritual leader of the Markham Clauster? They've heard about his training in New Beniford and think he should come here when he's finished."

"He's young but he seems to be a bright fellow with a good heart. You'd be lucky to have him," Orban says.

Damon thinks back to the optimism they all felt at the Gathering in Fayredell, where Meridia was acclaimed not only as Calumet of the Melfar, but as Prophet of the Mundani as well. Saami Pherson had addressed the Gathering, too, and proven remarkably well spoken for one so young, valiantly rejecting the violent ways of his older brother Warreth. Damon hadn't allowed himself to think much about how Meridia's absence might impact the stability of the whole country, how important her return could be. He'd only thought of how important she is to him. But things are still uncertain, and, if it were known, Meridia's continuing absence could shift the balance back toward Palinjians who still crave the power of a Warreth Pherson in preference to the peace of a Saami Pherson.

"Don't you think so, Damon?" Teagan says.

"I'm sorry, what did you say?" Damon thinks it was something about Lambert Quint. He'd been lost in his own thoughts.

"We were talking about Lambert's role as spiritual leader in Fayredell. Don't you think they'll soon be calling him Prophet, too? There's no reason why there can't be more than one, as there have been in the past. His teachings on the Sidaya are drawing in a lot of old Sidayens."

Damon agrees, but his lack of enthusiasm betrays his distraction. There's no point in continuing to pretend to follow their conversation. He excuses himself and walks outside into the garden. Teagan's house is only a short distance from the Markham Clauster and he catches a faint whiff of incense. He wonders what kind of prayer the incense is meant to convey. A prayer for peace or a prayer for dominance? *Oh, Meridia, I want you here. You're my one true love and life partner, but I know others need you as well.* He lets his own prayer drift upward with the incense. *If you come home safely, I promise I won't try to distract you from being the Calumet. And a Prophet, too, if that is what's needed. I trust you. I just want you back here in my arms and in my life. I want our family, our precious nens. Our home.*

She's coming, Damon.

Abél's response is unexpected. Damon has felt so distraught, his Revelant powers submerged and unreliable. But Abél has pertanged his thoughts.

Soon Meridia will, too. Keep reaching out, Damon. We'll find her.

33

Limn was relieved to intercept a general dispatch to all ships, ordering them to abandon pursuit of the fugitive vessel Pequod, which they summarily designated as "lost at sea." She was also able to access a partially garbled message from Menza Uhr to Tarja Ssu, placing Tarja in charge of Limn's former responsibilities. Limn knows how pleased Tarja must be with her promotion. She knows that, as far as Menza Uhr and Tarja Ssu are concerned, Limn Ssu no longer matters. No longer exists. The people of Port Sillick have a knack for forgetting things and people for which they have no further use. Limn can't decide if she's feeling liberated or only sad. Maybe both. As much as she dislikes Port Sillick and the Protocols, that is the only life she's ever known.

That life is over for Limn Ssu. She may not know what lies ahead, but what she does know is that she's now free to indulge her curiosity without fear of repercussions. As they continue their journey southward, Limn presses Yuli and this other woman she can't see to tell her more about the history and customs of their country, asking question after question and listening with rapt attentiveness. She taps vigorously on her computer, often feeling as if she must be writing fiction. How could all of this be true? Do these people really possess an extra sense organ? In her deepest dives into relic computer files and old books Limn had found that the pineal gland, deep inside the brain, was sometimes referred to as a "third eye." Could this gland be what has developed among Melfar into what they call their "gnosic orb"? And is it possible that they really have developed some sort of active control over the production of biophotons via sound waves from vocalization? Her scientific mindset is overtaxed by the stretch required to put all of what they're telling her into familiar frames of reference. But...sound and light...it's all vibrations, right?

"Why did you want to know what color radar is?" she asks.

"I pertanged a pulsing field of red," Meridia says. "When I verberated the green notes of the Song of the Calumet, it seemed like it was being pushed away. Canceled into a dull brown."

"So... you could see the radar?"

"I guess that's what I pertanged. It's not the same as seeing, of course. Images form in my mind that don't come from my eyes."

Yuli affirms that she pertanged it as well. "But it was a different sort of red from what I'd pertanged on the ship we arrived on. Was that radar, too?"

"Radio waves. You pertanged radio waves. Of course you did." Limn chuckles and turns back to her computer, deep in thought. She types vigorously: *It's true that what we react to and process are the images our brains compose from narrowly perceived visual and aural stimuli. We never see or hear everything exactly as it is because our sense organs are limited. Our eyes are only sensitive to a very limited range of the light spectrum, and that definitely does not include the infrared part that extends into radar and radio waves. I wonder if they can pertange X-rays and gamma radiation as well?*

Later that night, after Yuli and Odi have gone to sleep (and Limn supposes that Meridia and the other baby have done the same), Limn connects one of the external data storage units she brought with her and begins scrolling through lines of words on her screen. Her sense of leaving her familiar world behind, of venturing into an unknown space, has caused her to remember something that she had felt was impossible when she first encountered it. Now she's not so sure. She finds what she's searching for and begins to read:

"June 12, 2087. This will be my final entry. I don't know why I bother. Everyone's gone. I may very well be the last *Homo sapiens* left, so who do I think will read this? Maybe someone from elsewhere. They're out there, you know. They've passed through once or twice but never seemed interested enough to stay and talk. Maybe one of them will find this.

"It's such a beautiful little planet when you look at it from out here. Just a blue-swirled sphere cradled in its jeweled cloak of endless space. Well, it used to be blue. We thought we were its finest achievement and instead we're its death knell. Stranded up here, we've been able to follow the reports of how bad the disease outbreaks became, reports of the conflicts and violence as one nation blamed the next, if not for the disease, then for the drought or the poverty or the famine or the floods. All too often, they blamed the refugees. There were so many refugees and nowhere left for them to be. No peace and no one left to make peace. No one who even believed peace was possible. And so the people with power brought out every weapon they'd ever created and proceeded to destroy one another. We had a lot of weapons and I'm pretty sure we used every damn one of them. From our heavenly exile, we watched the little puffs of smoke and pops of light when the bombs fell and saw the accumulating clouds of toxic and radioactive dust and gas and then, later on, the volcanic eruptions and quakes as the whole surface of our precious planet was torn apart. It's still shrouded in a gray cloak so that I can barely see what remains. But when a gap forms, it's a window onto an unfamiliar continent or archipelago and I know beyond any doubt that it's all over for *Homo sapiens*.

"The Anthropocene has ended.

"As our rations run out along with our hope, one by one we just step out into the void, into endless space. Tomorrow it will be my turn."

Limn checks the boat's instruments and walks to the window, staring up into the cloudless expanse of stars. *Once upon a time, our ancestors knew how to travel into space*, she thinks. *That's what this report is about. It's about what we used to be. And it's about the end of us.*

But it wasn't the end. Not yet.

34

Every day I reach out with my orb, searching for Damon and Father. We must still be too far away. This small boat may take more days to travel the distance to Selbourne than the great ship that took Yuli and Odilia from Selbourne to Port Sillick.

Or maybe it's not the distance. Maybe it's me. I lack the energy I need for clear verberation and I don't know how to restore it. I can't help but wonder if this strange condition I'm in is beginning to take its toll. I eat and drink nothing, and although Omi suckles several times a day, she likely takes in nothing more than the comfort of my nipple in her mouth, my heart beating next to her tiny ear. Limn calls my condition being "out of phase." I have no idea what that means. She's tried to explain about some work that her people once conducted at Swarthpol, but she uses too many words I don't understand. She also tries to explain that the researchers were not her eldpeople, that she has no eldpeople in the usual sense. I don't understand that either.

Odi seems increasingly disturbed by my condition as well, searching for me with her eyes when I talk to her or sing to her. I think she may pertange her sister twin more solidly, though I can't be certain of that. It's only that they sometimes coo and gurgle to one another in blurred images that almost compose into simple songs. They cry together, too, long breathless shrieks of blue and orange, breaking my heart. I've tried taking Odi into my lap, and, for no more than an instant, it's almost real. Almost satisfying.

I'd hoped that drawing closer to home might begin bringing me back into a normal state. Back into phase, as Limn says. Instead, I seem to be experiencing the reverse. I feel less substantive and more prone to wander. I've had glimpses of Amergin and his Naomi at their home in the mountains with their children. I think there are three of them now, a "now" so very long ago. Lazaro is a father, too, but he has only one child. Oh, Lazaro, I'm sorry about your partner's passing.

I remember the photograph Damon tried to make from the Song of All Songs.

Did he find the photograph of the ship with wings?
Yuli, would you sing for me? I'm not feeling well.
What song should I sing, Meridia?
The Old Amethyst. Sing me the Song of Hope.

35

Their first day's journey out of Markham goes smoothly, as Damon and Orban follow Umet along a southerly path that never strays far from the western bank of the Lubak River.

On the second day Umet suddenly announces: "I've lost the path Teagan recommended." His shoulders slump and his eyes are dull. "Also, I can't find Abél."

Damon had suspected that they were wandering, heading vaguely southwest, but in a ragged pattern that he had not found reassuring. The river had been out of sight since midday. Damon is annoyed, thinking they should have kept closer to the river. "If we continue heading west, we're bound to find the seacoast," he says. "Sooner or later."

"I've tried to follow the river, but I keep getting pulled off course. I think maybe you or Orban should take the lead, Damon."

"I have a good sense of direction," Orban says. "I'll do it."

Umet steps back to follow the two Mundani men, grateful to be relieved of a burden he no longer feels capable of bearing. He didn't want to say it, but now he thinks he should. "We may be getting close to Swarthpol."

"Do you think so?" Damon says. Abél's descriptions of the dreadful effects he attributed to Swarthpol come unbidden to mind. "I wish we knew exactly where Swarthpol is, so that we could be more deliberate about avoiding it." He tries to think: Did Abél mention anything about structures or landmarks near Swarthpol? Damon knows the place is not inhabited. Or has he only assumed that? The only landmark he recalls is a dark pond surrounded by broken black stones. Damon reminds himself that the road Teagan recommended was something frequented by Mundani, who wouldn't have minded how close they came to Swarthpol. He's sorry they've put Umet in danger; he wonders vaguely if Swarthpol might have any effect on Mundani Revelants.

Damon has thought little about his supposed Revelant capabilities lately. He's used them hardly at all. He's sure that being Revelant was what enabled him and Meridia to communicate without words in the past, even over great distances. Some distances are too great. Meridia said their ability to pertange one another's moods and thoughts drew also on the strength of their love for one another, their heart connection. These days Damon's heart holds nothing but sadness.

The hills Orban leads them through are low and covered in tall stands of golden grasses interspersed with expanses of tiny, bright yellow flowers growing low to the ground. The three men wind their way around and through the hills with little effort. Even where they're forced to climb over them, these hills are as nothing compared to the mountains that Abél and his companions must surely encounter.

"Can you smell it?" Orban says.

Damon inhales deeply. There's an ocean breeze, blowing humid and salty against his face. "We must be getting close," he says.

They stop on the summit of the next hill. Below them the land evens out into a more gently rolling plain and in the distance the sun sparkles off the surface of the ever-moving sea.

"From here we should be able to follow the coastline northward all the way to Selbourne," Orban says.

"Can you tell how far that might be?" Umet is breathing hard and beads of sweat roll down his face.

"Are you okay, Umet? Let's sit down here and rest for a while." Damon offers his water sheath to Umet, who has drained his own.

"No, I'm not okay," Umet says. "I feel weak. I've been struggling to keep up with you and I'm getting a headache." He rubs the back of his hand across his forehead. "I seem to have forgotten where we're going."

"We can stop here for a while until you're feeling better." Orban exchanges a worried look with Damon.

Umet shrugs and sits.

"I don't think staying here will help," Damon says. "This route may have come closer to Swarthpol than we thought. I'm afraid we may have to pass even closer as we turn more to the north. I'm sorry, Umet."

Umet's face is drawn into a distracted frown as he looks out to sea, mumbling something about Yuli.

Damon sits down next to the young man and hands him one of the fresh guavacots from his pack, a fruit Rio picked from their garden in Markham.

"Did Abél say Swarthpol was on the coast?" Orban says. "I guess I assumed it was farther inland."

Damon doesn't know and it would do no good to ask Umet anything at the moment. They rest a while longer, drinking more water than they probably should, given that their journey may now take longer than expected. They'll have to watch for a spring or stream where they can refill their water sheaths.

The flat plain is not so easy to traverse as it appeared from above. It's studded with clumps of stiff grass and soft mounds constructed by insects. Damon hopes they're not ants. Orban says they probably are. There are also occasional burrows of some kind of animals. Orban says they're probably conies. Damon hopes they're not snakes.

"There's a stream up ahead," Orban says.

As they draw closer to the stream, Umet begins to utter strange sounds. He wheezes and stumbles as they approach the trickling water.

Damon hesitates. There are no plants growing along the stream and the sand beneath the water is very dark. It's strewn with glistening white pebbles. "I don't like the looks of this," Damon says.

"Okay. Maybe we'll find something farther on." Orban looks at Umet and then meets Damon's eyes with a shake of his head. Umet doesn't look well at all.

They round a bend in the coastline past the stream and stop in their tracks. Just in front of them, there's a tumbled pile of huge stones, blacker than the beach sand. A row of posts leads inland; it looks like the remains of what was once a fence. Damon turns to face Umet. "Is this it?" he asks. "Do you think this is Swarthpol?"

Umet is unable to speak. The blankness of his expression and the lethargy of his stance provide all the answer Damon needs.

"Let's keep moving," he says to Orban. "We have to get Umet past this place."

The two Mundani men almost carry Umet as they hurry past the tumbled stones and up the beach, not slowing their pace until their muscles begin to seize up with the added weight and relentless pace. They find a spot near a cluster of stunted trees and they sit Umet down, giving him what's left of the water in their own sheaths. The sun is obscured by a bank of dark clouds and the breeze from the ocean is suddenly chill. Umet shivers. Damon and Orban gather sticks and build a small fire.

After a while Damon asks, "Are you any better, Umet?"

He doesn't answer. He sits with his knees drawn up to his chest, hunched toward the fire, eyes half-closed. "The Song of the Sea is right," he says. His voice has a colorless rasp to it and he seems to struggle for a moment, almost choking. "That place is dangerous." He couldn't utter the name of Swarthpol.

Damon and Orban are determined to get their Melfar companion as far away from Swarthpol as possible. They're not sure what the power of the place might be, but they can readily see its effects, so they douse their small fire with sand and guide Umet another half fellspan up the coast. Despite the young man's physical weakness, it takes all of their strength to keep him headed in the right direction. They find a trickling stream of fresh water amid some rocks that look less forbidding and afford a semblance of shelter. They can rest here for the night.

Despite Damon's weariness, his aching heart and unsettled mind consign him to another sleepless night. Umet's experience has reminded him of Abél's tales of his time at Swarthpol and of its devastating powers. Swarthpol is there in the Song of the Sea and the book Damon found confirms that a boat very like the Elossa sank near Swarthpol in Mundani passage 472.

Damon reaches again and again for Meridia, finding her still too distant. By the time the sun rises, Damon has arrived at what he acknowledges may be an irrational decision. He doesn't care. He's going back to Swarthpol to see exactly what's there.

"Are you sure that's wise, Damon?" Orban says, speaking softly so as not to awaken Umet.

Damon is pretty sure it is not wise, but he can't help feeling that going to Swarthpol might provide him with some insight into this whole convoluted situation, so much of which seems to connect with that strange place. Ignoring Orban's question, Damon only says, "I won't be long. You stay here with Umet and let him rest. I'll be back by midday."

36

Yuli startles at a grinding noise that she doesn't recognize. *Did you hear that, Meridia? What do you think it was?* The noise is followed by a frustrated shout from Limn and a clatter of rapid footsteps going back and forth on the deck above, then down some stairs and up again.

A few moments later, Limn comes halfway down the stairs leading into the cabin and leans over the railing toward Yuli. "We're stuck," she says through the translator. She looks as if she's on the verge of either tears or a tantrum. "The damn boat has run aground."

"What will you do about it?" Yuli says.

Limn turns as if to go back up the steps but then her head drops forward. Even without verberations, Yuli can see that Limn knows of nothing she can do about this turn of events.

"Well, as long as we're not going anywhere, come sit down with us and tell us more about this being stuck." Yuli pats the faded cushion on the bench next to her.

Limn descends, each footstep falling heavily on the wooden stairs. She sets her translator on a table. She sits.

"What does 'run aground' mean exactly?" Yuli asks.

"I was trying to navigate between a couple of rocky islands, but we were running low on power and the sensors malfunctioned and failed to report exactly how shallow the water was. We've lodged on a sandbar or some rocks or something. The good news is that I've inspected the lower hold and I don't see any evidence of the boat leaking." She tilts her head, watching Odi as the nen wriggles and coos in Yuli's lap.

"Meridia says we're caught on some rocks," Yuli says, glancing toward the last place Meridia had been, though she's not there now. "But not big ones. Just a kind of loose pile of stones and debris."

"Why doesn't she tell me that herself?" Limn continues watching Odi in fascination.

"She tried to, but you didn't hear her."

"As bad as that, is it? But you're still able to communicate with her, right? I guess that'll have to do. How do you know what we're stuck on?" Limn isn't sure how this information will help, but she's curious as to how these women purport to know such things.

"We can pertange the arrangement of the rocks from the living things that cling to them or swim among them." Yuli begins humming softly to Odi. "Were we at high tide or low tide when we got stuck?" Yuli asks this question for Meridia.

"I wasn't keeping track of that. We do seem to be sinking lower." Limn looks out the window. "Oh, lord. We're a lot closer to shore than I thought we were and for sure closer than I intended. It was getting dark. And the instruments were going all wonky. Not enough sunshine yesterday."

I drag my attention away from the flurry of small creatures swimming below us. A number of flower-like things were crushed as the boat scraped against the rocks that they clung to. I need to tell Yuli more about tides and moon phases. Does she understand me?

"High tide might raise us out of the rocks," Yuli says. "Also, we're in a waxing phase of the moon." Yuli isn't sure why a waxing phase is important, so I show her the bridge of steppingstones that stretched from the land right across to the island of Selbourne at a full moon low tide. I'm certain that if low tides are lower, high tides must be higher.

Limn seems confused. "What is a 'waxing phase'? And what difference would it make?"

"Tides are more extreme at full moon," Yuli says.

"So you think we might be able to just float out of this?"

"At high tide on the full moon. Possibly."

Limn taps at her wrist communicator and scowls. "No information on the moon," she says. "Not a thing the Protocols say we need to know about, I guess." She shakes her wrist, as if that might help the device to provide her with the answers she seeks. "Do you think Meridia will be okay?"

Yuli doesn't respond.

I want to reassure her, but I don't know what I could say. I clutch Naomi and lean heavily against the wall behind the bench. Finding the contact less substantial than it ought to be, I lean forward again. I'm weaker. Or maybe it's just that everything around me feels less solid. I say that, knowing that all these things are perfectly solid to Yuli and Odi and Limn. It's me that's become less solid. I stroke Omi's face. At least Naomi still feels solid to me. I worry about how this existence is affecting her even more than I worry about its effect on me.

Limn is speaking. "Tell me again about how Meridia came to be here," she says. "All the details. Meridia told me that the pieces of the broken mirror were facing one another and that she sat between them. What else was in the cave at the time?"

I close my eyes against the tears that want to well up as I relive the strange experience. I show Yuli and then Yuli tells Limn about the mirrors—the ones that Amos Quint fabricated in addition to the ones that were there from before—and about the song I was singing. It was the Turquoise Song of the Canopy of Time, or at least the section of it that's contained in the Song of All Songs. I resist it now, fearful of the effects it might have on my fragile state. Then I show Yuli the rest of the space—the cask of artifacts that Amos collected from farther back in the cave, the rough floor with the blood stain. I wonder if Limn regrets that, regrets the injury to Amos Quint. I also show Yuli the channels along each wall filled with water and with stones covered in luminous slime.

I begin to drift, remembering Damon's search for the glowing snails that feed on the slime and how the snails helped him produce photographs like the ones Fannan made. I think of the nacreous fever, the billbugs, the medicine from the furtivine. I see some of Damon's pictures. He found the photograph of the ship! My hand goes to the Quartz bead that hangs on a cord around my neck, the bead Damon gave me at our partnering.

Meridia? Are you still there? Yuli's concern tugs at my awareness.

I think so. I was just remembering things.
Meridia?

37

"If we can make it a little farther," Abél wheezes, "we can shelter in a cave." He pauses for breath. "There's one just on the other side."

Both Vidvana and Salma have urged Abél to rest, concerned about his labored breathing and faltering steps. Only Zara is also aware of how rapidly his heart is beating, of how it occasionally skips a beat.

Vidvana isn't sure how Abél knows about a cave, but she'll trust him. "If it's close," she says, "we can take it a little slower. We'll get there, Abél."

The path has been steep and difficult and they can see that there are more twists and turns, more steepness ahead. But at least there's a path. At first, they kept expecting to run into dead ends, impassable slopes, impossibly narrow ledges. None of those materialized and now they're high into mountains none of them has visited before.

They slow their pace for the final ascent and find, just below and around a turning, the mouth of a cave. It's partially obscured by basket vines, but inside it's spacious enough to offer protection, though Vidvana and Salma find the ceiling rather low. They're surprised to find a stack of wood along one wall. It's old and a little moldy, but Abél insists it will burn.

It does. They cluster around the warmth and light to share a meager but welcome supper.

You shouldn't push yourself so hard, Abél, Zara says.

I don't know how long Idös will be able to guide us. Without her aid we surely would have lost our way. Abél hasn't seen the bluebill for the last hour or so. His experience suggests that such birds seldom cross from one side of the mountains to the other. Of course, this is his first experience with this particular bird.

Zara tries to reassure him. *The path looks clear enough now, even to me. If we pay careful attention, I think we should be able to follow it all the way down.*

Vidvana offers Abél the last of the wilderfruit they collected from the orchards of Old Túl and insists he take it. "Have you been able to contact Meridia again? Can you tell if she's getting closer?"

"Nothing," Abél says, frowning even as he sucks the sweet juice from the fruit, one of the season's last.

The old man knows he should rest. His body has been screaming that message at him all day long. But when he finally stretches out, wrapped in his blankets, his mind refuses to let go of the miserable state of affairs in which he finds himself. His daughter is impertangible and he doesn't know where she is. Since midday, he's also been unable to find Umet. He knows the young man has been guiding Damon and Orban toward Selbourne, the same destination Abél aims for. But they've taken a different route. Abél almost wishes he'd done the same. The mountains are hard. Misery enshrouds him.

When sleep finally comes to Abél it's not a restful sleep. He awakens repeatedly, gasping for nourishment from the thin air of the high mountain. His heart has quieted a bit, but he knows its pace is still too rapid.

His heart breaks for his daughter.

38

Damon approaches the site he assumes is Swarthpol in the early morning light. He left his companions before sunrise and, traveling by himself along the beach, he made quick progress. He can't decide if the golden light glinting off the cold black stones is ominous or only awesomely beautiful.

He climbs along the edges of the tumbled pile of stones, moving inland. He needs to see what else this place holds. He clambers to the top of one of the rocks and peers down at his own face, reflected in a pool of still water. Dark water. Almost black. He shivers, remembering what Abél said about Swarthpol, what the Song of the Sea says about the dark waters of Swarthpol. He has to see more.

Cautiously, he skirts the edge of the pond. The surface of the stones is slick as glass in some spots and after slipping twice he goes down on his hands and knees to continue his exploration. He finds a gap in the stones, a spot where he can approach the water more closely. He scoots down toward the pool.

The light from the rising sun no longer offers him a reflection. Instead, rays of sunlight penetrate the surface of the water, glinting darkly off submerged stones and more intensely off something that Damon thinks might be a mirror. There's no movement in the water—no fish, no insects, no life of any kind.

Next to the place where he sits, the ground is littered with fragments of a material that is not from these dark stones. He picks up a pebble and raises it to the sunlight. Its milky translucence glows blue and green with hints of orange. Damon recognizes it as one of the substances Abél shared with him to use in recording images on his photographic papers, images from song. It's an ingredient used in the crafting of Benisons. It's ecphorite.

The Song of the Sea said there was ecphorite at Swarthpol, said it was something the empty people wanted. For what purpose? The song doesn't say.

Still holding the pebble of ecphorite in his right hand, Damon's left hand goes to the Quartz bead that hangs on a strand around his neck. His heart opens out toward his missing partner, his beloved Meridia.

I'm coming home, Damon.

Damon sits up straighter, leaning toward the dark pond, squeezing his eyes tight shut, and pressing the Quartz bead against his heart. He clutches the pebble of ecphorite more tightly. *What can I do to help you, Meri?*

He waits. He listens intently. No answer comes.

39

I'm so afraid. I refuse to lay Naomi down at all. Without her strong connection to her sister twin Odilia, I might drift away to some other time-space or even cease to exist altogether. I spend long moments with Amergin and his Naomi or with the terrified people of Aldbeck, who watched the Old Mica pushed out into the Endless Sea. Sometimes I'm with Lasaro and his stolen pebble of ecphorite. Earlier this morning, I was sure I was with Damon. But where was Damon? Does he know I'm coming home?

Limn can no longer communicate with me directly. I can hear her voice, but she doesn't hear mine. Yuli is still aware of me. At least she is whenever she's holding Odi.

Ask Limn to tell us more about Swarthpol, I say. *Ask her about the ecphorite and the dark pool.* Why would Damon go to Swarthpol?

Limn doesn't answer Yuli's question immediately. She's set up her computer here in the little room below deck and she turns to it and begins tapping keys. She's searching for something. I wish I understood how this object works. I know that it holds words and numbers like a book, but with pictures similar to the ones Damon and Fannan printed. Moving, living pictures. And it has sounds, too. Not like the sounds contained in a Benison, though. These computer sounds have no verberations. The images and sounds are separate things.

"Here it is," Limn says. She squints for a moment at the screen, leaning forward with her hands clasped between her knees. She turns toward Yuli and says, "Swarthpol was the reason I came to your country in the first place, you know. I was curious about the research that these reports said was once conducted there." She pauses for a moment and her expression suggests that she's having a quarrel with her own thoughts. "It was research that was never picked up and used in Port Sillick. Never part of the Protocols. Never even mentioned in anything other than these relic reports."

"What were they doing at Swarthpol? What did you learn?" Yuli asks. She starts to put Odilia down but I implore her not to. I don't want to miss whatever Limn is going to tell her.

"They were working on fabricating a substance they called ecphorite. Or at least ecphorite appears to have been the outcome of their research. They were trying to find better materials to use in building and programming computers. You know, machines like this one." Limn presses some buttons and the lines of words on the screen move up, revealing more lines of words, more drawings. "I wasn't the first of my people to ask questions about what had been done at Swarthpol," she says. "Almost two hundred years ago another person—someone like me, someone afflicted with curiosity—set out to investigate Swarthpol, to see if they could recover some of the ecphorite. They never came back."

I'm fading again. Phasing? I see more screens, a whole line of them. I recognize them as computer screens. The people sitting in front of these screens are not Elossa, not Mundani, not Melfar. They're brown-skinned people with straight dark hair. They're short and sturdy like Melfar, not so dark as Mundani.

One of them is Lasaro's mother.

She's crying because her son has been sent away for interfering with their work. They say he stole a piece of ecphorite. She refuses to believe it. She grieves the injustice. But he did take it. He thought it was beautiful and he didn't understand what it was. So he was sent away into the care of the Sisters at Saint Odilia's Refuge for Children. If Lasaro's mother had been at Swarthpol when the bombs fell, she might have survived. But she'd already gone away, gone out in search of her missing son.

Many of the people who worked there, deep underground, did survive, just like Amergin and Naomi survived underground. Some of them became Melfar eldpeople.

How am I pertanging so much all at once? So many images and sounds, fleeting and yet precise in their clarity, even when they overlap and overlay one another.

Who is Idös?

40

Meridia remains beyond the reach of Abél's orb and he isn't sure if it's her or perhaps his own ill health that makes him unable to find her. He hasn't pertanged Umet since the day before yesterday. Idös's bird was apparently unable to cross over to this side of the mountains, so her guidance is no longer available. Brân is available. He wants to help but he's as mystified as his brother twin about what to do. Even the Migrant feels somehow withdrawn and unreal to Abél.

It's altogether too much like Swarthpol.

Abél has no idea how many Elossa might be with Meridia when she arrives. If she arrives. He's assumed that Yuli and Odilia are with Meridia and Naomi, but he can't know that for certain. He sighs deeply and turns his attention to something practical. "How long will it take us to reach Selbourne from here?" he asks.

"It's hard to say how long it will take," Vidvana says. "A couple of days, more or less." Abél's state of mind makes her think he'll push for less. The state of his health makes her think it ought to take more.

Zara is even more painfully aware of how this journey is taxing Abél's aging body, how his physical weakness is causing him to doubt himself. But what can she do about it? One way or another, they have to get through these unfamiliar mountains. Zara reaches out to Bekanz with her concerns.

Bekanz responds almost immediately, as if she's been following their journey, as if she's been monitoring

Abél's condition. She shows Zara some flowers that can be steeped to make a tea helpful to an aging heart. *I'm not sure they grow on that side of the mountains,* she says. Bekanz also mentions voyma leaves, a plant Zara knows well.

I think I saw some of those yesterday. Zara thanks Bekanz for giving her the tones associated with these plants as well as their images, the texture of the leaves, and the scent of the flowers.

Abél wants to set out immediately, but Zara and Vidvana convince him to wait. "This fog will clear in another hour or so, and then we can be more certain of our way," Vidvana says.

Abél sits down again. He knows they're probably right. The path they're following is treacherous and elusive under the best of circumstances. Maybe that other fog, the one inside his head, will also dissipate. Abél eats what Zara gives him while his orb searches for Meridia, for Yuli, for Odilia and Naomi. And for Umet, who is supposed to be guiding Damon and Orban to their common destination.

Damon finally tears himself away from Swarthpol, letting go of the hope that his brief contact with Meridia might repeat itself. He dwells on the memory of how, when he and Brân were building the raft to transport the Mica Benison, Meridia would somehow walk with him along the beach, her hand in his, even though she remained across the water on Selbourne. He wants that now.

Meridia said she was coming home. Is that what she said? Or did she only say she wanted to come home?

Damon can't remember. It wouldn't make any difference, would it? If she's coming home of course it's because she wants to. But what if she wants to come home but something... No, Damon won't allow his mind to go there. If Meridia wants to come home, if she's ready to come home, then she'll come home. Meridia is strong. Even when Damon saw her stammering in that shop in Temur before he even knew who she was, he knew she was strong. She'd spurned his help then. Why does he think she needs it now? She's the Calumet. She's hailed as a Prophet by Mundani Chanters. She's coming home. She has to be coming home.

Damon is gripped with a renewed determination, a rekindled faith in his partner's power to manage these circumstances, to manage somehow to come home again. Tears fall, but they're no longer tears of sadness or despair. They're tears of hope.

I'm awed by Damon's faith in me and my fingers clutch at the Quartz bead around my neck. *I do want to come home, Damon. We've been detained, but we'll find a way. And this time I may need your help.*

I pull away, not wanting Damon to know my weakness. It saddens me that I can't touch his hand the way I long to. I want him to know I'm aware of him. I want him to be aware of me.

Damon tells Orban and Umet what he can about his experience at Swarthpol. "I'm sure Meridia is coming home," he says, "though I think something has detained her." Where did that thought come from? Is he only making up an excuse for why contact remains so elusive? He turns to Umet. "You seem to be feeling better."

"Yes, I am. Thanks." Umet is grateful that Damon's desire to visit Swarthpol gave him more time to recover from the enervating effects he experienced the day before as they passed too close to that strange place. He's glad Damon contacted Meridia. Glad and a little envious.

The three men gather their belongings and set out, with Orban again leading the way. He promises that the beach will be easier going than the rough coastal plain they traversed yesterday.

Damon is soothed by the soft sand, the gentle waves breaking on one side, the breezes ruffling brittle grasses on the other. He lets his thoughts wander toward Selbourne. He was there only a few sixes ago. Meridia was there with him, tending Amos Quint's wounds. Damon thinks again about all the moments when he or Meridia could have done something different, something that would not have led to this difficult moment.

"No point worrying over what's past," Umet says. "We're doing our best."

Damon is pleased that Umet's ability to pertange his thoughts has recovered. "Have you found Abél and Zara yet?" he asks. He won't ask about Yuli.

Umet slows his pace, falls a few steps behind, and then hurries to catch up. "Abél is still up there in the mountains. That's a hard climb for an old man. It will likely take them another two days to reach Selbourne. Maybe more." *At least he didn't have to deal with Swarthpol.*

"Do you think Meridia will be okay once we get back to our own country?" Yuli asks, hoping Limn might have an answer. She's concerned about the changes in Meridia, about how sometimes she almost seems to evaporate altogether. She's back now.

No, gone again. Yuli thinks she's trying to contact Damon. Of course Meridia would want to do that. Yuli's orb searches incessantly for Umet.

"Maybe," Limn says. "I'm not entirely certain how she phased into this time-space to begin with. Or how that relates to the time-space where she originated. Or how this time and that space intersect…" She trails off, lost in thought.

"Have you found out when full moon will be?" Yuli says. She didn't grasp Limn's comments about time and space. Moon phases are something she understands. What she doesn't understand is how someone like Limn, who lived so close to the ocean, knows so little about its tides. Yuli had never seen the ocean before her abduction, so it's understandable that the interaction of the moon and the sea would come as a surprise to her. She trusts Meridia's prediction that the high tide will free their ship from the rocks where it's lodged itself.

Limn thinks about how sometimes disparate events have to come together just so in order to produce specific outcomes. "Tomorrow should be full moon," she says, staring at a series of circles on her computer screen. "Well, actually the day after, since the moon won't rise until just past midnight. Will the darkness make any difference?"

Meridia tells Yuli that it won't, that the light from the sun has no impact on the business of tides. But Yuli doesn't hear her and Limn seems more concerned about the weather than the tides.

"Why are you always so worried about whether the sun is shining or not?" Yuli says.

"Oh. I guess I should've explained that to you. It just seems like one of those obvious facts to me. It's the solar power. Our sails are solar collectors that store power from the sun to run our engines and all of the devices."

Yuli nods as if she understands.

Limn turns back to her computer, offering no further explanation,

Yuli watches Limn's facial expressions as the woman scrolls through lines of words and unrecognizable pictures. Sometimes she scowls with displeasure. Right now she has a faint smile as she stares at a picture of a blue-swirled circle against a black background.

"Limn," Yuli says, "what would've happened to us if we'd stayed in Port Sillick?"

Limn doesn't want to answer. She's ashamed of what her people had planned. Slowly she turns toward Yuli. "They would've put you into a museum," she says.

"What's a museum?"

"Oh. Well, it's a place where they put things on display so people can come and enjoy looking at them."

"What things? What people?"

Limn is suddenly struck by the fact that Yuli and Odi were to become only "things" in a museum display. And they're not things. They're people. She does her best to explain. It's never easy to explain the inexplicable. She refuses to confess that it wouldn't even have been a living exhibit. "Anyway, I knew it wouldn't be right," she says. "So I decided to take you away."

"What will they do to you when you go back? Won't they be angry with you?"

That's something Limn has been reluctant to think about. Of course they're angry. Well, they were at first. Now they've erased her. Forgotten her. She doesn't want to go back to Port Sillick, but where else can she go? She has several decades remaining in her expected life span. Where will she spend them? Port Sillick is the only city Limn knows. There used to be a few other coastal cities, with ships going back and forth between them. Those cities no longer exist. Until her recent expedition, Limn had been convinced that Port Sillick was the only remaining inhabited place on the whole planet. It as much as said so right there in the Preface to the Protocols: "All was destroyed and it fell to us to preserve *Homo sapiens* for all time." Obviously, that was wrong.

Port Sillick is a big city. Maybe she could lose herself in it somehow.

Yuli gets the answer to her question from the shifting expressions on Limn's face. Yes, the people of Port Sillick are angry with Limn for what she's done. Yuli's aurynx radiates a golden pulse of gratitude for Limn's selfless action.

"Are you hungry?" Limn says. The provisions she packed for the journey ran out the day before yesterday and the ship's stores are meagre. Limn thinks it must have been in port for restocking.

They make their way to the galley and Limn heats a couple of prepared meals inside a box that produces no heat although the food comes out piping hot. Yuli thinks it's using something like radar. Only a bit higher pitched.

"How come the rest of the people in Port Sillick are not like you?" Yuli asks as they sit down across from one another to eat. Yuli doesn't know what the food is and she's stopped caring about that.

"They're the way they're supposed to be. I'm the one that came out wrong." Limn can tell that this answer doesn't make sense to Yuli, so she tries harder to explain. "We're all clones," she says, reminding Yuli of what clones are. "There are six clone sets and each set was designed to fulfill a specific function—technocrats like Menza Uhr, technicians, guards, police and so on. And entertainers like Jack. There were originally ten sets, but four of them have been lost. They went extinct for one reason or another." Limn doesn't attempt to explain that they were eliminated when, over too many generations of cloning, their root genomes became nonviable. "Other clone sets had to take over their functions. I'm Ssu clone set, which are considered technicians now, but were originally designed to be artists—painters and writers and poets and musicians. But when the original technician set—the Sahns—went extinct, the people in charge gave their function to Ssus and tried to suppress our creativity with a daily supplement. Well, a drug really. But I'm mostly immune to it because of a mutation. So, as I said, I came out wrong."

Yuli notices that Meridia has stabilized somewhat, drawn to this bizarre explanation that briefly pulls her mind together as she struggles to understand. "Are there any others like you?" Yuli asks. It's Meridia's question.

"Yes, but not many. They get eliminated if they're discovered." Limn is almost certain she was on the verge of being discovered. She turns away, hoping Yuli won't ask what she means by "eliminated."

Thinking of mutations and DNA reminds Limn of the genetic analysis she ordered of Yuli and Odilia and the old Mundani man on Selbourne, the analysis she intended to study in further detail once she had time. *Well*, she thinks, *I certainly have time now.*

42

Abél breathes more easily as they descend, devouring the richer air in great gulps. He's also sustained by the blue spirals of song that he knows are coming from Bekanz. He keeps his orb as open as possible, hoping for something more from Meridia. He tries to tell himself that if she's still too far away to contact in the usual way, that should mean that he'll be able to arrive at Selbourne before she does.

His brother twin Brân is still there on the island with Amos Quint. Does Brân know that Meridia is coming home?

Yes, brother. You told me.

I was hoping that Meridia might be more pertangible as they come closer, but I'm finding no change at all.

Brân acknowledges that he senses the same stasis.

Abél sees that Brân and Amos Quint have moved the broken mirrors, the ones that produced the breach through which they lost Meridia. They've put them in the back of Quint's meditation chamber and laid them face down, well apart from one another. Brân thinks that until they can learn more about them, the mirrors need to be kept where they can do no further harm.

Abél agrees. *As long as Meridia is coming home without using the mirrors, we may as well destroy them.*

"How are you feeling this morning, Abél?" Vidvana can't be certain of such things without asking.

"I'm stronger, thanks," he says. "No need to worry about me. I'll make it."

Vidvana has had some doubts about herself. She'd had no problem with the long days traveling on foot to Brightlea and then on to Túl but climbing in the mountains is hard work. She's a scholar, after all, a woman who works with her mind and her hands. She's a little envious of Salma, who has handled the rugged terrain with unflagging energy.

Zara has lagged behind for her own reasons. When she catches up, she calls out to Abél to get his attention. She's found some of the plants that Bekanz showed her. Zara hands Abél a small handful of leathery leaves. *Bekanz says these will be good for your heart. There's no preparation necessary. Just chew the leaves, one at a time. No more than two in a half-day and another at night.*

Abél accepts the leaves and pops one into his mouth. His eyebrows shoot up and his lips pucker as he bites into it. He keeps chewing as he sends stuttering golden arcs of gratitude to both Zara and Bekanz.

"Can you tell where Damon is?" Vidvana asks.

Abél exchanges a quick glance with Zara before answering. "Yes. Umet had some trouble getting past Swarthpol. They got too close and he felt its effects. He's okay now." Abél thinks maybe Damon went back to Swarthpol, but he isn't sure.

He did go, Abél. Meridia contacted him there.

Abél bites down harder on the leaf, asking it to heal him. He thinks Umet just told him that Damon has been in touch with Meridia, but he doubts himself right now so he says nothing. He chews the leaf more vigorously, swallowing its bitter juice.

43

"What can you tell me about the babies' parents?" Limn stares at lines of numbers and configurations of letters on her computer screen, trying to sort out what she's seeing in the DNA analysis of Yuli and Odilia and Amos Quint.

"The nens are pure Melfar like me," Yuli says. "Both of my parents were Melfar. It's not possible for a Melfar woman to become pregnant except by a Melfar man."

"Really?" Limn scrolls back to another set of diagrams. "Are you telling me that both of the nen's parents were also, as you say, 'pure Melfar'?"

Yuli hesitates, looking for Meridia, seeking her permission to talk about the circumstances of the twins' conception, of Meridia's parentage. She's felt Meridia's presence more strongly this morning, but she still can't see her. "Well, no," she says at last, hoping Meridia will approve or at least forgive her. "Meridia, the nens' mother, is only half Melfar. Her mother was Mundani."

"So Mundani women can become pregnant by Melfar but not the other way around?"

"That's right. It's always been that way."

Limn questions the "always" but she lets it pass. "I thought you told me that Meridia's partner is Mundani. So that can work?"

"Well, no. And Damon is not the nens' father. Not physically. Though he's truly the best father any nen could ask for."

"I'm confused," Limn says. Granted, she's unaccustomed to thinking about sexual reproduction, but this seems unduly complicated.

Yuli takes a deep breath, trying to figure out how to say what she needs to say. "Odilia and her sister twin Naomi were conceived in an unfortunate incident between Meridia and another like her. But Damon is their father now."

"Oh." Limn sits in silence for a moment. "Oh," she says again. "And when you say, 'another like her,' you mean the man also had a Mundani mother and Melfar father?"

"Yes." That's all Yuli is willing to give Limn. She won't say that Malaki's father and Meridia's father are themselves brother twins.

"So if both of their parents were of mixed parentage, why do you say they're 'pure Melfar'?"

"It was what one of our most skilled healers told Meridia about them." Yuli won't apologize for the hint of belligerence in her voice. She touches Odilia's tiny iridescent hand. How could this nen be anything other than pure Melfar?

"Well, I'm sorry to say that your healer made a mistake. Odilia has several genetic markers that are the same as the old man's and different from what I find in your genome, Yuli."

What? Yuli, what is she telling us?

Yuli is surprised by the sudden vibrant presence of Meridia. *She says they're not pure Melfar. That somehow they're part Mundani. Meridia?* She's gone again.

Limn turns back to her computer. She toggles back and forth between the detailed genomic analyses of Yuli, the baby, and the old man, wishing there was some way to take a sample of Meridia's DNA. That thought makes her smile. She rests her chin on her left fist as she stares at one particular comparison, tilting her head first to one side, then to the other as potential interpretations compete for her attention. "Oh," she says at last, sitting up straighter, both hands returning to her keyboard. "Yes, that could explain it."

What she'd been seeking to explain was why Melfar and Mundani genomes were so nearly the same even though the people themselves were so distinct. She could easily account for such unimportant differences as skin color and body form. That's just a matter of alternative genes at a few key loci. What she couldn't account for was the existence of any separate organs, any aurynx or gnosic orb. Yuli said these were distinct organs that Melfar had and Mundani lacked. The hypothesis that Limn proposes is that these are not in fact distinct organs, but rather inherent physiological capabilities in both groups, with the only difference being a particular genetic sequence that is switched off in Mundani, switched on in Melfar.

Another idea occurs to Limn and she taps away again, waiting impatiently for additional data to appear on her screen. She's looking for two things: First of all, the original genome readout for her own clone set. The designers claimed a new subspecies designation for their clone series—*Homo sapiens fictis*. The second thing she waits for is a genomic analysis from one of the relic data sets she'd gained access to—an analysis of the genome of *Homo sapiens sapiens*, the ancestral population of all humans now living. Well, "all" as far as she knows. She smiles at that very scientific caveat. It's always, "as far as we know" and "based on available data." Firm conclusions about anything are illusory. Things can change in light of the next question that nobody had thought to ask before.

There it is. She scrutinizes the new material and succeeds in bringing all five genomic readouts onto her screen at the same time—Yuli's, the baby's, the old man's, her own clone set genome, and the relic genome of *Homo sapiens sapiens*. She scans them first, looking for gross comparisons. There's one chromosome-level distinction between Yuli and the old man that doesn't seem to have anything to do with being Melfar or Mundani. It's the pair of chromosomes that, according to records, accounts for much of the difference between males and females in sexually reproducing populations— XX for females, XY for males. She notes that her own pair is XX. She's looked at this previously and knows that all the clone sets are universally XX. It's because of the need for eggs to use in the cloning process. Males became unnecessary.

Next Limn focuses in on the set of genes that she believes differentiate Yuli and the old man in another way, the genes that she thinks might account for what Yuli calls the Melfar aurynx and gnosic orb. Limn studies the sequences intently and then sits back in her chair. For perspective. The genetic sequence that's switched on in Melfar and off in Mundani was there also in the relic *Homo sapiens sapiens*. And in this example, it was switched off. Was it usually switched off? She'd need more data to know that, but she hypothesizes that Melfar ancestors must have included at least some key individuals with that sequence switched on. And for reasons she still cannot fathom, in the populations that became Melfar, those individuals were more successful at surviving to produce and raise offspring. Offspring who could produce and raise offspring.

What Limn sees in her own DNA brings tears to her eyes. The genetic sequence that accounts for Melfar's unusual abilities isn't even present in her genome. It's been pruned away and she knows why: Her designers decreed that any genetic sequence that was switched off ought to be eliminated. For efficiency. What other human potential had they also deleted from her genes?

Limn glances toward Yuli, drowsing there next to the window with baby Odilia nestled in her arms. Tears course down Limn's face unrestrained.

44

Amos Quint scans the beach and then squints toward the mountains through the lens of his farglass. He's not certain where Abél's group might emerge. Brân has told him only that they're coming over the mountains. Brân says that Damon's group will arrive along the beach, coming from the south. Amos thought he saw movement in the mountains, but it was probably just the wind. He turns his lens to scan the water toward the north, looking for some sign of the ship that Brân tells him is bringing Meridia back home. Who else will be on the ship? Yuli and the nens, of course. Hopefully. If there are Elossa, Brân won't know about them any sooner than Amos will. Even Melfar have to see these people with their eyes.

"Brân." Amos motions for his Melfar friend to join him on the terrace. "I think I saw something." He offers the farglass and points northward, across the sea.

Brân takes the implement from Amos and struggles to keep one eye closed as he scans the pulsing blue water. And then he sees it. Or he sees something. He fumbles for the part of the device that turns, the part that makes images clearer. He laughs. "Well, if this is what you saw, my friend, it's definitely not a ship. All I saw was a large fish of some kind leaping out of the water. I see no ship."

Amos Quint looks disappointed as he accepts the farglass from Brân.

"I still can't find Meridia," Brân says, answering Amos Quint's next question before he asks it.

"But Abél has been in touch with her, hasn't he? And she told him she was coming home?"

"So he says. But it happened several days ago and he's had no contact since. I can't explain it." Brân has no idea where Meridia and Yuli and the nens have been and thus no notion how many days it might take them to get back. If indeed they are coming back at all.

Amos says what Brân doesn't want to. "Do you suppose something might have happened to them?"

"We'll find out soon enough."

Amos turns his lens once again toward the mountains. After a moment he emits a low chuckle. "Unless that's a pack of pudus up there on the mountain, it looks like your brother will be arriving soon," he says.

Brân already knew that. He thinks Damon will arrive first.

45

Sometime in the night Yuli and Odi awaken to a loud scraping noise as the boat tips and jerks. Yuli picks up Odi and climbs the stairs, looking for Limn.

"Are we moving again?" Yuli asks.

"Yes and no," Limn says. She's hunched over some panels of buttons and glances back and forth between the buttons and the computer screens. "I think we're not stuck anymore, but I can't get the engines to engage. I may need some help."

Yuli's heart skips a beat as she scans the cabin, seeking some source of such help. Of course there's no one there—really there—except herself and Limn. "I don't know anything about ships," she says.

"That's okay," Limn says. "Come here. You see this button? The white one right below the line of small black ones? I'm going down into the engine room to see if I can adjust some things to get us going. When you hear me shout 'go' that means I need you to press that button. Press it hard and hold it down until you hear the sound of the engines. Or...or until you hear me shout 'stop'. We can't use the translator, so you'll have to recognize those words." Limn repeats the two words. "'Go' and 'stop'. Got it?"

"Yes, I think so," Yuli says. She points toward the white button. "This one, right? And you'll say 'go'." She voices the word exactly as she heard Limn say it, not using the Mundani equivalent that came out of the translator. "And I'll listen for 'stop'."

"Right. Let's hope this works. Keep your fingers crossed!"

Yuli looks down at her hands and moves her fingers back and forth.

"No, that's just an expression. Okay, here we go. No, not yet."

Limn scurries away and Yuli hears her clattering down one set of stairs and then a few more, going down into a part of the ship Yuli has never seen.

Can you think of anything else we could do to help? Meridia? Are you there?

I'm here, but not here. I'm in several places and maybe different times. I sense that Omi and I are insubstantial in all of them. But if I move my thoughts toward a given person or place, there I am. Here I am.

Most recently, I've been with Damon. Wherever I go, whenever I am, I keep coming back to Damon or to Odi. They're my touchstones, my anchors. I'm not sure I could do this without Naomi here with me. Damon seems to understand that I'm coming home on a ship. He wants so much to believe that when the ship arrives all will be well. I wish that were true.

I've been with Brân and Amos Quint, too. I see what they've done with the broken pieces of the mirror. I know they're trying to prevent further accidents. Doesn't Brân know that my being as I am was no accident? It makes me uncomfortable, what they've done. When Brân returned, he arrived back right there between the mirrors. But I'm coming back on a ship. Perhaps I don't need the mirrors.

I've also been with Father. I pertange all of these individuals, but none of them pertanges me. Father is pushing himself far too hard, trying to get to Selbourne so that he'll be there when we arrive. I want to tell him that there's no need to rush, that we're stuck. We're waiting for the moon.

Odi is crying.

Now Naomi is crying, too.

Yuli bounces Odi on her shoulder, trying to quiet her. She needs to listen for Limn to call out to her. All she's heard so far is some banging and a few shouted words that are not "go." The words sound angry.

There's a screeching sound, like metal scraping on metal. Another bang.

Silence.

"Go!"

Yuli presses on the white button as forcefully as she can and holds it down. There are more noises from below and then a steady hum and a shout from Limn. Should she let go of the button? Is that noise the engine running? Yuli takes her finger away from the button and the hum continues. She hears footsteps pounding up the stairs.

"We did it!" Limn bursts into the room, beaming with satisfaction. Yuli thinks the broad grin makes Limn's thin lips and small teeth almost pretty.

Odi cries louder with the sudden shouting and Yuli bounces her some more, crooning soothing words. "Are we moving again?" she asks.

"We will be shortly," Limn says. She's moved back to the panel of buttons in front of the computer screens. Her smile fades. "We're low on power, but I think we'll have enough to get the boat into deeper water. Enough to get us to morning."

"Do you need me for anything else?"

"No, you can go look after Odi. Thank you, Yuli. I couldn't have done this without your help. And Meridia's. Is Meridia here?" Limn glances around the cabin. "I heard two nens."

"Yes, she's here." *Mostly. Sometimes.*

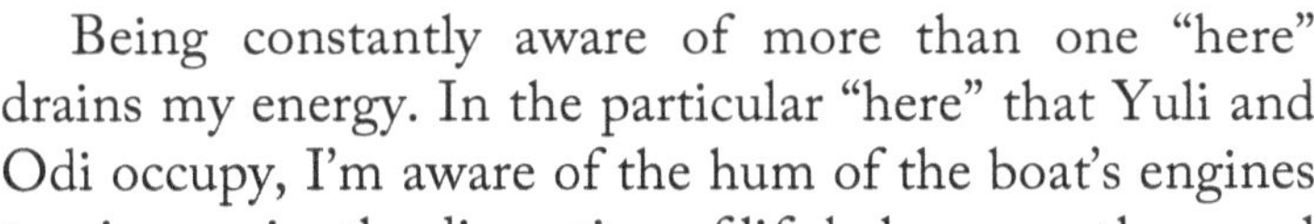

Being constantly aware of more than one "here" drains my energy. In the particular "here" that Yuli and Odi occupy, I'm aware of the hum of the boat's engines turning again, the disruption of life below us as the vessel begins to move.

Damon remains stalwart. He knows I'm coming home, but he wants proof of me like he had when I was on Selbourne and he and Brân were building the raft on the other side of the bay. We walked together then, holding hands. I try to take his hand now, but he doesn't acknowledge me. He doesn't feel my presence.

Father is better. I think he's chewed some voyma leaves to strengthen his heart. It was a long and tiring journey over the mountain. I wanted to tell him there was no need to hurry.

What was it that Limn told Yuli? She said that Odi is not pure Melfar after all. She's part Mundani. I don't understand. Emba told me the nens were pure Melfar. How could she have been wrong? I want to ask Limn if this unexpected mixture is because both of Odi's parents were half Melfar, half Mundani. Her physical parents. I want Limn to explain more about how this DNA works. Odilia and Naomi both look Melfar. They have the iridescent skin that all Melfar nens have. I think they still do. It's hard to be certain of such things at the moment. It's hard for me to fasten on physical, material things.

46

By the time Abél and his band make their way around the last mountain standing between them and Selbourne, Damon and Orban and Umet are resting on the beach below, in the company of Negyed and Vedö. The two Mundani men had set up a camp near the beach, where they have kept watch over Brân and the old Prophet Amos Quint, who remain across the water on Selbourne.

"Abél wants us to join him up there," Umet says, gesturing toward the rock shelter above the beach.

It's an easy ascent and Damon and his companions arrive almost simultaneously with Abél and his three women escorts. Damon is taken aback at how pale and tired Abél looks but he leaves it unremarked, only greeting his partner's father with a fond embrace. Their amiable words can't disguise the vortex of mingled hope and fear that engulfs both men.

"Umet told me that you were in touch with Meridia only two days past," Abél says. "You know, I'd begun to wonder whether my contact with her had been nothing more than an illusion. Did you learn anything from her?"

Damon recounts his experience, trying his best to hold the images vividly in mind as he speaks. "Although she said nothing about how she was coming back, I got the distinct impression that she was coming on a boat of some kind."

"Are Yuli and Odilia with her?"

Damon peers over Abél's shoulder toward Umet. "I don't think she'd come if Odilia wasn't with her. And I'm sure that means Yuli, too."

The two groups gather around a hastily kindled fire to share what they've learned, to share their hopes for the safe return of Meridia and Yuli and the twins.

Damon shows Abél the book he acquired from Elvrid with its picture of a ship like the Elossa. "The book says that this boat sank off the western coast in Mundani passage 472," he says. He reads the words that identify the event with "a village called Swarthpol" and then the part about "a land far to the north where people flew about in machines driven by power sucked from the sun."

Abél shares what he learned from Noita and Idös. "The story we entered into the *Book of All Time* as the Song of the Sea contained some unfortunate errors and omissions," he says.

Umet nods thoughtfully. *I thought the words recorded in the book seemed a bit different from the song as I learned it from my eldfather. Did you know my eldfather was from Túl, Abél?*

Abél hadn't known that. He wishes he could share with the young man the intensity of the original song's imagery as he'd experienced it in the presence of Idös and the Ancient Jasper Benison. But he doesn't want to exclude Damon, so he uses words. Abél begins by telling about the boat that came on great wings and sank into the sea. He tells how some of the sailors were rescued by Melfar, how they spoke words that no one could either comprehend or pertange. "They took ecphorite from a place the empty people called Swarthpol," Abél says. "Then the Melfar built a boat for the empty people. But it was small and they only went as far as Selbourne and stayed there. And then the song says, 'The place called Swarthpol harbors great danger in the depths of the dark pool. Let this song be a warning.'"

"That certainly makes better sense than the version recorded in the *Book of All Time*," Damon says. He glances apologetically at Vidvana. "No mention of mirrors?"

"Mirrors were there in the imagery of the song as Idös sang it, but I'm not sure where they belong in the story. The Túl Melfar are much better at verberating complex images than we are," Abél says. "But I do know that Idös showed me how the empty people took mirrors from the dark pool at Swarthpol." It's a pool he knows only too well.

"When I went to Swarthpol, I saw a pool like that," Damon says. "I think there may still be mirrors there."

Damon and Abél and their companions settle for the night in the shelter above the harbor. Damon is beset by dreams in which he and Meridia have to rescue their two daughters from a dark pool. Abél is haunted by visions of the same dark pool, but in his dreams, he is the one who is drowning and there is no one there to rescue him. Umet dreams of Yuli.

Abél yields to wakefulness long before morning and rises to walk along the ledge outside their shelter. The moon is just past full, dropping slowly toward the west. Its reflection dances across the waves below. Abél is tormented by loss and loneliness. His orb strains toward those who are gone—his mother, Avienne; his estranged partner, Maddie; and now his daughter Meridia and her twins. *But Meridia is coming back,* he tells himself. Is she? If she is, why can't he find her?

She's okay, Abél. We're on our way.

Oh, thank you, Yuli.

Relief surges through Abél like a warm breeze. Meridia is okay! But as he draws in his next breath, another thought follows: *If they're close enough for Yuli to be pertangible, why can't I find Meridia?* He seeks out his brother-twin across the water in Selbourne. Brân, too, has given up on sleeping.

I'm sure it was Yuli, Abél says.

Yuli? Not Meridia?

Not Meridia.

Brân offers no insight, only sending Abél an Amethyst wave of reassurance. *If Yuli says not to worry, we shouldn't worry.*

～～

Perhaps it's just as well that I'm not able to contact Father or Damon, better that they can't pertange me. They would only find me consumed with the worry that Yuli is trying to guard them against.

47

"Yuli says they're okay." That's the message Abél conveys to the others when he tells them of his experience.

Yes, she found me, too, Umet says. *We were together.* The young man's freckled cheeks redden.

Damon knows he ought to find this message, this contact with Yuli, reassuring. He doesn't. He's tried to be confident about Meridia's return. But if she's okay, truly okay, he wants to hear it from her. He's eager to cross over to Selbourne, convinced that the island is where Meridia will arrive.

After brief discussion, it's agreed that Orban will ferry Damon and Abél and Umet across to the island while the others remain encamped. The waters are smooth and the crossing peaceful, almost soothing. Brân and Amos Quint are there to welcome them as the raft approaches.

Abél and Umet accompany Amos Quint up the stairs to the dwelling chamber. Brân and Damon linger on the terrace outside the hall of mirrors. "There's something I need to give you," Brân says. He reaches into a pocket and then extends his hand toward the younger man.

Damon knows at once what it is. "You mean she didn't take them with her?" His optimism wavers. Meridia has not had her pouch of waifs with her.

"She helped me find my lost waifs once, and I've been holding these for her ever since I found them there in Quint's dwelling chamber. I'm sure she'd want you to take care of them. And, no, I didn't have my waifs with me either when I was taken from between the mirrors. Or rather...I had them, but they were left behind. And I can't explain why that was."

"So you mean even if Meridia had been holding them...?"

"Yes, I think somehow the stones would have stayed here anyway. But she'd left these under her pillow in Amos's room."

Damon's hand goes to the Quartz bead around his neck. Does Meridia still have hers?

Brân pertanges his concern. "She must still have it, Damon. Otherwise we would have found it there between the mirrors."

Damon is slightly relieved, confident that the Quartz beads he and Meridia shared at their partnering may still hold some power to connect them. "Is there any way we could use her waifs—any of them—to help get her back?" Damon tries to remember which stones are in Meridia's pouch. He thinks first of the Old Jade, the stone he himself found in the old photo bag he got from Brân. That seems so long ago. He knows there's also her Quartz with the map that led them to Woodclasp and an Amber containing the Song of Turning that she used to save him from harm in his later travels.

"Maybe," Brân says. "I don't know. But whatever connection they may have with her I'm sure will be strengthened by putting the stones in your hands."

Damon nods in acknowledgment. He holds the pouch of waifs in his hand for a moment, recalling how Meridia always carried them on a loop at her waist. He wants to carry them closer to his own small collection of waifs, closer to his heart, and so he pulls the cord holding the pouch over his head and tucks the precious packet inside his shirt. It feels slightly warm and he almost hears a cascade of soft tones vibrate against his chest.

After supper, Damon and Umet volunteer to spend the night below stairs in Amos Quint's workshop, leaving the three old men in relative comfort in the living chamber.

In truth, Damon craves time alone. He knows Umet does, too, so he's confident they will respect one another's peace if they can find any. So much has happened so fast; Damon needs to let it settle into his mind and heart without having to interact with anyone.

Quint's workshop, where they intend to sleep, stinks of fahm, the oily black stones the old Prophet burned in fashioning his own mirrors. Without speaking, Damon and Umet arrange their blankets on either side of the doorway so that they can breathe the fresh salt air. So that they can see outside. Damon is grateful to be resting a bit closer to the ocean.

"Are they okay?" Damon asks.

Umet nods with a faint smile and turns away.

Damon's heart wrenches with the certainty that Umet is now in almost constant contact with his beloved Yuli. Damon wants to be happy for that, but the knowledge only makes him miss Meridia more. Through the night, his fragmented dreams are haunted by visions in which he and Meridia are still together. He hears the plaintive blue and orange cries of Naomi and Odilia. Each holding one of the nens, he and Meridia sway together, singing a tender lullaby, singing and swaying until there is nothing but love-drenched silence.

The moon is only a few days past full and sometime beyond midnight it reaches a point in the clearing sky where it shines directly into Damon's closed eyes so brightly that he's awakened. He looks across the undulating waters at the moon's reflection. There's another reflection there, too. He sits suddenly upright. The second reflection isn't a reflection, but rather a small spot of white bobbing on the far horizon. Could it be…?

Damon rises, taking care not to disturb Umet. He creeps up the stairs and into the chamber filled with the snores of the two Melfar brothers and the old Mundani Prophet. He finds Quint's farglass and hurries back down to the terrace. He sits there the rest of the night, watching as the white speck grows larger, as it becomes a boat, a ship with great white wings like a butterfly. It doesn't seem to be as big as the Elossa. But surely this must mean that Meridia is coming home. *Please be there, Meridia.*

Just as the sun begins to pink the sky above the eastern mountains, Damon is joined by Amos Quint. Damon hands him the farglass and points. Abél and Umet and Brân arrive, too, but they need no visual assurance about the approaching boat. Umet gazes longingly toward it. His thoughts are filled with Yuli.

The five men stand there on the terrace shoulder to shoulder, watching the ship as it grows steadily larger, each man engrossed in his own thoughts, his own hopes and fears.

Amos dwells on memories of his encounter with the empty people from the ship Elossa that arrived so unexpectedly little more than a tide past. He doesn't trust these Elossa people. They kidnapped Yuli and Odilia.

They stole one of his mirrors, broke another, and left him gravely injured. But someone also tended to his wounds. Are they really coming back just to bring their captives home? How many Elossa might be on that boat?

Umet tries to ask Yuli about that, but he finds her agitated, worried about Meridia. Umet glances toward Damon, sending an Amethyst pulse of comfort that arises from his own hope that all will be well as soon as the ship arrives.

Damon fidgets, shifting his weight side to side, periodically leaning forward, silently pleading. Meridia told Abél that she was coming home. And he's sure that he, too, was in touch with her in that brief moment at Swarthpol. She told him she wanted to come home. And didn't Yuli tell Abél that Meridia is well? Umet is in contact with Yuli, but Damon's own partner remains painfully absent. Meridia has to be there on the ship. He delves into his pocket and wraps his fingers around the pebble of ecphorite he brought from Swarthpol, his talisman from that moment of contact with his beloved. If Meridia is there on the ship, why can't he contact her? Have his Revelant sensibilities finally abandoned him? "Do you pertange anything?" he says, turning first toward Brân and then toward Abél and Umet.

Abél and Brân remain silent, keeping their eyes trained on the distant ship. Their eyes and orbs.

Umet knows Damon is asking about Meridia. He doesn't want to share Yuli's concern about Meridia's wellbeing, so he, too, says nothing.

Damon heaves a deep sigh of frustration. "Maybe Meridia and Yuli are using some kind of canopy," he says, grasping at hope. He refuses to believe that something awful might have happened on their journey home. Meridia has to be there. There has to be a reasonable explanation for why they can't find her.

"Yes, maybe a canopy," Brân says. The three Melfar men know that isn't the case. There is no canopy and they pertange Yuli and Odilia with increasing clarity. Occasionally Abél senses Naomi as well and when he does, he reaches for Meridia. He doesn't find her. They all shield their concerns as best they can from Damon, not wanting to shred his fragile hope for Meridia's safe homecoming. They won't put their trepidations into words. When the ship arrives, then they'll know. Then they'll all know.

The men wait. As the ship comes ever closer, even Damon's Revelant sensibilities can detect Yuli and Odilia's presence. He desperately wants more. He wants Meridia and Naomi.

The ship drifts uncertainly into a spot near where the Elossa dropped anchor. This ship is definitely smaller and it has a different name: Pequod. The vessel bobs there, tilting rhythmically with the pressure of the waves. Someone—an Elossa someone—hurries onto the deck from the boat's interior and, working awkwardly, manages to push the heavy anchor into the water. She shouts something over her shoulder.

"There they are!" Amos's hand trembles as he points. "Yuli and the nen are there!"

Damon smiles a tight, tearful smile at the sight of his tiny daughter Odilia safe there in Yuli's arms, but he holds his breath. Waiting. Waiting for Meridia to emerge. Waiting for Naomi.

The Elossa woman holds Yuli's hand as they step into the small boat that will bring them ashore. The boat detaches from the Pequod and begins its short journey to Selbourne.

The five men make their way down the stairs to meet the boat. Umet takes the stairs in reckless leaps. The three old men follow, moving more slowly. Damon comes last. He's dazed, disbelieving. His breath comes ragged and his heart thuds in his chest, heavy as stone.

And then he feels it. It's just a faint touch. Did he imagine it? The fingers that just stroked his cheek? They stroked it exactly the way Meridia does. Damon stops dead still on the stairs as the three old men move cautiously onward. It happens again. He closes his eyes. This time it's Meridia's palm that rests warm against his face. An amethyst sob bursts from his throat, strangling his words as he voices her name, as he names their other child, the one Meridia holds in her arms.

And then she's gone.

No, not gone. Only just beyond his grasp. But now Damon knows she's here. Somehow, she's here.

He brushes away his tears and hurries down the remaining stairs. When he reaches the narrow beach, he runs toward Yuli and Odilia. Umet releases Yuli from his embrace as she turns toward Damon and places Odilia into his arms. "She's here, isn't she?" Damon whispers.

"Yes," Yuli says. "She's with us. But we have to figure out how to get her all the way back."

Damon nods. He hugs Odi to his heart and turns toward Brân and Abél and Amos, who are conversing with the Elossa woman. He's surprised that they seem able to understand one another.

"Her name is Limn," Yuli says. "She learned some Mundani from me. She can speak it a little bit." They'd had ample time to practice during the days their ship was stuck on the rocks.

Damon attunes to the conversation.

"It was you, wasn't it?" Amos says. "You're the one who patched up my arm." Amos Quint also knows that Limn was one of the party of Elossa who stole his mirror.

"My sorrow what my people did," Limn says. "Better we never come. My idea. My fault. My regret. I bring Yuli and nen home. Same Meridia and other nen."

Amos Quint appeals to Brân and Abél for assistance in trying to understand what Limn is saying, but then he remembers that Melfar can't pertange Elossa, can't understand their meanings any better than he can.

"Who else is with you?" Amos says, squinting toward the ship.

Limn laughs. "No person. My alone. Yuli explain better."

"But Meridia..." Amos scowls. "You said Meridia is here. Is she still on the ship?" He turns toward Damon. "Should we go get her?"

"She's already here." Damon speaks softly as he gazes into Odilia's face. It's now Odi's tiny hand that rests against his cheek. "Yuli knows. Ask Yuli."

The group mounts the stairs again toward Amos Quint's residential chamber, and as they settle in the cramped space with glasses of tea, Yuli does explain. Everyone—even Limn—listens with rapt attention. Limn smiles occasionally, pleased at how much she can understand, amused to hear Yuli's account of events she experienced differently. And sometimes Limn scowls, knowing that what Yuli is telling isn't the whole story.

Amos turns toward Limn. "None of this explains why you came here in the first place. Perhaps you ought to tell us about that." He didn't intend to speak so harshly.

Limn looks down and takes a deep breath. She'd tried to prepare for this moment. She knew the question would come. "My your language not good. My computer better one, please?" She opens the satchel she carried with her from the ship and takes out a device with a screen and keyboard.

Abél and Brân exchange a glance. They've seen such devices before.

After a moment, Limn begins speaking into the computer in her own language and her words are translated into almost perfect Mundani. "We came searching for ecphorite. It was my idea. I'd read about ecphorite in some old records and I was curious to find out if it was something real."

Damon holds up the pebble he brought from Swarthpol. It gleams softly.

"Yes, we did find it and we took some back with us."

"And the mirror?" Amos asks.

"The mirrors contain ecphorite," Limn says. "I hadn't known about the mirrors before. We were only looking for the ecphorite."

"And that's what led you to my cabin," Damon says. "It was the mirror fragment."

"That's right. Our dioristimators were calibrated to search for what I believed to be the chemical profile of ecphorite and so of course they homed in on the shard of mirror."

They understand most of what Limn says in spite of the occasional words for which Mundani has no equivalent.

Abél is thinking about the fact that there were also pieces of ecphorite in his own cabin. Probably in Zara's, too. And in Damon's workshop. Why did these devices not lead the Elossa to those places? Was it because of the pointing-stone that they habitually keep with ecphorite? He's convinced that must be it.

"But why did you take Yuli and the nen?" Brân asks the question that's in every mind.

Limn closes her eyes for a moment, her thin lips pressed together. "That wasn't supposed to happen. The ones who went over the mountains acted on their own. When they returned with the girl and the nen—with Yuli and Odi—I thought it was too late to take them back. And I didn't want to just leave them there on the beach." She doesn't say that she'd been afraid to let her people know how horrified she was at the abduction. "I'd seen how the old man had tried to fight us off and feared others might soon arrive. I just wanted to take the ecphorite and go, to return to a laboratory where I could study it."

Abél squints at Limn, trying to understand what's going on in the mind of this very strange little woman, seeking something to pertange. Does that look in her dark eyes mean she regrets her decisions? "Can you tell us what you found in your records about ecphorite?" he says. "And why that information led you to come here?" Abél is trying to put things together, but there are many missing pieces.

"Long ago there was a scientific research station near here, located underground to shield it as completely as possible from ambient sound and light. The station was called Swarthpol and the focus of its research was the fabrication of a composite silicate to use in building and programming computers." She starts to explain how her own people's computers still use the legacy technology of silicon chips, but she quickly sees this information is of no interest to her listeners. "They were working with a theory integrating their knowledge of both photons and phonons—light and sound particles. Vibrations. Their aim was to be able to program computers via sound. I think the theory actually emerged from some biological research conducted earlier that focused on a local species of diatomaceous algae. And snails."

"Snails?" Damon is suddenly alert. "Glowing snails?"

"Yes, I think so. You know something about those?"

Damon explains briefly about how a substance from the snails works to produce especially vivid photographic images from songs.

Limn taps on her keyboard.

"What became of the research station?" Brân asks.

"Like everything else, it was destroyed in the Tantum." It's a word that the translator can't render into Mundani, so Limn tries to define it. "That was the terrible time when almost everything was destroyed—people, cities, living things of all kinds. We were surprised to find that human beings—people—had survived in this area."

"But your expedition wasn't the first, was it?" Abél says.

"No. There was a previous expedition launched in 4308. I'm not sure what year that would be according to your timekeeping. It was 194 years ago."

Amos frowns and then says, "That would've been the passage 472."

"Only two returns before the dedication of the Ancient Jasper Benison," Abél says. "The Song of the Sea."

"So you were aware of that first expedition?" Limn's eyes glow with anticipation. "Please. Tell me what you know about that."

And so they tell her about the Song of the Sea, about the Melfar of Túl, and about the entry Damon found in the book from Elvrid's shop that also mentioned the Mundani passage 472. Abél wants to mention something about his own experience at Swarthpol but decides that can wait for another time.

"Were the mirrors I found here part of their research?" Amos asks.

The only thing Damon wants to know is what all of this has to do with the problem of getting Meridia back.

I try so hard to listen. But then I think too longingly of Damon and I lose myself in a past where none of this has happened yet. Where it's only me and Damon and the twins in our little cabin in New Beniford. Or before that when Avienne and Mother were still alive.

I reach out to touch Damon again, begging him to acknowledge me.

You need to sing, Meridia. You must sing the Song of Turning.

Who is this? Someone is aware of me, but it isn't Damon. It isn't Father. Is this the Migrant? It's a woman. A woman manifesting through the Migrant.

Avienne?

Avienne is here with us. We want you to sing.

It's Idös, this woman I've never met. *Why the Song of Turning?* I know how I've used that song before. I don't see how it could be helpful now.

That song is not just about deceiving Mundani, about losing them in an altered landscape, although it can have that effect. It's also about the colors and tones of your own mind. Yours have become disarrayed and that weakens them. They've grown pale and chaotic. You need to sing!

And so I do as this woman asks. What harm can it do? I sense that she is able to understand the songs not only in the details of their images and effects, but also in a more absolute way that I find mystifying. Idös says Avienne is with her and I sense that this is true. Avienne said she couldn't help me because she is no longer where I wish to be. Idös is there. Idös is still alive.

I sing. And as I sing, my mind moves and turns, colors and notes settling into place, falling into stronger patterns. I breathe more deeply, sensing air rushing through my nostrils, inflating and deflating my lungs. Naomi looks up at me with a smile and a squeal. I hold her close and send flower-bright thanks to Idös. I don't know her, but she knows Avienne. I'm grateful for her advice. Her support. Other than Naomi, no one else is here with me—not really here.

Are you a Calumet? I ask.

Yes, Meridia. I am a Calumet. Like your eldmother. Like you.

I verberate gratitude and continue singing.

Yuli's mind has been wandering ever since she finished her summary account of her sojourn among the Elossa. She tried to listen as Amos and Brân and Abél questioned Limn about details. Truly, she wants nothing more than to quietly rest her head on Umet's strong shoulder. She doesn't know why she's suddenly started humming the Song of Turning. She's not trying to turn anything. It's almost as if she herself is turning, her awareness shifting slowly from Limn and the others to the teeming life in the water beyond, then back toward Selbourne and to Meridia.

Meridia! There you are!

You can pertange me?

Almost. Much better, anyway. Your image and verberations are stronger. Abél, she's here! "Abél!" Yuli's voice is breathless and urgent.

Abél and Brân both turn toward Meridia, their eyes wide as their orbs find her.

48

Limn insists on visiting Amos Quint's chamber of mirrors, curious to know what else might be there among the artifacts he spoke about. Brân and Abél accompany Amos and Limn. Damon remains in the dwelling chamber with his daughter and Yuli and Umet.

Limn is exhilarated by her own uninhibited curiosity. She carries her computer along in its satchel and relates, through the translator, more details about the Tantum, about the worldwide nuclear explosions and subsequent earthquakes and volcanic eruptions and violent storms and how the coastlines and landscapes everywhere shifted and changed. Nobody had made new maps, of course, so her journey southward in search of ecphorite had been guided only by outdated information, vague hope, and insatiable curiosity.

"Where are the mirrors?" Limn had expected them to be here near the entrance to the cavern where she'd last seen them, but all she sees are the newer mirrors, the ones crafted by Amos Quint.

"We didn't trust them," Brân says, "so we put them in the back after Meridia disappeared."

"And the relics you mentioned?"

Amos retrieves his chest of artifacts. Without waiting for permission, Limn begins sorting through the objects. She handles the oddly shaped pieces of glass, shards of ceramic, chunks of petrified rust, and lumps of fossilized plastic with impatient disinterest. An untranslatable exclamation accompanies her retrieval of one peculiar item. She holds it up to the light of Amos's lantern to examine it more closely.

"What is it?" Abél asks.

"A data drive," Limn says. "I suspect it's from the scientists who were here in the early forty-fourth century. You said that was in your passage 472? It's in a remarkably good state of preservation for something nearly two hundred years old."

"You mean there could be information inside it?" Abél, of course, is hoping for the kind of information that will help get Meridia back. He can't quite relate to Limn's desire for knowledge as if that were enough. In fact, he finds that fixation bothersome. He's concerned about recovering his daughter. What good is knowledge if it doesn't help solve a problem? Of course, Limn can't possibly understand how important Meridia is to them. Meridia is their Calumet. She's needed. She's loved.

"Yes, I'd say it's possible that there's recoverable information," Limn says. "Though we shouldn't be too optimistic. One advantage of our strict adherence to the Protocols is that nothing changes. Well, almost nothing. Mistakes are made, of course, but surprisingly few. I've accessed some very old data from similar devices that I found locked away in museum vaults in Port Sillick." She examines the object more closely. "Yes, I'm pretty sure this will attach to one of the receptacles on my computer. Hopefully the storage language is one that my computer can read. As to whether the data on the drive remains uncorrupted... We'll just have to see." She places the object in her pocket and continues sorting through the remaining items. There aren't that many and she finds nothing else that captures her attention.

                                    49

Holding Odilia in his arms again only intensifies Damon's longing for me and for Naomi. There are things he would like to ask me about the conversation Abél and Limn shared with one another before they went down to the mirrored chamber. He keeps thinking there ought to be something in all of it that will help them bring us home. His mind is full of questions. *How did those researchers at Swarthpol manage to go from making computers to interfering with time-space? That's what they ended up doing. How did they do it?*

I heard everything that was said, Damon. I have the same questions.

I want more than anything else to be here with Damon and Odilia, but since I can't be here—not the way I want to be here—I'd just as well go to Swarthpol and see what I can learn there.

I'm oddly confident that in our present state Naomi and I will be immune to whatever unpleasantness it was that Father experienced from Swarthpol. Besides, I don't intend to visit the time when Father was there. I'm looking for something much older. I want to find the sinking ship and see for myself what those earlier Elossa did at Swarthpol. Why do I think the place was known by a different name before they came?

I'm shifting, feeling for the notes and colors that are where I wish to go.

Yes, there's the ship.

Melfar call to one another, fearful of this strange ship with its torn wing, uncertain what manner of people are on it. The people on the broken ship speak empty words and verberate nothing, but the Melfar can see that they're in trouble. These Melfar are fishermen, well acquainted with the sea, and so some of them dive into the water and swim toward the empty people. Other Melfar launch small fishing boats. They can't rescue everyone, but before the strange ship sinks finally beneath the waves, many of its occupants are safely on shore.

They're definitely Elossa. Their hair is cut exactly the same as the people of Port Sillick and they wear the same plain-colored garments. Several of the ones wearing green look disconcertingly like Limn.

What was it these people wanted here? The ecphorite. And the mirrors that came from a dark pool. I seek such a pool and find none, only a pile of huge black boulders. Is there water beneath the stones? I think there is. I think there's a huge underground cavern filled with water. But it's not a natural cavern like the one Amergin and his Naomi traveled through. No, this one is all straight passageways and squared-off rooms.

I watch a while longer but see nothing more that interests me. I shift Naomi from one shoulder to the other, grateful that she's still sleeping peacefully.

I want to know about the research. I think about the computers I saw in my travels with the Migrant. Were any of those here in Swarthpol? My presence shifts again, attuning to other notes and colors, phasing deeper and deeper into the past until I find what I seek.

I find Lazaro's mother. She's working with one of the computers, singing a song she learned from her own mother long ago. It's one of her son's favorites.

"Chisa!" The man's voice is sharp. He's standing amid a complex of objects and devices at the center of the room. The only objects I recognize are the mirrors. They're larger and of a more regular shape than the ones from Amos Quint's chamber. "Chisa," he scolds, "I've told you: No singing when we're running tests on the materials."

He has told her several times, but she keeps forgetting. Singing is second nature to Chisa. Her people sing all day long, at all their tasks. It was the clarity of her voice that earned her this job in the first place. "I'm sorry, Jefe," she says, calling him Chief. Boss. I know this from her verberations. She falls silent, but I can hear the song still verberating in her mind. I think I ought to recognize it.

The one that Chisa calls Boss is trying to explain to someone else—someone he also addresses as Boss— about the progress they're making with their experiments. "The mirroring is intended to filter and concentrate the photons that are generated in consonance with the phonons. Certain frequencies pass through while others are reflected. The employment of two of the filters facing one another, reflecting onto each other, should intensify the effect."

"I see," the Boss's Boss says. He doesn't really see; he just doesn't want to appear ignorant. "And you're ready to test it?"

"Yes, we're ready." The first Boss glances toward a man operating a computer next to the mirrors. He's using a keyboard, but it's not like Limn's keyboard. This one has regular groupings of interspersed white and black keys, all arranged side by side in a long line.

The first Jefe signals to the second Jefe to stand away from the mirrors. They watch as the computer operator begins working the keyboard. He doesn't tap the keys the way Limn does on the little square keys of her computer. He holds them down and when he does, there are sounds. Nice sounds. Empty sounds. No, now they've begun to generate images. But the images are nothing recognizable. Just patterns of light and color dancing there between the two mirrors. Nevertheless, I'm fascinated that they would have built a machine to do something so similar to what Melfar do with our aurynx. Naomi stirs and I see that she's awake, smiling at the music, the patterned light.

My attention is drawn back to Lazaro's mother, Chisa. She seems unconcerned with the experiment, engrossed instead in her own work. She's begun to hum again.

There's a sudden shout from across the room.

"Stop!" Jefe One said that. "Did you see it? Am I imagining things?"

"Yes. No. I saw it, too. It was there and then it wasn't."

Naomi is disturbed by the shouting and I pat her reassuringly. I know I've missed something important, so I focus my attention backward in time a few moments and instead of watching Chisa, I watch the mirrors. As the operator generates colorful sounds with his keyboard, a lizard skitters out from behind one of the mirrors and runs onto its face and then...it vanishes.

Oh. They weren't trying to do this. They didn't mean to do it at all. It was an accident. My heart flops heavily in my chest. Was my disappearance also an accident? And Brân's? Did they ever figure out how to control this?

I believe they did, Meridia.

Idös? Did you see what happened?

Yes, it was Chisa's song that caused the breach and the breach took the lizard away. Thank you for showing me this. Did you recognize the song?

And all at once I know where I heard it before. *It's part of the Turquoise Song of the Canopy of Time, isn't it? It sounds almost like the section that became part of the Song of All Songs.*

You need to tell Abél about this.

Can't you tell him for me? I'm uncertain about my father's ability to pertange me. But Idös is already gone. She left me with a pulse of gratitude for having brought her to this place as a witness.

I need to experience the moment again, the moment when the lizard disappeared. I step backward in time once more, refusing to be amazed at the facility with which I'm able to do this, grateful that Naomi is unperturbed by such shifts. There was something about the lizard that sparked a tingle of recognition, of familiarity. I watch again. I listen. I reach toward the small creature at the precise moment in which it dematerializes.

Yes, that is how I felt when Naomi and I transited from Selbourne to Port Sillick, my body more space than substance.

The tiny particles within my vastness vibrated with the notes and colors of song, shifting, slipping through mirror and stone and time like a bird gliding through forest canopies. No, not like a bird. Like the wind, like particles of light. Photons? No, not even that. Substance ceased to exist as my spaciousness slipped easily through all the spaces that form leaves and branches and stones and then and now until, once again, I began to catch the light. Catching it, slowing my vibrations. Becoming almost solid once again. Solid and elsewhere.

How will I tell all this to Father?

50

I find Father sitting next to Damon in Amos Quint's living chamber. He's holding Odilia.

I hum the Song of Turning in an effort to intensify my presence. Then I join with the melodious strands of blue and orange light that connect the nen in my arms with the one in Father's arms.

Father. Father, I need to tell you something.

"Meridia?" He speaks my name and clutches at Damon's arm. "Damon, can you pertange her?"

I show Father two intersecting spheres, one amber, the other turquoise, showing him the space within each, within both, as I continue to sing the Ancient Amber's Song of Turning. Then I take Damon's hand and guide it toward Odilia.

His eyes grow wide. He glances toward Abél and nods to confirm that he knows I'm here, that he feels my hand on his. His eyes flit around the room, searching, wanting something more. His awareness of me is fragile.

Odilia begins to cry. She cries for her missing sister. And for me.

This can't go on. How can I be Odi's mother in this strangely altered state of being? *Father, please. We have to try. The two songs. The mirrors.* I verberate as intensely as I'm able, but I'm not certain he understands. The effort of communicating is too much and I begin to drift again. I'm more aware of vibration in my body—this spaciousness that I experience as my body—as I rove backward and forward among potential realities. No, not potential. They're all real. Just not all here. Not all now. If I had physical substance I'd cry. I miss being able to cry. I clutch Naomi closer to my breast, wondering what she's experiencing. She hasn't suckled today. I don't know how much longer we can sustain this.

Abél sits quietly, barely breathing as he tries to make sense of what Meridia verberated. Damon leans toward him, gazing into Odilia's anguished face, stroking her arm to soothe her cries, murmuring comfort. He knows Meridia was here. He sensed her presence in his tormented Mundani heart. If she had some specific message, he has to trust that Abél received it and will be able to convey it to the others.

"Meridia wants us to set up the mirrors again," Abél says.

Limn raises her head from the computer where she's been working all morning. "You touch Meridia?" she says. She toggles on her translation program as she turns to face Abél. "Please tell me."

"It wasn't much," Abél says. "She seems convinced that the mirrors are needed for her to return. And I think she wants us to use the Song of Turning and the song of the Canopy of Time. Somehow."

"I think she's right about the mirrors," Limn says. "Tell me about the songs." She leans forward, her hands clasped, shoulders hunched in concentration.

Abél explains that the Song of Turning has always been used to alter or distort perceptions of the landscape. He has an uncomfortable feeling that it may be more than that, but he continues his explanation. "The Canopy of Time lets us experience the past. It puts us into the past as if it were now. Not bodily, of course." He's not certain that's how Mundani perceive it.

Damon's hand goes to the two pouches of waifs under his shirt. His own pouch contains only a few waifs, but one of them is an Amber than contains the Song of Turning. Meridia gave it to him. He knows that her own pouch contains a waif of that same Benison.

Limn is lost in thought, her almost nonexistent eyebrows knitted tightly together. "What I'm learning from the data stored on the relic drive suggests that the ecphorite did prove to be a successful material for storing photonic images via impressions made by phonons. Sound into light. It's all vibrations." Limn finds the process mystifying, though intuitively sensible. "I've found nothing about the mirrors so far. Or about traversing time-space. But if Meridia thinks those two songs might activate the mirrors and get her phased back into our space and time, then I don't see why we shouldn't try it." She cocks her head to one side. "You say your Song of Turning is about spatial perception." She inclines her head the other direction. "And your Canopy of Time is about temporal perception. Hunh. Yes, let's definitely give it a try."

At the moment, Abél and Brân, along with Yuli and Umet, are the only Melfar available on Selbourne. *Will our voices be enough to accomplish this?* Abél asks.

When I left, when Meridia left, we had nothing more than our own voices, Brân says. *And we had no idea what we were doing.*

"Nevertheless, let's wait for Zara to get here," Abél says. He knows she's already on her way. *We don't want to make any mistakes. Surely more voices will be better.*

Damon is impatient. He's suspicious of the powdered supplement Yuli has been mixing for Odilia. The nen doesn't seem to mind, as she nestles into Damon's arms and sucks hungrily on the odd-shaped nipple and bottle that's been her only source of nutrition ever since her abduction. Damon knows that whatever the supplement is, it couldn't be as nutritious as milk from her own mother. He pushes aside once again the thought that keeps wanting to intrude: *What if we're never able to get Meridia back?* He didn't think that. He won't. But the possibility scratches at the margins of his consciousness.

The cramped space of Amos Quint's living chamber becomes unbearable and Damon carries Odi down the stone stairs to watch for Zara's arrival. He's done everything he can. He has, hasn't he? He found Fannan's picture of the ship, the one the old photologist must have made from the Song of the Sea. He also found the brief reference to the first Elossa arrival in the old book from Elvrid's shop. All of that seems to have fallen into insignificance with Limn's arrival. Of course the Elossa people had been here before. Of course they travel in ships powered by the sun. The Song of the Sea contains a true, albeit abbreviated, history of that first encounter.

None of that gets them any closer to getting Meridia back. She didn't leave on a ship and now they know that she can't return that way. She has to come back the same way she went. They have to use the mirrors. Damon tries to think about the two songs Meridia wants them to sing—the Canopy of Time and the Song of Turning. He's heard Meridia sing them. He's seen their effects. He understands a little of how Brân used the Canopy of Time to protect him and Meridia when they were traveling to Beniford for the first time. Only a few notes resound in his memory, but they elicit a dizzying sense of tall trees and an elusive scent of lemon and florapple. He recalls how Meridia used the Song of Turning to protect him when he was being followed on his way back to New Beniford with his photography equipment.

Odilia dozes as Damon wanders down the shore. He goes farther than he'd intended. When he comes back, Vidvana is there, tying up the raft to keep it from floating away. Zara is already on her way up the stairs.

"Can I help you with that?" Damon says as he approaches Vidvana. It's a pointless offer. His arms are occupied by a sleeping nen.

Vidvana smiles as she finishes knotting the second rope. She brushes the sand from her hands before tucking a stray strand of hair behind an ear. "Zara says you've figured out a plan for getting Meridia back."

Damon explains about the two songs as they climb up toward Quint's chamber of mirrors. "At least that's how I understand it," he says. "Limn thinks it makes sense. One song to maneuver space, the other to adjust time." He tries to relay Limn's concept of being "out of phase" with time-space. "They're setting up the mirrors now."

"Are you sure the Elossa person—this Limn—is trustworthy?" Vidvana says. "Wasn't she part of the expedition that took Yuli and Odilia in the first place? And weren't they responsible for Amos Quint's injuries?"

"Limn was also the one who tended Quint's wounds and carried him to his living quarters. And she did bring Yuli and Odilia back home."

"True. But won't others try to follow her here?"

"No. Surely not." Damon hadn't thought about that possibility. Limn has told them she was already in trouble back in her home country. "She doesn't think so, anyway. She seems pretty certain that they're glad to be rid of her."

The worry creasing Vidvana's face doesn't change.

They stop outside the entrance to the mirror chamber, uncertain whether they should go in. It's not a spacious room. They listen for a moment to the conversation going on within, voices muffled by the stone walls. Damon explains to Vidvana that one of the voices comes from Limn's translation device.

"Is that how the mirrors were arranged when Meridia left?" the voice asks.

"Yes," Abél says. "Yes, I'm sure this is exactly how we found them after Damon witnessed Meridia's disappearance."

"Well, then." There's a shuffling of feet as the singers position themselves. "Now you sing?" Limn stands just inside the entrance.

"Now they sing." Damon murmurs the words and clutches his sleeping daughter more tightly.

Limn turns to see who spoke. "Do you want to come in, Damon?"

Damon does want to go in, but he isn't sure he should. The vision of Meridia and Naomi shimmering into absence between those mirrors still haunts him. The power of the mirrors frightens him.

"Go, Damon," Vidvana says. "Didn't you tell me that Meridia continues to be linked to Odilia through Naomi? Wouldn't it be good to have Odilia close by?"

Limn moves aside and Damon takes a few hesitant steps into the dark chamber. He blinks. Abél and Brân are there. Also Yuli and Umet and Zara. Five Melfar singers. Damon pats Odi gently, resting his cheek against the softness of her pale golden curls.

Abél voices a few notes to begin the song, to focus their verberations. Soon Yuli and Umet join him in singing the Canopy of Time. They play with a few different images and then settle on a verse Meridia herself composed about the discovery of the Mica Benison on Selbourne. Brân and Zara begin the Song of Turning, at first humming quietly, weaving their notes harmoniously among the tones and images and cadences of the Canopy of Time.

Damon's breath comes tense and shallow as he waits, staring into the dim. The glowing stones along the walls seem to dance. He watches their reflections in the mirrors. "Please come home, Meridia!" His words are barely more than a whisper, but Odilia startles and raises her head, looking first into her father's face and then directly into the space between the mirrors. Damon looks, too. There's a shimmer there that begins to suggest a shape. A human shape.

The singers continue with increased vigor, singing the same phrases over and over. There's excitement and wonder on their faces.

Damon catches his breath as Meridia's form flickers there between the mirrors. He takes a few steps toward her and feels a tug on the child he holds in his arms.

This isn't right. I'm here, but still elsewhere. My vibrations feel thwarted by the vibrations of this place.

Damon and Odilia and Father are there, ready to welcome me, wanting to welcome me. I struggle to adjust, to vibrate differently. I sing the Song of Turning but my mind is still askew. I sing phrases from the Canopy of Time, phrases contained within the Song of All Songs. The phrases Father and Yuli are singing are different phrases. Wrong phrases. It's all wrong. Naomi is crying, screaming a chain of deepest blue links, casting it toward her sister twin. Odilia shrieks strands of brilliant orange that wrap tightly around and through the blue chain and I know. I know what's happening and I thrust Naomi into Father's arms as my own vibrations fade and I slip away, tumbling into a Turquoise memory in which I'm leaping from a cart and running toward an empty cabin and I'm engulfed in a suffocating brown sadness.

"Meridia, no!" Damon clings to Odilia and grasps after the dissipating vision.

The songs falter and then cease, overwhelmed by the lusty cries of the two nens. Abél looks toward Damon and then back at the child in his arms.

Naomi is back.

Odilia is still here.

Meridia is still gone.

51

Damon's tears are at last exhausted, but he can't get enough of holding Naomi, knowing that she was only a short while ago held in Meridia's arms. He watches Odilia sleeping in her basket. She's bigger than Naomi. Not much bigger, but it's noticeable.

Brân and Abél are engaged in animated discussion with Limn. Something about the information she's found in the relic storage unit recovered from Quint's chest of artifacts. She's been poring over it ever since their failed attempt to retrieve Meridia. "Do you have any kind of musical instrument that would be able to replicate the specific tones that are indicated here as the mechanism of activating the portal? The output speaker on my computer is not functioning properly. I can hear the tones, but they're broken up with static. I think we'll need pure tones to make this work."

"We can sing the tones," Zara says.

"Yes, you could. But when you sing, my audio analysis program picks up interference from additional vibrations. It may be what you refer to as verberations, but whatever it is, it interferes with the purity of the tones."

Brân retrieves his backsack from near the door and fumbles around inside it. He draws out a wooden flute.

Abél stares. "Is that...?"

"Yes, brother. It's Malaki's flute. Do you have something better to offer? It's a good instrument, though we'll have to remove the reed drone that Malaki added."

"Do you know how to play it?" Vidvana asks.

"I can try."

"Well, if you'd like, I'd be willing to try," Vidvana says. "My father played the flute and he taught me when I was a child. Of course, I haven't played in many passages. Meeds, even."

Brân is amused by Vidvana's mixing of Mundani and Melfar time frames; he holds the instrument out toward the Mundani poet with a smile. "By all means," he says.

Vidvana sits next to Limn, listening intently to the sequence of notes emitted by the computer. Tentatively, she reproduces them on the flute.

Amos Quint busies himself laying out some of the food that Vidvana and Zara brought from across the bay. There's fresh fish and pickled mooli-root.

Abél listens intently. If this is a song, it's not one he's heard before. Or is it? It has no images, but it tugs at the edges of his awareness, nudging his gnosic orb. After listening to it a few times, he hums it quietly to himself. "Oh!" he says. He turns toward Brân. *Do you pertange it, brother?* He hums the notes again and the image intensifies, an image of a bright road extending endlessly. It pulses deep orange.

I do. It's a phrase from the Song of the Wide Path. The Ancient Carnelian song. But there are other notes that Vidvana is playing. Listen.

Together, the old brother twins listen, nodding as the notes from the Carnelian song pass and other notes take their place. Brân catches the new notes and begins to hum. Abél joins him, and together they verberate deep blue images of swiftness, spaciousness, buoyant flight. They recognize the phrase from the Old Lapis Benison's Song of Liberation.

Suddenly, the imagery they pertange is joined by simple orange and blue notes from the other twins, from Naomi and Odilia.

Vidvana stops playing. "Do you recognize these notes, Abél?"

"We do," Abél says. "It's just that there are no images from the flute or from the computer. It's only when we sing the same notes that they verberate images."

Brân's thoughts have gone to the first time he heard his son Malaki play the instrument. *When Malaki played that flute, it wasn't the instrument verberating the images. It was Malaki himself.*

Abél explains which songs they've identified. "What I don't understand is how Brân was able to go and return without knowing any of these things."

Limn turns abruptly to face Brân. "You experienced the portal, too?" No one had mentioned that to her; she stares at him with unabashed wonder, unguarded curiosity. "Please. Tell me about your experience. All of it, beginning with exactly how you transited."

Brân would prefer telling the story in images but Limn requires words. "It happened while Amos Quint and I were chanting together among the mirrors. It was just the two of us. We were chanting the Song of All Songs."

"Tell me about that song." Taking her computer into her lap, Limn sits on the floor in front of Brân and Abél and Amos, giving them her full attention.

"Meridia brought us that song. It's called Song of All Songs because it incorporates sections from so many of the songs the Melfar know." *Though not, in fact, all of them.*

"And that would include..." Limn consults her notes. "The Song of Turning and the Canopy of Time?"

Brân tries to remember exactly which songs are there, woven into the song Meridia brought new from the Migrant. "Maybe," Brân says. He recalls that the Amber waif within the pattern Meridia designed for the face of the Benison is a Preterit Amber, containing the Song of Raising the Waters. Is the Ancient Amber Song of Turning the one in the song itself? Did they make a mistake in composing the pattern of waifs for the design on the Benison? "The Song of All Songs does include the Canopy of Time," Brân says, "as well as the Song of the Wide Path and Song of Liberation." He explains that he'd identified those two songs from the notes Vidvana played as she copied the notes from Limn's computer. "But I'm not sure about the Amber Song of Turning." He appeals to his brother.

Abél sits quietly, reviewing the Song of All Songs silently in his mind. There's the Mica Song of Reflection, the Amethyst Song of Hope, the Jade Song of the Calumet. He shivers at the notes from the Obsidian Song of Embracing Death, the song he'd sung through his tears at the cremation rituals for his mother Avienne and then for Meridia's mother Maddie. The Song of All Songs moves on, resonating in his mind. There's the Ancient Quartz Song of Reconciliation, the Carnelian Song of the Wide Path, the Turquoise Canopy of Time. A lump comes to his throat as his aurynx silently forms the notes of the Preterit Granite Song of Regret. The Song of All Songs contains a medley of all the Marble Songs—Flowers, Seeds, Falling Leaves. The Amber should come next and Abél struggles to let it be what it is and not what he wishes it to be. He listens. The notes pass quickly. It's only a brief phrase and he realizes with a start that it's a phrase contained in both the Preterit Amber Song of Raising the Waters and the Ancient Amber Song of Turning. The song continues through the Jasper Song of Burning and the soaring notes of the Lapis Song of Liberation.

Abél emerges from his reverie and is chagrined to see that all eyes are on him. He nods at his brother Brân. *You heard it, too, didn't you, brother?*

"Yes," Brân says. "The Song of Turning is there in the Song of All Songs."

"Damon made a picture of the Song of All Songs," Vidvana says.

"Wait. What?" Limn presses the fingers of both hands against her forehead. "Would this be one of those photographs made using snail slime? What did that picture look like?"

"There wasn't much to it," Vidvana says. "It was kind of a swirly blue circle on a black background."

Limn inhales sharply and turns back toward her computer. She taps furiously for a moment. Then she points toward the screen. "Like this?" she says.

"That's it," Zara says. "Do you know what that's supposed to be?"

Tears well up in Limn's eyes as she tries to make sense of the ideas that are finally coming together in her mind, leaping together as if drawn by a magnet. She has to find translatable words to explain space travel to these people who had never even contemplated ocean travel prior to her arrival. Space travel and high frequency radio signals, though she suspects the Melfar may know more about such signals than she does.

"How did you acquire the picture on your screen?" Vidvana asks.

"Long ago," she says, "before the Tantum, people used to store all kinds of information in remote...far away computers and other devices that were all connected by means of electromagnetic waves." There's a pause as she scrutinizes her listeners' faces. It's clear to her that they have no idea what she's talking about. She takes a deep breath and continues. "Anyway, I've been able to access some of those computers and examine the information that's stored there. Satellites, with similar computers on board, were sent into space to circle our planet like the moon does. Some of those are still up there and a few of them have continued broadcasting the information stored in them for more than two thousand years because they're run by solar power. And I think also because they're the ones that were built using the ecphorite technology." She scowls deeply, shakes her head, smiles. "Who knows? Maybe that technology generates some kind of light waves from sound or sound waves from light and somehow Melfar people..." Her eyes glisten with wonder.

I keep singing the Song of Turning with great vigor in an effort to fix my attention steadfastly on this conversation. How did I find the Song of All Songs anyway? Where did it come from? I'm certain my father is right; the Song of Turning is there in the Song of All Songs.

My gnosic orb twitches and tingles. I think Limn is trying to tell us that these songs we've always said come from the Migrant are...what? Vibrations from devices set up many meeds ago using ecphorite? And the sun? What color are their vibrations? What songs do the vibrations form?

I reach out. I listen.

"How does all this help us get Meridia back?" Damon is slightly annoyed at Limn's elation over these discoveries. None of it matters to him unless it brings his partner back.

"Maybe," Abél says, "maybe what we need to do is sing the Song of All Songs. Not just a few of us. Not just a few fragments of the song, but the whole thing, exactly the way we sang it at the dedication, so that all the different songs can verberate through the mirrors."

Brân murmurs agreement.

"There's another thing that I've been wondering about," Amos Quint says. "What if the mirrors are losing their strength? There was a powerful shaking when Brân went away. Much less when he returned. None at all when Meridia left."

"There are more mirrors at Swarthpol," Damon says. He's sure that must be what he perceived in the depths of the dark pond. Those glinting shapes have to be mirrors.

"Really?" Limn says. "Well, if you're thinking of gathering a large group of singers, doing it at Swarthpol might be better. Amos-ji's chamber is rather small."

Abél recoils in horror from that thought. He knows Swarthpol.

"That's not a good idea," Damon says. He knows Abél's story and he personally witnessed the effect the place had on Umet. "That place is dangerous for Melfar."

"Oh," Limn says. "Well, now that I think of it, that place might be bad for all of us. According to what I've learned from the data left behind by the first expedition, Swarthpol is radioactive. At least it was when they were here nearly two hundred years ago. Surely less dangerous now. They suggested that some interaction of a nuclear explosion and volcanic eruption had produced pockets of radioactive obsidian."

"What's radio action?" Abél knows what obsidian is, although he hadn't known anything about how it was formed.

Limn explains. "I've assumed that members of the first expedition eventually died from their exposure to the radioactive obsidian. Their reports indicate that they were ill. And they expressed concern about the native people who had recovered the ecphorite for them. According to what you've told me, it seems likely that the radioactivity affected Melfar differently." She holds her hands palms-up near her shoulders, smiling. "You people are quite the ticket."

"Do you think it would be safe for some of us Mundani to go to Swarthpol and recover whatever mirrors might still be there?" Damon says.

"As long as you're only there for a short while it should be no problem. I'm sure the radioactivity is less now than it was when the first expedition came there. I'll see if I can calibrate my dioristimator to monitor radiation levels." She wonders if the members of her own team that went to Swarthpol for ecphorite recorded any notes about radiation.

"Well, I'm willing to risk it," Damon says. He tries to think who might be still available across the water to accompany them. Surely Orban will be willing to go. And maybe Salma, who was with Abél's party.

"I'm sure my brother Negyed will go," Vidvana says. "He's still waiting across the way. Vedö, too."

"We can set the mirrors up across there on the coast," Brân says. "And we'll let others in New Beniford know that we need their assistance here to sing our Calumet back to us."

52

I listen to their plans. I have no idea if it will work. I think about what Limn said about computers flying around overhead, circling what she calls our planet Earth. She said the devices revolve around us like the moon. Is that what the moon does? I turn my orb toward the moon, listening.

At first I find nothing. What am I listening for, anyway? I've brought whole songs from the Migrant in the past. Is that the kind of thing Limn meant?

I open my orb. I ask Avienne and Idös for guidance, but I don't call upon them as "Avienne" or "Idös." I ask only that their presence within the Migrant guide me.

Breathe with your mind, Meridia. I'm remembering what Brân told me when he first tried to explain how the gnosic orb works.

I breathe.

I breathe more deeply.

There. Tones. Faint images flickering. Colors coalescing from the notes of a song. This time I don't seize the music or try to make sense of the images. This time I search for the source.

What I find is unexpected. When Limn said the songs might be coming from a computer inside a... What did she call it? A satellite? I had no idea what all of that meant. I think this must be what she was trying to tell us about. It's constructed mostly of some kind of metallic material, but inside it there's a complicated structure built almost entirely of ecphorite. It's the ecphorite that sings. The ecphorite flings its tuneful images out toward Earth and moon and stars, singing its song continuously, again and again. Within its song, I recognize some of the songs I know. Parts of them anyway, although the imagery is less specific. There are other bits of melody, fragments of imagery that I don't recognize. Songs I don't know yet.

I listen. I breathe.

All at once I'm aware of other devices, each one floating, looping at great speed, each one singing its own song, telling its own story. I almost lose myself in the overlapping swirls of color and song.

Somewhere I pertange something greater than any of these devices and as soon as I know it's there, I arrive.

Surprising.

This is huge compared to the song devices. It's like a house floating in the air. There are people inside. Not Elossa. These people verberate as they speak and think. Not as vividly as Melfar do, of course; more like Mundani. I rest among them to observe.

This one is speaking something into his computer. His spoken words make no more sense to me than Limn's, but at least with this one there's something to pertange. He's thinking of another person in front of another computer as he speaks. *Just be calm, friend. No, nothing to be done. We'll hold out as long as we can. We want to come home. We can't. It's not your fault. Are you there? Friend? Sadness. Anger.* He looks back at the other person sharing this strange floating house. *No hope,* he says. *Destruction. So much destruction. No supplies coming. Failure. We could go together,* he says. *Out there among the stars. Okay, tomorrow.*

I turn toward the other person and I'm surprised that she's also turned toward me. As if she knows I'm here. *What sort of place is this?* I ask.

It's a tomb, she says. *It's an observatory of the end of the world. No, not the world. Just humanity. And so many other living things. Are you the angel of death?*

I think about Sister Maggie Marie praying for the children to be saved by angels. I'm certain those were not angels of death and so I say, *No, an angel of life.* I'm not really an angel of any kind, of course, but I say that anyway.

She chuckles a dull lavender pulse. *Where do you come from, angel of life?*

How do I answer that? Maybe "when" I come from would be a better question. I think these people are in the past, at the time of Limn's Tantum. Does that mean I'm from the future? My questioner has moved more deeply into her own thoughts now, thoughts about things that carry no verberations for me, or at least no meaning.

I survey their small room. There are windows. Outside one of the windows I see stars brighter than any I've ever seen before. I watch the stars. Sometimes I think there are songs that come from the stars, too. Maybe someday I'll go look for them.

I turn toward another window and my orb is inundated with the vision that meets it. I see a sphere floating in a star-sparked darkness and the Song of All Songs rises within me in a rush of glorious memories that take me to the day we raised the New Marble and I'm carried back to my own people and my own time.

This is where I want to be. This is *when* I want to be.

53

Limn informs the assembled crew that the radiation levels at Swarthpol are no longer dangerous. Damon and the others had already begun working. They weren't going to let something they couldn't even see deter them from doing what was necessary to bring Meridia back.

The task of getting the mirrors up from the depths of the dark pool is harder work than Damon anticipated. They locate two mirrors, but both are deeply embedded and have to be dug out before they can be brought to the surface. None of the Mundani party are great swimmers, so it takes many dives to accomplish their task. All five of the participants—Damon, Orban, Salma, Negyed, and Vedö—take turns diving and digging and eventually they're able to pull out the two large mirrors undamaged. It takes two days of diligent effort to complete the work.

Limn watches everything and continually prods them with questions. She's walked the full extent of what remains of Swarthpol several times and poked her dioristimator into every nook and cranny of the place.

It's late on the second day and everyone is exhausted and ready for rest but Limn is still full of questions. She sits on a rock with her computer in her lap. She prods Damon. "Tell me more about what you saw down there under the water."

"Well..." Damon hesitates. He knows Limn is just curious, whereas he and the others are singularly focused on doing what is necessary to get Meridia home. "There might be a deeper chamber behind some rocks. I'm afraid it would require more expert swimmers than we are to enter it."

"Could you see if there was anything in it?"

"No," Damon says. That's mostly true. He thought he might have seen some flashes or sparks of something behind the rocks, but he's not going to give Limn any reason to suggest that they stay and investigate.

What Limn is trying to figure out is this: If radioactivity is no longer a problem at Swarthpol, what is it about the place that has such a negative effect on Melfar? Umet was here only a few days ago and seems to have been as strongly affected as Abél was more than thirty years past, as debilitated as the first Melfar who were here when that first expedition arrived in search of ecphorite. Could it be the ecphorite itself? Could there be much larger quantities of it somewhere under the waters?

"They're heavier than they look," Damon says next morning as he takes hold of his end of one of the mirrors. Each mirror is roughly trapezoidal and not quite as tall as the average Mundani, which is considerably taller than most Melfar. Orban has cleaned the mirrors as best he could and wrapped each one separately in mats and blankets for transport.

Negyed struggles to lift his end. "I don't think I can do this," he says. "I'm not feeling well."

Vedö steps forward to take over. "That's okay, Negyed."

"When did you start feeling ill?" Damon says.

"I began to get a little dizzy shortly after we arrived," Negyed says. "At first I thought I was just tired from the long trek getting here." They'd made the journey in only one day, though it should have taken at least a day and a half. "But it didn't get any better. Today I have an awful headache. I haven't been able to eat anything since yesterday."

"Wasn't your father part Melfar?" Salma asks. She knows that Negyed is Vidvana's brother. Vidvana had told Salma about her mixed heritage.

"That's right. I guess that could make me at least a little susceptible to whatever it is at Swarthpol that's harmful to Melfar. Perhaps I should've expected this." He only wanted to help.

"I didn't know you were part Melfar," Damon says. "How?"

"My mother was Mundani, but Father was mixed. Like Meridia." Negyed steps closer to Damon and speaks in a quieter voice. "I didn't know if I should mention it or not, but my father's sister, who was, of course, also mixed, partnered with a Mundani man. They eventually had a child, Damon. Their own child. It is possible."

Damon grabs the mirror more tightly because his muscles have suddenly wanted to go slack. "So Meridia and I..." A grin creases his face. "Thank you, Negyed. Thank you for sharing that with me."

Burdened by the mirrors, their return journey requires a full day and more than a half. By the time they arrive at the beach across from Selbourne, preparations are well underway for the event that they hope will sing Meridia back to them, back to this place and this time. They've cleared and levelled a space among the dunes and Abél guides them to the spot where the mirrors are to be erected.

"We're planning to sing this evening," he says. "We don't want to delay any longer than we have to. The people coming from New Beniford camped overnight at Aldbeck and should be here shortly. You should go get some rest, Damon."

Damon doesn't have to be told twice. Every muscle in his body aches from the walking, the diving, the digging, the carrying. He wanders away toward the shelter above the beach, remembering when he camped there with Meridia. He thought he'd be alone, but he's pleased to discover that Yuli and Umet are there before him. And the nens. Yuli shushes him unnecessarily; both Naomi and Odilia are asleep in their baskets. Odilia has almost outgrown hers.

"We brought them across this morning," Yuli whispers. "We wanted to make sure the nens would be here to welcome their mother home."

Damon smiles in grateful acknowledgement and stretches out next to the two baskets, curving his body protectively around his two daughters. Eyes closed, he sighs deeply, begging for a few moments of rest.

Exhaustion grants his wish. As he drifts away, he pertanges faint bursts of light coming from within the baskets, orange from Odilia, blue from Naomi. Within each burst, a tentative note of song. A song in Meridia's voice. *How can she sing both the Wide Path and the Canopy of Time at once?* No, it must be the Song of All Songs. *She knows,* Damon thinks. *You know what we're doing, don't you, Meri?*

In his deepening slumber, he reaches out for his partner, but she's faded from insubstantial to absent. Was she there at all?

When he opens his eyes again, it's Yuli who is singing. She's feeding Omi from a bottle as Odi presses her feet against the bottom of her basket and whimpers. Damon takes Odi in his arms and Yuli hands him a second bottle.

"Is this more of the stuff Limn brought?"

"Yes, but we're running out. We'll need to get some cabra's milk soon." She glances up quickly. Damon says nothing, but she adds, "No, of course you're right. Soon they'll have the real thing."

Damon wanders out to the ledge and peers down toward the beach. "They're here," he says. The people from New Beniford have arrived. There are Mundani as well as Melfar. Damon recognizes Gerd and Fergus and Ann. Vidvana's partner Willem has come, of course. Lambert Quint is there, too, along with a few of his students. They've come all the way from Fayredell. How did they get here so fast? A Melfar woman Damon doesn't recognize joins them. She appears to have arrived from a different direction, coming up from the south. Damon doesn't know any Melfar women from that area. Whoever this woman is, she knows Zara.

Without a word, Damon, still holding Odi, climbs down toward the beach. Yuli brings Naomi and Umet follows with the two baskets. They know it's time. Soon they'll sing. Soon Meridia will be back. Damon's legs quiver with anticipation as he climbs down to the beach.

Gerd and Ann are overjoyed to see the twins again. Gerd takes Naomi in her arms and croons eldmotherly words to her. Ann coaxes a smile from Odilia.

"There you are, Damon." Zara approaches, accompanied by the stranger. He introduces her as Boovez breth Noita. "She's come all the way from Túl to help us sing Meridia back. Her eldmother is Calumet in Túl."

Damon means to tell Boovez how much he appreciates her coming, but as he gazes into her face he's caught in a whirlwind of disjointed images and snippets of sound. He stands facing Boovez with his mouth open.

"I apologize, Damon," Boovez says. "Zara told me you were Revelant and I thought... Never mind. It's wonderful to meet you. I know Meridia thinks the world of you."

Does she know Meridia? Damon is confused. "Thank you for coming," he says at last. He's thankful when Zara urges Boovez away to greet someone else. The woman's presence is exhausting. When he looks down at Odilia, he sees that her eyes are following Boovez.

Vidvana sidles up to him and lays a comforting hand on his arm. "The people of Túl are more intensely Melfar than anyone I've ever met," she says. "Even Abél says that they can be overwhelming."

54

Wisps of cloud and fog move onshore as arrangements are finalized for the singing. Days grow short at this time of year with the approach of Sixth Stint. Melfar call it Fogtide.

Orban and Vedö have placed the mirrors retrieved from Swarthpol at the center of the clearing facing one another, precisely parallel, and braced in position with branches and stones. Abél, who felt it would be unwise for Melfar to work in too close proximity to the mirrors, expresses his gratitude to the Mundani workers. Melfar have different work to do.

Orban tests the stability and alignment of the mirrors one more time and then steps away, joining the others as they form an irregular circle about four spans distant from the mirrors. Fog thickens, swirled by breezes from the ocean. There are a few coughs and throat-clearings as the company still themselves in preparation.

Without visible signal of any sort, Abél and Zara begin the song simultaneously, singing the opening notes of the Song of All Songs in ringing unison.

Abél feels the weight of the song more profoundly than he did when it was first sung at the dedication of the New Marble Benison. That was not even eight moon-tides past. He thinks about how rapidly life flows, how it bends and changes and how Melfar and Mundani have come into new alignments with one another in that short time. He thinks of beloved ones who have died and new beloveds who have been born. He shivers, immersed in the song as other singers add a rich drone of harmony in deep Mundani voices. One of the voices is Amos Quint's.

Amos knows only a few notes of the song and he lets them carry the words that have become such an important touchstone for him: "We are the myriad expressions of the singularity of existence," he chants. "We are one." He glances toward his son, Lambert, who chants the same words in equally resonant tones.

Lambert Quint is entranced by the notion that these mirrors in front of him might have the power to breach time and space and bring Meridia back into their midst. He thinks of the compelling pull of the mirrors he collected and placed on one wall of his quarters in Fayredell. But those are only ordinary mirrors. Not like the ones standing at the center of their circle here. Lambert repeats the words again, listening to how the tones meld with the melodic embellishments Zara and Yuli are singing.

The songs within the Song of All Songs entwine and overlap one another—the Song of Reflection, the Song of Hope, the Song of the Wide Path. Damon tries to follow Abél's lead as the voices move into a section from the Canopy of Time. The notes are in an easy register for Melfar voices, but Damon strains for the high notes. He wants to sing all the things that will bring Meridia home. *Meridia...*

I'm here and I yearn to join you. I pertange passageways, but they're narrow and brief. I move toward one but it closes before I reach it. Another opens and then another over there. It makes no sense. I listen. I

want to sing but I can't find the right tones. Just as my voice engages, the tones shift. I move in slow motion or else too quickly, I can't tell which. The Song of Turning. Idös told me I should sing that. Perhaps it will bring my mind into synchrony with your song.

Gerd watches Damon and the two motherless nens. She doesn't trust her singing and hums quietly whatever notes she can find. She notices Limn sitting there on the ground at the edge of the group, fussing with her computer. *Can't she leave that ashing machine alone for a few minutes and join us?* Gerd shrugs off her irritation and begins singing more vigorously.

Limn is not ignoring them. She's scanning for radio signals, searching for a broadcast from one of the ecphorite-equipped satellites that might match the patterns developing in the song. She straightens up suddenly, her eyes wide. She touches a couple of keys and inclines her head toward the machine, listening. She touches another key and holds it down for a moment. Notes emerge from her machine. The substance of the sound is strange and of course devoid of imagery, but the sequence of tones matches the song that they're singing. Limn nods along with the song, enchanted. Entranced at how the notes match perfectly. Almost perfectly.

There's something amiss. Limn listens more intently. The mismatched sequence of tones repeats. And repeats again. She frowns and picks up the computer and walks hesitantly toward Yuli. "Hear this," she says. "Little not same." She's forced to speak Mundani without aid of the translator.

Yuli listens. She frowns, uncertain. How could she possibly be so bold as to alter something as important as a Benison song, especially this one—the Song of All Songs? She feels something brush her shoulder.

Yes, Yuli. Sing the notes this way.

Yuli takes a deep breath, hoping Meridia is right, and begins to sing lustily these notes of the Ancient Amber Song of Turning, notes not included in the Song of All Songs as they know it. The singers falter and turn toward Yuli. Why would Yuli do this? Why would she disrupt the singing? A second singer joins Yuli. Zara recognizes Boovez's voice.

This is right, Boovez says. *Idös agrees with Meridia.* Boovez places a hand on Zara's arm and the two women join in the enlarged segment from the Song of Turning, wrapped in a glow of honey-colored light. In a flash the change is accepted by all the Melfar singers.

The colors intensify. Yuli feels Meridia's presence grow stronger.

Move. You need to move.

Yuli immediately sends Meridia's request to all the Melfar singers. They begin walking slowly, nudging their Mundani companions along as they go.

This change feels right. The movement is right. It's like a vine. No, two vines. It's like Omi and Odi crying together, winding their colors in and out as they reach for one another.

There's a moment of confusion as Zara and Boovez reverse direction, weaving in and out among the other singers. Others follow their lead and soon there are two circles of singers braiding their song and colors together as they move around and through one another in a graceful dance.

Damon doesn't understand what's happening, but he follows as best he can, his heart bursting with amethyst hope as his fingers grasp the Quartz bead where it lies against his chest between the two pouches of waifs that have begun to vibrate with the rising song.

At the center of the space between the mirrors, bursts of colored light and then wavering beams appear, gathering and weaving together into a whitening, brightening space opening there, glistening there, exploding brilliance and sound and every color as Meridia materializes, fades, shimmers, gleaming more and more distinctly into view as her voice joins theirs as Naomi and Odilia cry out in rapture as tears flow from every eye as they look at one another as if to say—still singing: *Do you see it, too?*

The earth beneath their feet trembles.

"Meridia!" Damon shouts and runs toward her, stopping just before he reaches the bright space she occupies. He holds out a hand and Meridia extends hers. Their two hands—equally solid and real—grasp tightly. Laughter flows into the song as Meridia steps toward him and they embrace.

The song continues a few moments more, the singers unwilling to close off this thing that—they're certain of it now—has brought their Calumet, their Prophet back among them. And then Zara's voice overtakes the fraying Song of All Songs as she begins to intone the Song of the Calumet, her voice clear and strong and joyful.

Through jubilant tears, Meridia notices a small gray bird with deep blue wing and tail feathers that alights briefly atop one of the mirrors and then soars toward the mountains.

55

Everyone wants to speak with me, to touch me. They need to verify that I'm really, truly here. I think I am. My mind still drifts, filled with the memories of what I've experienced, the memories of elsewhere, of spaciousness. There's a certain allure when I recall the confidence I felt as I began to master the technique of shifting my vibrations to encounter different time-spaces. I think I want to try that again. But not now. Right now all I want to do is hold my nens—both of them at once—while Damon's arm rests with welcome heaviness across my solid shoulders. People stare, their eyes grasping at me as if I might suddenly vanish again. I focus on Naomi and Odilia and Damon. And Father. He's here by my side as well, accompanied by Brân. I think Damon said we can sleep tonight in the shelter above the beach. Sleep! How long has it been since I've slept the insensible sleep of this solidly physical realm?

Brân tells me that I was gone barely a tide. It seemed like more. And less. Brân understands the disorientation of my experience, the disengagement from time as it was experienced here. I think his disconnection during his own travels must have been more profound since he traveled more widely than I did. As long as Naomi was with me, I was firmly tied to Odilia, and through her to the same time that she and Yuli and Damon and the rest were experiencing. Once Naomi was safely delivered back into this time and place, I traveled more freely. How will I explain to them about the song devices and the great floating house? Maybe Limn can help with that. My heart warms and tingles—my emotional, love-filled Mundani heart. My desire to care for my children and to be with my partner has never felt more intense.

Someone is speaking to me, someone whose verberations overwhelm my thoughts. Images fly past in a jumble, like leaves in a storm. The woman's face is not familiar.

Father understands my confusion. "This is Boovez breth Noita," he says, using words to steady me. Then he shows me where she's from. He shows me the old Calumet who is her eldmother.

"You're Idös's child," I say. *She helped me. She showed me how to use the Song of Turning to arrange my mind. Please thank her for me.*

You've done that yourself.

And then I see how hesitant Idös had been regarding my return. How untrusting she was of the Elossa she knew only as the empty people from Túl song. She still doesn't trust Limn.

No, we don't trust her. That's Boovez saying that. *But if you wish to work with her, we respect your choice.* Idös speaks to me directly then, in a smooth cadence that overlays Boovez's verberations. *As for the Melfar of Túl, we will continue, as we always have, to guard the deepest ways of the Melfar. We send you benediction. We maintain ourselves apart.*

As Zara and Boovez move away, I close my eyes, verberating gratitude toward Idös. I'd like to tell them to trust Limn, to reassure them that Limn is a good person who brought us home against the will of her own people.

I open my eyes and see Limn approaching. She looks me up and down, her head cocked to one side.

"You not so fat," she says. "I think you same shape Yuli."

I have to laugh as Limn reaches inside her satchel to turn on the translator.

"Sorry, was that impolite?" the computer voice says. "You're thinner than I thought you'd be."

"I'm thinner than I used to be. I guess all that time spent out of phase, as you call it, when I wasn't eating or drinking anything, ended up affecting my body." It affected Naomi, too, which I find far more concerning. I don't mention this to Limn. Now that my breast milk is real again, I'm hoping Omi might catch up with her sister. Odilia thrived on the formula provided by the Elossa. I verberate gratitude toward Limn for her compassion, for her assistance in bringing all of us home. And then I remember her total imperviousness to verberations and use words. "Thank you for helping us, Limn. I don't think we would have been able to get me back without your help."

She shrugs. "Oh, I don't know about that," she says. "You Melfar folks are pretty crafty."

"It wasn't just Melfar that made this happen," I say. "Mundani effort, Mundani voices, Mundani heart vitality helped, too. It was something we all did together." I smile at Limn. She understands smiles. "What will you do now? Will you go back to your city?" I'm sure the ship we came in could easily make the return journey as long as Limn steers clear of the rocky, shallow places. I think again about how beautiful those great sails are. Limn calls them solar sails. They still remind me of butterfly wings.

"I can't go back," Limn says. "I don't want to go back. What I'd like to do is stay here with you. With your people."

"Of course you're welcome to stay in New Beniford. Maybe you'd be willing to teach us about some of your science. The solar sails and the computers and such. Won't you miss all of that? We live so simply here. And none of us knows anything about science. We don't even have a word for it. We must seem very ignorant to you."

"No. You're not ignorant. My people back in Port Sillick are the ignorant ones."

"But they know science. They have so many amazing devices."

"They know technology. They know math and chemical formulas and how to build things. But that's not science. They've forgotten how to ask questions. How to do research."

"Your people invented ecphorite," I say.

"It's not the inventions, the things and materials that matter, Meridia. It's what you make of them. And your people have made of ecphorite something beautiful."

I think she's talking about the Benisons and the songs but also, perhaps, the way we share them with one another.

Limn's eyes sparkle as she continues speaking. "There were once millions—billions—of human beings and we had so many inventions. So much science. But in the things that really mattered, we failed. We destroyed ourselves and one another. I find your people—all of you,

Melfar and Mundani—to be very open and curious. I like that."

She hasn't met all of us yet. Not all of us are like the ones gathered here. I think about the Palinjians. And I think, too, about the Túl Melfar. Among both groups there are people unwilling to change, afraid of working with people they consider to be different.

"Well, then, come back with us to New Beniford. We'll build you a house." What I verberate probably should have been rendered as "We'll make you a home."

56

I don't think I've ever been happier. Naomi and Odilia are strong and healthy, even though Odi is still bigger than Omi and has already begun to lose her iridescence. Her eyes may be starting to change color, too. Or at least one of them is.

Damon returns to his photographic work one or two days in six. He's teaching Limn about his process and she explains what she knows about photography. About the science of photography. And about ecphorite. Limn says that ecphorite was fabricated out of silica and that the ancient researchers extracted the silica from what she calls diatomaceous algae. I think she means luminous slime.

Yuli asks us if we want her to help look after the nens. I accept her help only during the hours when Damon is away at his workshop. When he's with me, we want the nens only for ourselves. Besides, we're sure Yuli is happier spending time with Umet. They've decided not to delay their partnering any longer and are planning the ceremony for the next full moon. Yuli wants me to guide the ritual and of course I've agreed to do it, even though the only partnering ritual I've ever participated in was my own. Zara says she'll help me.

Limn has befriended Umet, drawn by his expertise in creative arts. She reminded us that her clone set was originally designed to be artists. She says the longer she goes without the daily supplements, the drugs she took in Port Sillick, the more she feels the impulse to create something. Even though she was partially immune to the effects of the drugs, she's relieved to be completely free of them. One of the things Limn has created is a new set of clothes for herself. I think her frilly blouse and brightly colored trousers with flaring hems are a bit strange, but they're certainly more interesting than the monotonous garments everyone wore in Port Sillick. She's offered to make me some new clothes.

I rarely go anywhere except to my green glen, but I'm never at a loss for company. People come here to our house every day. Some come for healing, as they always have. Others come for advice from their Calumet.

Some people just come to look at me and at Naomi and Odilia and to drink in our experiences through their eyes and orbs. At first, I found this a little annoying. Now I don't mind so much. Sometimes they ask for a song and I always insist that we sing together. I encourage them to sing the three songs I received from my eldmother Avienne—the Old Amethyst Song of Hope, the Ancient Jade Song of Pacification, and the Old Granite Song of Firm Resolve.

Father comes often, of course. And Brân. They're here now. It's an unusually warm fall evening and we've gathered outdoors to eat supper. We converse in words so as to fully include Damon in our discussion. When we talk about Limn, words are necessary for all of us.

"Did you know that Limn had never seen trees before?" I say. I remind them of what Port Sillick was like. "There were no trees there. None at all. She says she'd read about trees and seen replicas in a museum."

Speaking of trees reminds us all of Ann breth Keira, Lambert Quint's daughter's daughter. "Ann has invited

Limn to come to Fayredell and speak at her school," Brân says. "Did you know that Ann and Fergus are talking about partnering? Not right away, of course. They're still young."

Damon takes my hand in his as our two hearts share a rosy glow that envelopes Naomi and Odilia as well.

"Limn was trying to explain to me about how Elossa differ from Mundani and Melfar," Father says. "I'm afraid I didn't understand most of it. It seemed as if she was trying to say that she has some kind of disability, something missing that all of us have."

"She came looking down my throat yesterday," I say. "Trying to find my aurynx." My throat bubbles orangey waves of amusement. "She says it's really just something more developed in Melfar, but that Mundani... Oh, I don't know. You can ask her about it." I wonder if I should tell Limn that sometimes there's a pertangible wisp of color at the crown of her head.

"Did she tell you that birds have something called a syrinx? That's in addition to their larynx, which birds and humans—Melfar and Mundani and Elossa—all have." Brân thinks a syrinx and aurynx are probably similar.

"I'm still uncertain about something, Father. Limn has tried to explain to me that what we've always called the Migrant can be described in terms of what she calls physics. She says it's all just vibrations. Waves and particles and... strings? And of course we all saw how the..." I search for the right words, the ones Limn used. Her words have no verberated images, only the ones she shows us on her computer screens. "We saw how the sound patterns she captured from the song devices—the satellites—into her computer were the ones needed to activate the mirrors and bring me home. Well, they worked once they were sung and verberated. But we didn't know that pattern when Brân disappeared. Or when he came back. Or when I left. How were we able to get the mirrors to work then?"

"I asked her about that," Father says.

We all look toward him expectantly.

"She didn't really know." Father verberates Limn's face, her expression a mixture of confusion and curiosity. "But she thinks our Song of All Songs was probably precise enough to activate the mirrors because Meridia had received the song itself from one of those ecphorite computers up there in the sky. Beyond that, she's willing to say it was mostly just Melfar being Melfar." *Maybe what she actually said was 'Melfar being human.'*

"She told me that she's trying to figure out how to test the capabilities of our gnosic orbs," Father says. "Umet is working with her on that. He and Yuli."

We sit in amiable silence for a while as the orange and blue light of the fire dances and crackles.

"Limn asked me about what I saw at Swarthpol." I glance at Father. "She was curious to know what it was like before the first Elossa came there. I tried to describe it to her." Describing things to Limn is even harder than describing things to Mundani people. "She kept asking about the pool and I kept telling her there wasn't one."

"Really?" Father says. "How did the pool get there?"

"I think the place where they did the research was underground. Didn't Limn tell us that? Limn says it probably collapsed and filled with water in the Tantum. Then the first Elossa dug it up and when they did, they disturbed things. It was their digging that made the place dangerous for Melfar. And for the Elossa who did the digging. Before they came, it wasn't dangerous for anyone. Melfar were living right there." I try to remember what Limn said that their town was called before it was called Swarthpol.

"Limn told us she thought the Elossa who came here the first time died from some bad effects coming from Swarthpol. What did she say it was?" Brân furrows his brow, searching for the unfamiliar word that has no accompanying image.

"Radioactivity," Damon says.

"That's it. So it was their own digging that killed them?" Brân shakes his head sadly. "I asked her about another thing I've been studying on. I asked her: If those first Elossa explorers died on Selbourne, why haven't we found any of their bones? She said they must have thrown their bones into the ocean. But I ask you, how does a dead person throw their bones anywhere?"

There's a murmur of laughter around our circle.

"What do you think happened to them, Brân?" I already know what he thinks but I want to hear him say it anyway.

"I think they figured out how the mirrors work."

There's an audible intake of breath as we consider that. Father nods sagely.

We continue talking until the fire dies away and the air grows uncomfortably chilly. Father and Brân take their leave and Damon and I go indoors. We've been holding the nens wrapped warm against our bodies, Damon with Naomi and I with Odilia. We probably hold them too much. They're old enough that they should be allowed more time to move about, rolling from back to belly and back again, clutching at objects. Or at the shiny orbs rolled their way by me or their eldfather. We bundle them into the wooden crib that was a gift from Orban. They never stir, but I think Damon and I both see the soft blue and orange tones that weave into a flowery pattern to envelope the nens like a blanket as they sleep.

"Damon," I say as we stretch out side by side in our own bed. I lay my hand along his upper thigh. "Damon, you know it's okay. I'm real now. I'm here. We can make love again."

And so we do. It's wonderful. The physical joys of this existence are not equaled by anything in that ethereal realm I inhabited during my absence. Here I'm completely happy.

We settle, breathing deep breaths of contentment.

"I learned something recently from Negyed," Damon says suddenly.

I can't imagine what could be important enough to interrupt our current state of beatific peace. "Yes?" I say.

And he explains something he'd learned about Vidvana and Negyed's aunt, a woman who was half Melfar, half Mundani like me.

"He knows that for a fact?" I say, joy bursting all rainbow colors from my aurynx and heart. "She was pregnant by her Mundani partner? So we... Oh, Damon. That can happen? For us." I gaze fondly at our sleeping nens, imagining already for them a younger sister or brother as I reach again for Damon.

This evening I went to my green glen and found Limn there. She stumbled upon the spot by accident one day and seemed so happy there that I invited her to come back anytime she wanted. She's mostly there in the evenings, whereas I'm most likely to go in the mornings. Occasionally we meet one another there. When we do, I think it's on purpose.

I step quietly. Limn has her computer sitting on the ground in front of her, but she's staring up into the sky. "I was hoping you'd come," she says, switching on her translation program. She uses it less and less these days.

I sit down next to her and wait, verberating curiosity. She remains silent and so I decide to ask a question that's been on my mind. "You told us that what we've always called the Migrant can be explained by vibrations and such. I'm not sure I understand that." Or maybe I just find the explanation inadequate. These are hard questions to formulate.

Limn tilts her head and gazes into my eyes, as if she sees something there. "Yes, I could tell that my explanation didn't satisfy you," she says. "Perhaps I also should have mentioned that, in the past, what you experience as the Migrant was what many people called God."

"God?" I say. The word was untranslatable by her computer.

"It was just another way of talking about experiences," she says. "Experiences of something vaster than our ordinary world. But in the past, naming it God, people tried to turn it into more of a person, complete with a personality, with likes and dislikes."

Should I tell her about the Mundani Creator? Their Restorer? I continue listening.

"Sometimes this God had a very demanding personality. But your people... You don't ascribe a personality to your experience so much as assign a vocation, a vocation of movement, of being here and there, then and now. Your Migrant isn't a person. It's a presence and it's everywhere."

I think that sounds right. "But when we say that our songs come from the Migrant, it appears that we're wrong. The songs are really coming from the floating devices and we never knew anything about those."

"Everything comes from somewhere," she says. "And you did know the most important thing." The mechanical words from her computer can't convey the deep feeling I hear in her voice. "You knew that whatever is offered up in the bounty of this fragile planet, whatever we encounter, ought to be used for peaceful ends. For healing and not for destruction and domination. I've learned that lesson from you. What is it they call you? A Calumet? A peace-bringer."

We sit in silence for a while. I'm thinking about the history of Melfar and Mundani and what they expect of me as Calumet and Prophet. Limn's words give me courage. "Was there something else you wanted to talk about?" I say.

"If you don't mind, I'd like for you to tell me again about what you experienced when you located the satellites that are still broadcasting through their ecphorite computer systems."

I know she's talking about the floating song devices, so I tell her about those. She'd been surprised when I told her that the song devices emanated imagery in their tones.

"I hadn't expected that they'd broadcast images as well as sound in their wave patterns. That's the work of the ecphorite. The only reason my computer received nothing but tones is because my computer isn't made with ecphorite." She frowns as if she would scold her device for its inadequacy. Or perhaps she's wondering how she might construct a new computer using ecphorite. She doesn't need that, of course. She has Melfar to help her now.

"And then you said you found...what did you call it? A floating house?"

"That's right."

"It was actually called a space station. Not that that matters anymore. Tell me about that."

"There were two people inside it and one of them was talking to someone somewhere else on his computer. They were very sad about...about destruction. Was that the Tantum that you've told us about?"

"Yes. Go on."

"One of the people was a woman and she seemed to be aware of my presence." I share my recollection of what felt like a conversation with the woman.

Limn picks up her computer and taps a couple of keys. "I want to read you something," she says. "It's something that was written down by the last survivor on that space station." She looks up at me for approval.

I nod. As she reads, I try to visualize the people I pertanged in the floating house. This was written by the woman.

Limn's voice grows thin and quivery as she continues reading. "'As our rations run out along with our hope, one by one we just step out into the void, into endless space. Tomorrow it will be my turn. Yesterday I think I was visited by the angel of death, although she claimed to be the angel of life. I'm probably just hallucinating because of too much time in space, too little nourishment. But whatever this presence was, I think she was from the future, and if she was, then there's hope. We don't destroy everything. I'll look for this angel when I step into the void tomorrow.' So you see, Meridia? She knew you were there. You really did enter her time-space."

I sit in silence for a moment. I find this interesting, but after all I've been through, I don't find it surprising. It has moved Limn to tears. I know I ought to say something, so I say, "That's remarkable. Thank you for telling me."

Limn pushes her computer aside and sits for a while, gazing into the sky where stars are flickering into view. "In Port Sillick," she says, "I used to go for long walks by the ocean. I miss the ocean." She turns briefly toward me with a wistful look before focusing once more on the emerging canopy of stars. "But the sky will do. Actually, the sky is even grander. Even more endless."

"Do you think there might be others out there, somewhere beyond Port Sillick, beyond the Endless Sea?"

Limn smiles her impertangible smile.

"I'm sure of it Meridia." She's looking at the sky again. "And someday they'll arrive. They're curious, too. Even now they may be on their way.

Donna Dechen Birdwell

Appendix 1
Experiencing Time

MELFAR do not think linearly, but rather conceptualize all time in terms of cycles. They utilize a lunar calendar overlaid on a solar one, measuring time in *tides, returns,* and *meeds.* A *tide* is a full lunar cycle. The only consistently named tides are Darktide, Brightening Symmetide, Suntide, and Darkening Symmetide (corresponding to periods encompassing winter solstice, vernal equinox, summer solstice, and autumnal equinox, respectively). Other tides receive descriptive labels, which can vary from one return to the next (e.g., Fogtide, Fruittide). A *return* is a cycle of all the solar seasons, with a new return always beginning on the full moon closest to the start of Brightening Symmetide. There are twelve named returns corresponding to the twelve types of stone from which a Benison is crafted to mark the start of each return (see below). A full cycle of returns comprises a *meed,* and meeds are named in the same sequence as returns. The completion of a full cycle of meeds is known as a *Great Turning.* Returns of the current cycle are called New, with previous cycles referred to as Old, Ancient, and Preterit, in that order. To the Melfar, "Preterit" means both "before" and "after." To "date" a particular event, one might say that it happened during the Darktide of the Amber Return of the Old Turquoise Meed.

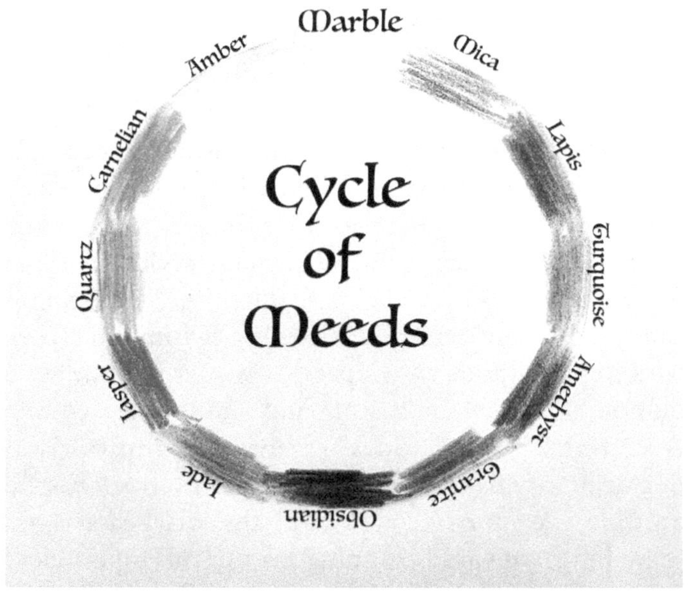

The most important *Benison Songs* mentioned in these texts are the following:

Preterit Meeds: Marble Song of Flowers, Lapis Canopy of Protection, Turquoise Song of the Sun (Gathering of Clouds in Túl), Amethyst Song of the Migrant (Song of the Forest in Túl), Granite Song of Regret, Amber Song of Raising the Waters.

Ancient Meeds: Marble Song of Seeds, Mica Song of Calling the Rains, Lapis Song of the Floods, Turquoise Song of Refuge, Granite Song of Solitude, Obsidian Overwhelm With Splendor, Jade Song of Pacification, Jasper Song of the Sea, Quartz Song of Reconciliation, Carnelian Song of the Wide Path, Amber Song of Turning.

Old Meeds: Marble Song of Falling Leaves, Mica Song of Reflection, Lapis Song of Liberation, Turquoise Canopy of Time, Amethyst Song of Hope, Granite Song of Firm Resolve, Obsidian Song of Embracing Death, Jade Song of the Calumet. The Jasper Meed had its Song of Burning, but no Benison. In the Quartz Meed, waifs were crafted containing maps. In the Carnelian Meed, beads were crafted from the Ancient Carnelian and given as talismans to Mundani Chanters. There was no Benison and no waifs for the Amber Meed.

New Meeds: As described in the first book of this series, the start of the New Marble at the Great Turning was marked by raising a Benison containing the Song of All Songs.

MUNDANI utilize a rigidly linear solar calendar. Their equivalent of a Melfar return (our year) is a *passage*. Passages are sequentially numbered, beginning with the birth year of Razak Caloyer, a revered prophet. Each passage is divided into twelve *stints*, each with exactly thirty days, comprised of five *sixes*. These stints are not named, only numbered. To regularize their calendar, they observe a period of five (sometimes six) days at the conclusion of Twelfth Stint. These days are called the *Binder*. The new passage begins on the longest day (our summer solstice), which they call Full Sun.

ELOSSA people have preserved the Gregorian calendar system and count time in weeks and months and years and centuries just as we do in the Twenty-First Century. According to this calendar, the Mundani Prophet Razak Caloyer (see above) was born in the year 3836 and the apocalypse (Tantum) occurred in 2087.

Appendix 2

MAP

THE MAP on the following page represents the world as known to Mundani and Melfar. Melfar don't use maps as such, relying for guidance on the old Melfar Ways recorded within waifs of the Old Quartz. For the benefit of readers, the map shows the approximate locations of the following places that are important only to Melfar:

1) Beniford
2) Aldbeck
3) Lindmor
4) Woodclasp
5) Gorshfen (on the lake of Glasllyn)
6) Selbourne
7) Túl
8) New Beniford
9) New Túl
10) Swarthpol

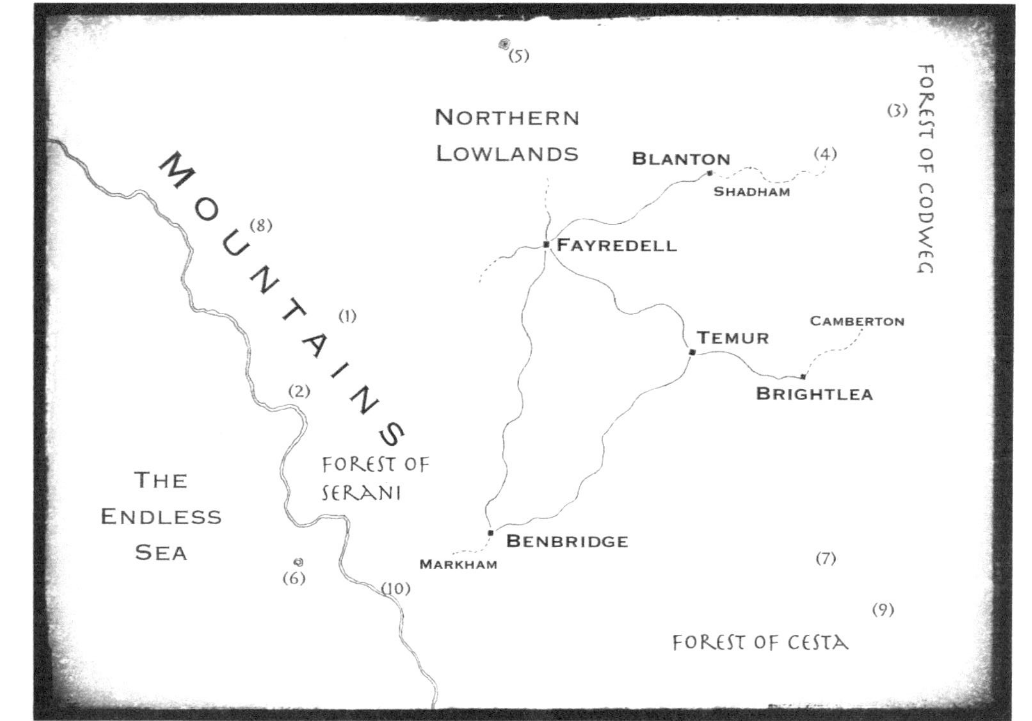

(5)
NORTHERN LOWLANDS
FOREST OF CODWEG
(3)
BLANTON
(4)
SHADHAM
MOUNTAINS
(8)
FAYREDELL
CAMBERTON
(1)
TEMUR
BRIGHTLEA
(2)
THE ENDLESS SEA
FOREST OF SERANI
BENBRIDGE
MARKHAM
(7)
(6)
(10)
(9)
FOREST OF CESTA

Appendix 3

Glossary

Archaeozón: Among the Elossa, a museum dedicated to the display of relic life forms.

aurynx: The Melfar organ that sonically verberates biophotonic patterns. It is located in the throat near the larynx.

Benison: A stone monument crafted by Melfar to commemorate the end of one meed and the start of the next. Each Benison contains the imagery of a song.

billbug: A biting insect similar to a mosquito or horsefly.

cabra: A goat-like mammal sometimes kept for milk.

Calumet: A "peace-bringer" who serves as a respected social and cultural leader among the Melfar.

Chanter: Among the Mundani, a student of Melfar song and poetry.

clauster: A sacred space often associated with a Mundani temple.

dioristimator: Among the Elossa, an instrument for detecting the chemical composition of materials.

Elossa: Term used by Mundani and Melfar to refer to an invasive people from the north. Also called "empty people."

equid: A horse-like mammal kept as a draft animal.

fahm: Coal. Deposits of fahm are found mainly in the remains of ancient storage facilities.

fellspan: The distance to the horizon on relatively flat ground. Approximately 4.2 miles.

fireblock: A fabricated fuel made from waste material soaked in some oily substance.

gnosic orb: The Melfar sensory organ that pertanges photonic and sonic patterns. It is located in the center of the brow just above the eyes.

kinren: Any of the employees, servants, clients, apprentices, and women attached to a particular Sidayen.

lamin: An alpaca-like animal kept as a beast of burden and draft animal.

Melfar: A "race" of people native to the forests who communicate without spoken or written language. They are generally short in stature, stoutly built, with curly light or reddish hair, skin tawny to ochre, and eyes generally yellow or green.

Migrant: The ineffable presence that, according to Melfar belief, motivates and empowers everything.

Mundani: A "race" of people living primarily in towns and farms with written codes and formal religion. They are generally tall and slender, with wavy dark hair and dark skin and eyes.

nacreous fever: A potentially fatal illness marked by iridescent blisters.

Palinjian: Among Mundani, a devotee of Zibal Palinj.

patkány: A very large and vicious species of predatory rodent.

pertange: To sense in a tangible way the photonic and sonic verberations of people and natural things.

pointing-stone: A mineral with magnetic properties, perhaps magnetite or hematite.

Protocols: Among Elossa, the rules and commentaries on rules that specify what can be done.

pudu: A type of small deer found in the mountains.

Revelant: An individual who has died and come back to life in the same body.

Shoon: A derogatory term Mundani use to refer to Melfar.

Sidaya: A code of moral conduct among the Mundani.

Sidayen: One who adheres to the Sidaya. Alternatively, a high status exclusive to Mundani men.

Tantum: Among Elossa, the apocalypse that destroyed all human civilizations and most of life on Earth in the year 2087.

verberate: To emanate biophotonic images and sound.

vital nexus: Among Mundani, the energetic network centered around an individual's heart.

waif: Among Melfar, a stone associated with a Benison and sharing some of its properties.

weftred: Among Mundani, a clandestine network of women and other kinrens.

Acknowledgments

By the time you reach book three in a series, there are far too many people who have participated in the process and product to thank them all individually. There are the ones who first set you to thinking the thoughts that eventually became the story. There are the ones whose words and actions gave you valuable insights into the breadth and depth of this intimate experience of being human and of all the myriad ways in which we can be that. There are the ones who taught you how to say it better, how to be a better writer. And there are, especially, the ones who believed you had stories worth telling and gave you little nudges of encouragement along the way. So huge "thank you" to the whole crowd. And extra special thanks to beta readers Cheryl Rooke and Claire Villarreal and to editor Katherine Catmull of Yellow Bird Editors.

I hope all of my readers will find the *EarthCycles* world as immersive as I have. Exploring Meridia's story has been an adventure.

I'm online at *donnadechenbirdwell.com* and you can also find me on Facebook, Twitter, and Instagram.

Also by Donna Dechen Birdwell

EarthCycles, Book One:
Song of All Songs
(2020)

EarthCycles, Book Two:
Book of All Time
(2021)

Not Knowing, 2019

The Recall Chronicles

Way of the Serpent, 2015

Shadow of the Hare, 2016

Flight of the Owl, 2016

COMING SOON: *Final Recall*

www.ingramcontent.com/pod-product-compliance
Lightning Source LLC
Chambersburg PA
CBHW051217190726
48288CB00006B/2003